THE SILVER SCREAM

THE SILVER SCREAM

Ed Gorman

HEADLINE
FEATURE

First published in Great Britain in 1998
by HEADLINE BOOK PUBLISHING

A HEADLINE FEATURE hardback

10 9 8 7 6 5 4 3 2

British Library Cataloguing in Publication Data

Gorman, Edward
The Silver scream
1. Horror tales
I. Title
813.5'4[F]

ISBN 0 7472 1685 1

Typeset by Avon Dataset Ltd, Bidford-on-Avon, Warks

Printed and bound in Great Britain by
Mackays of Chatham PLC, Chatham, Kent

HEADLINE BOOK PUBLISHING
A division of Hodder Headline PLC
338 Euston Road
London NW1 3BH

To some of the good ones: Ted Miller, Cindy Bell Linden, Fay Robinson, Mike and Marge Mead, Tom St. Clair, Tom Owens, Rolfe Beckheusen, Linda Wood, and in memory of David Markowitz

—Ed Gorman

Radio Interview conducted May 31, 1989

MB – Mitchell Baines, reporter for 'Iowa News Roundup'
TS – Thomas Sullivan, mayor, Parkhurst, Iowa

MB: You keep saying that Parkhurst is no different than any other town of 25,000 but when you look at the murder rate and the incidence of armed robbery and burglary—
TS: Those are problems we're working on.
MB: Now there's gambling to add to that. Parkhurst is situated close to several large truck stops and it's rumored that there are three or four different spots where truckers can gamble for some very serious money. And gamblers are coming downriver from Davenport and Dubuque and Rock Island, too. Parkhurst used to be a really great family town. Very quiet, very peaceful. Do you think it can ever be that way again?
TS: (sighs) I'd be a liar if I said we didn't have problems, Mitchell. We've got some teenagers who are out of control and we've got a few pockets of real serious drug addiction and we've got streets that just aren't safe any more. (Sighs again.) I hope we can turn it around. I sure do.

PART ONE

1

Her first night in prison, Darcy McCain took out her First Communion picture and stared at it for a very long time. She wondered how such a sweet little girl could ever end up in a place like this.

The night before her escape, three years later, she took the same picture out and stared at it again. She still had no answers to her question.

She didn't sleep well that night. All the what-ifs kept her awake. What if a guard saw her? What if the delivery driver saw her? What if she got shot?

The rain started about dawn, a slashing, cold March rain that soaked the farm fields in central Iowa where the woman's prison was located.

She dragged her way through most of the morning, first at breakfast in the cafeteria, then in the library where she spent more than an hour shelving books. Jackie Collins paperbacks were a big item here. All that Hollywood glamour, power and sex. Prisoners needed fantasy. It was one of the few things that gave them strength.

She also shelved one of her own paperbacks. They were very popular inside these walls. A lot of the women prisoners loved hearing Darcy talk about attending seminars where she'd met writers such as Dean Koontz and Mary Higgins Clark. Prisoners were just as star-struck as any other group of people.

This morning, she tried not to think about Ken's letter that had arrived yesterday. She hadn't answered any of her husband's letters for the past four months. Nor had she agreed to see him when he requested visits. She didn't want him to know of her plans. If he knew, he might be blamed for helping her, and then end up in prison himself. The only way – painful as it was – was to cut off all contact with him.

Every fifteen minutes or so, she'd slowly walk over to the back window of the library and look out for any sign of the delivery truck. There was a guard right outside the library door. She might get suspicious if he saw Darcy keep going to the window. Darcy had to be careful.

The plan was simple. The truck usually arrived just before lunchtime. Darcy would go out the back door the way she always did and start to walk across to the building where four cell blocks and the cafeteria were located. To reach her destination, Darcy had to pass the loading block at the back of the administration building.

Darcy had spent the past four months checking out trucks on the library Internet. While she still didn't know anything at all about engines, she knew a whole hell of a lot about undersides. There was a General Motors medium-duty truck that had what was called a tag axle mounted behind the drive axle. It helped hold the truck up. The size and shape of the tag axle was such that a small person could wrap arms and legs around it and ride out underneath the truck. She'd started carefully watching all the trucks that delivered goods to the prison. She'd finally found the make and model she was looking for.

The truck was just backing up to the loading dock. CHANDLER WHOLESALE OFFICE SUPPLIES it said on the black truck.

Darcy's heart started pulsing so loudly she could hear it in her ears. No matter how many times you mentally rehearsed for something like this, you still got scared. She started running through all the what-ifs again. And then stopped herself. Had to get a steely grip on herself.

She walked back to the small, battered desk where she sat checking books in and out. The library was one large room with ten large wooden bookcases and an ancient linoleum-covered floor. Some of the torn, yellowed magazines stacked on the floor dated back to the 1950s, golden oldies like *Look*, *Colliers*, and *American*. Darcy personally liked the *American* because it had a lot of great Nero Wolfe novelettes in them. Page for page, Rex Stout still gave her so much pleasure it was practically sinful.

But this wasn't a Rex Stout fantasy where four grown men lived in a New York brownstone and tended to exotic orchids and even more exotic women all day.

This was a women's prison where there were at least two murders a year, where the occasional guard knocked up the occasional inmate, and where the properly moneyed prisoner could buy just about any kind of drug her little heart desired.

'Hey, that new John Saul paperback come back in yet?' Myrna the guard said, stepping into the library just as Darcy was finishing up with her desk.

Myrna was one of the nice ones, a plump Iowa farm girl who looked right at home wearing a khaki uniform and a Sam Browne belt. She was also a fanatical reader of horror novels.

'Afraid not, Myrna. But as soon as it does, it's yours.'

'I like his characters.'

'He's good. No doubt about it.'

'You ever think of writing a horror novel?' she said.

Why do I need to write one? Darcy thought. I'm *living* one.

'Well, maybe I'll do one someday.' Then she glanced up at the dusty old sweep hand clock on the wall. 'Gosh, it's lunch time already.' She had to be almost elaborately casual about this whole thing. 'Guess I'd better get going.'

'You got any Robert McCammon books? I like him, too.'

'Tell you what,' Darcy said. 'There're still a lot of books I haven't put back yet. They're over there on that cart. You look through them and if there's anything you want, just tell me when I get back from lunch.'

'Hey, thanks.'

Hurry.

She came out from around her desk, banging her thigh on the sharp edge of it as she did so.

'Wow,' Myrna said, 'you all right?'

'Oh, sure, just a little bump.' Leading to amputation later on, Darcy thought. Otherwise, nothing serious at all.

'See you after lunch,' Myrna said.

Darcy smiled and walked out of the library.

She turned left and walked straight to the back door, which was approximately twelve feet away. Because she'd been an exemplary prisoner for three years, she had been granted certain liberties. Walking back and forth to lunch unescorted being one of them.

She was just about to put her hand on the doorknob, when a familiar voice said, 'You think I don't know what you're up to, McCain?'

She didn't have to turn around to match voice with face. This was Warden Judy Webster.

Darcy froze.

Warden Webster came up and, just as Darcy was turning around, waved one of Darcy's own books in her face.

'You gave me one so I'd get hooked on the whole series, didn't you?'

Darcy smiled, even though her knees were trembling so badly, she was afraid she'd drop to the floor. 'So you liked it?'

The book was *Midnight Whispers*. It was a suspense novel about a woman mystery writer who is framed for a murder she didn't commit. It was like an episode of 'The Twilight Zone.' You write a book about something – and it comes true. All during the arrest and trial, she'd wondered about the connection of book and reality. If she *hadn't* written the book would she have found herself accused of murder?

Darcy's photo on the back of the book was almost as dewy-eyed as her First Communion picture. Almost but not quite. Nothing could be. And, of course, Darcy would never be as good-looking as her elder sister, Anne. Or as intelligent. Or as socially skilled. Or as impressive. Growing up in the shadow of a classically beautiful sister who would some day be a world-class neuro-surgeon had sent the young Darcy desperately looking for something to impress her parents with. Luckily, she'd always been good at writing.

'I called the Barnes and Noble in Cedar Rapids,' Warden Webster said, 'and they said that your other three novels are out of print. Think I could sponge some copies from you? I'll bring them back, of course.'

Warden Webster was a stout woman who favored dark business suits. She had a soft and friendly face to off-set the impression her clothes made. The grandmotherly gray hair didn't hurt, either. She was not an excessive warden, neither too vindictive nor too forgiving. The inmates who'd lived through several wardens said she was the best of the bunch. Webster had only been here for three months.

'I'll dig them out for you this afternoon,' she said.

'Aren't you working on a new one?'

Shortly after coming to prison, Darcy had started writing a novel called *The Silver Scream*. Prison seemed an ideal place to write. So much time on your hands. But somehow she couldn't write in here – she was blocked. *The Silver Scream* was only one-third finished.

'Great. I really enjoyed this one.' Then, 'Say, are you walking over to lunch?'

'Uh, yes. Yes, I am.'

Darcy was sure that her face reflected her panic. Her heart hammered even louder than before. She felt a feather-touch of sweat start to bead on her forehead and arms and legs.

'Well,' Warden Webster said, 'why don't I walk with you, then? That's where I'm headed, too.'

It was all over, Darcy thought. If only she'd walked a little faster getting out the door. If only if only if only.

'That'd be great,' Darcy said, feeling like a school girl sucking up to a nun. 'But it's raining pretty hard.'

Warden Webster smiled. 'I imagine we'll survive, don't you?'

Darcy gloomily turned back toward the door and started to open it when—

The Warden's cell phone chirped.

'Hold on a sec, will you?' she said to Darcy. 'This damned thing is my lord and master.'

The Warden took the phone from her pocket, flipped it open, put it to her ear and said, 'Yes?'

'Warden, the Governor's office is on line three. It's about the budget and they say it's important.' The receptionist was an inmate trusty named Shirley Harris. Many of the prison jobs were filled by inmates. This was part of a broader attempt to prepare the inmates for life beyond prison, giving them at least marginal skills so they could find a job when they were released.

Warden Webster sighed. 'All right. I'll go into the supply office – I'm over near the library – and you can patch me in on that phone there.'

The Warden closed the little phone and put it back into her pocket. 'Well, so much for walking to lunch with you. This budget thing's very important. The legislature's in one of their really punitive moods. They think inmates should be put in a deep, dark hole and fed only beans and water. For once, the Governor is on our side. And he's Republican, which makes his position really strange.'

Because of the increase in violent crime – the *perceived* increase, actually, because most types of violent crime were down though the crimes that took place seemed unimaginably violent – the legislature was busy seeing who could most effectively pander to the electorate. So far this legislative term, the state house had proposed everything up to and including televised executions.

Darcy said, 'The Governor has a brother who's in prison in Colorado.'

'Really? How do you know that?'

'I worked on his first campaign. Helped him write some speeches. Nominally, I'm a Democrat but he was very pro-woman so I decided to support him.'

'That's very interesting, Darcy. Thanks for telling me that.'

Darcy looked out the window.

The truck was still there but it never took the delivery man more than fifteen minutes to off-load.

'Well,' the Warden said. 'I'd better go take that call. Nice to see you, Darcy. And I really did enjoy your book.'

Darcy waited until the Warden had reached the corner and disappeared before she opened the door.

Hail was accompanying the rain now. The stones pinged and banged and bonged off fenders and windshields and trunk lids and roofs. It dinged and danced and donged.

Perfect cover, Darcy thought.

She ran out into the storm. She was soaked before she was halfway to the truck. Her short red hair had been darkened and plastered to her head. Her running shoes already squished.

God, she hoped she knew what she was doing.

She sure hoped so.

2

Darcy glanced left and right before throwing herself to the concrete and rolling beneath the truck. It appeared that nobody was watching her. If they were, she'd know soon enough. Guards with rifles would come running up and surround the truck.

The underside of the truck smelled of oil, road tar and wet metal. She had rolled under the truck so that her feet were pointing to the rear bumper. Now she had to quickly locate the tag axle for her hands and feet to hold on to.

A shout: 'See you in a month, Steve!' a woman's voice called from the dock.

Footsteps slapping the wet concrete. Hurrying through the rain. She could see the driver's heavy engineering boots momentarily. He climbed up into the cab. The door made a *chunking* noise as it was slammed shut. The whole truck was jostled as Steve settled behind the wheel. As she remembered, he was a pretty good-sized guy.

He started the engine – or tried to, anyway. It wouldn't fire properly. Two, three times he tried. But it wouldn't start.

Dammit, Darcy thought. All her planning – all her fear – all her expectations – she would escape and find out the truth—

The the engine stalled again.

'You need some help?' one of the guards called.

Darcy knew it was over then, right here, right under the truck. The engine wouldn't start – the rain sure didn't help – and she would be caught.

'Lemme try it one more time,' Steve said. 'It always does this.'

He ground the key once, twice, slammed the gas pedal to the floor.

The engine caught. He shifted the gears, took off the brake and then started slowly away from the loading dock. For the next two minutes, all Darcy could see were the bottom thirds of tires –

other vehicles passing by in the opposite lane.

Then Steve hit the brakes hard and she knew he was at the gate.

'You got everything off-loaded real fast today,' said the guard at the gate kiosk.

'Bulls're in the playoffs,' Steve said. 'Their game starts at five. I wanna get home a little early today.'

'Lucky dog,' the gate man said. 'I don't get off till six.'

'That's what you get for havin' such a cushy job to begin with.'

'Smart ass.'

You're supposed to be in a hurry, Darcy thought. You want to see the Bulls, remember? Get the hell out of here.

A phone rang in the kiosk.

'Hang on a second, will you?' the guard said.

'Sure.'

The guard answered the phone.

She was sure she'd been seen. And now the Warden was calling the front gate to stop the truck.

'OK,' the guard said into the phone. 'I'll tell him.'

The guard hung up.

'You forgot to sign out when you left the dock this morning.'

'Oh, hell, I'm sorry.'

'The dock called the assistant warden and he ragged on their ass for not getting you to sign out.'

'I'll make a point of it next time.'

'Be sure you do. The inmates in the dock're always the one who catch the hell.'

'Thanks again.'

'You think the Bulls can do it tonight?'

'I sure hope so,' Steve said.

She heard the automatic gates of cyclone fencing part and open. The top of the fencing was covered with razor wire.

Until now, Darcy didn't see that holding on to the underbelly of the truck would be any special problem.

But then, the truck hadn't been going any faster than 10 mph.

Now they were on open road and her impression changed quickly. For one thing, she felt every tilt and sway and bounce of the truck. The tiniest crack in the pavement had a bouncing effect on the truck's shock absorbers. She had to clamp down much harder on the metal beneath her fingers. Already, the muscles in her hands were starting to cramp.

12

She saw country roadside. Dead brown winter grass. Smashed pop bottles and crushed beer cans. And beyond the edge of the asphalt highway, she saw the spring-dead fields. Even though the hail had relented, the rain was coming harder. She couldn't roll out from under the truck when it was moving for fear a rear tire would run over her; and she had to be sure to choose a place where people weren't watching. One glimpse of her prison uniform and they'd call the police.

In her two years in prison, Darcy had never gotten used to the drab and sometimes scratchy uniforms the prisoners wore most of the time. Nor had she gotten used to the endless regimentation and degradation that most of the women were put through. These were women without education, job skills, hope or self-esteem. Only a few of them were in for violent crime. Most of them were sad addicts of one kind or another. They had distrusted Darcy at first, of course. A pretty woman, middle-class upbringing, successful mystery writer. But Darcy had always had a real sense of being odd, of never quite fitting. She'd grown up – until she was seventeen – with esotropia, which meant that her left eye 'traveled' and gave her face a somewhat comic, slightly cross-eyed look. Kids, being kids, had been merciless. 'Which one've of us you looking at now, Darcy?' the boys used to tease her because she couldn't focus her eye. It had taken eight years and four operations to correct her vision and by then she was spiritually an outsider. She never identified with the pretty, successful girls and boys. She mostly hung out with the nerds, the overweight, the crippled, the unpopular – except when her friends Amy and Cindy took her around. She was like their mascot – the two most popular girls in school and their tag-along Darcy. But even when she was with them, she felt like a spy – an observer of a glittering world that would never be hers, a world she didn't belong in. Her early years stood her in good stead in the prison. Most of the women sensed that Darcy was enough like them to trust. She helped them write their letters home and compose poems for their kids' birthdays and to help them contact lawyers when they had a real grievance. She became one of them.

The truck was traveling at around forty miles per hour.

Steve had turned on a country-western station. Somebody was giving Reba shit again and the little gal didn't like it at all.

The first time the truck stopped, she was going to roll out from underneath, pitch herself off into a gully, and lie there until dark. Given the weather, dark wasn't too far off.

The truck started to speed up. Must be coming to a hill. One of her hands slipped off. She cursed and grabbed the tag axle again, cracking two of her nails as she did so.

He must be travelling around sixty now, she thought. The truck hit a deep, water-filled rut. Dirty road water splashed across her back and bottom. The axle got soaked and even harder to hold on to.

She let herself play a terrible, concentration-shattering game of what-if again. What if she slipped of and the back wheels of the truck ran over her?

He made the steep hill. But he didn't cut back considerably on his speed. He was probably thinking of the play-off game. Wanting to be home in plenty of time to see it.

They went on like this for maybe five miles. Though her hold on the tag axle was not as strong as it once was, she was starting to get used to the feel of sixty or so – the impact of bumps, the splashing off watery road holes, the whistling wind.

Then he started honking. It was funny the way horns reflected their owner's moods. He didn't honk long and he didn't honk often – drivers were told to practice road courtesy, and faced corporate punishment if they got a complaint – but you could hear the anger in the honk.

The truck slowed back to forty. Steve honked again. This time he laid on the horn. Darcy could hear him swearing. The truck abruptly swung into the opposite lane. The move was so sudden and so powerful that she was almost knocked from her precarious perch. Road goop – mud, water, oil – started dripping down in her face. She sputtered and spat when the goop got into her mouth. God, how could she possibly hang on much longer?

Fifty, sixty, seventy, seventy-five. Steve was really hauling ass now.

She could see the tires and the lower half of the rear of the car they were passing. It was a blue four-door of ancient vintage. It didn't seem to be moving more than thirty-five miles per hour. The driver was probably some old guy who didn't appreciate Steve's sacred need to get home before the game started.

Just then, Steve swung the truck back into the proper lane. Once again, Darcy was nearly pitched off the underbelly, her fingers like claws trying to rake purchase on the muddy metal of the tag axle.

Steve settled back to around sixty miles per hour.

From what she could see, the sky was darkening. She even glimpsed a few low-hung fog lights on the front of passing trucks. They burned like sickly yellow eyes in the gloom.

Bumps. Splashes. Cramping fingers. Dragging butt. He had to slow soon. He *had* to.

But he didn't, not for at least another finger-clawing ten minutes.

When he did stop, she peeked beneath the edge of the truck's underside and saw that he'd come to a stop light. Moments later he turned left, pulling on to the wide concrete drive of what appeared to be a convenience store. She could see the bottom of two glass doors – in and out – the legs of three different newspaper-vending machines – and several small self-serve gasoline islands.

Steve filled the tank and then hurried off to the store. Thunder rumbled; rain slashed down.

If she crawled out from under now, somebody would see her for sure. But maybe this would be her only chance.

She was deciding whether she should roll out from under the truck now when the dog appeared, coming from around the corner of the building and heading straight toward her.

She wasn't sure what kind of dog he was – he vaguely resembled a Dobermann – but he was big and angry.

He stuck his dark face below the rear bumper and started sniffing at her. His wolf-like ears flattened to his head as he started to crawl toward her. He sniffed her boots then her pants, moving inexorably toward the front of the truck and her face.

She kept herself as still as possible. She couldn't afford to anger the animal. Her face was a mask of fear. She didn't want to get attacked; she didn't want her position exposed.

God, when was Steve going to come back and drive out of here, anyway?

A low rumble in the dog's chest.

His jaws opening to reveal his teeth.

Oh my God, she thought. He's really going to tear into me.

She once again considered rolling out from under the truck, and then running.

But at a busy store like this one, somebody would see her. And within minutes, the police would have choppers in the air and manpower on the ground. And dog-power, too, hunting dogs that police used in tracking escapees. Dogs every bit as powerful and menacing as the one in front of her right now.

'Git, boy,' she said, 'git.'

The animal looked singularly unimpressed. The rumble in its chest made it all the way up its throat to its mouth this time, and emerged as a trembling rumble.

'Go on, git,' she said again, uselessly.

Steve came back. He turned the ignition on and tromped on the gas but nothing happened. Maybe he had flooded the engine. Or maybe it was more serious mechanical trouble. He tried ignition and gas pedal again.

The dog was sniffing her hand now, the one closest to its face. If he tore into her hand, she'd lose her grip and would be discovered for sure—

Get out of here, Steve, she thought. Get out, *now*.

The dog's cold, wet nose pressed against her hand. She was waiting for his mouth to open and for those dagger-like teeth to tear a large hole in the back of her hand.

She started to tremble both from fear and exertion. She watched as the animal continued to sniff. She formed the words of a desperate prayer. The dog continued to growl. Then abruptly he swung his head to the front of the truck, where her face was.

He crawled up to her. He sat flat for a long moment as if deciding what to do. And then, just as he had with her hand, he put his wet nose to her cheek.

She knew not to flinch. She just closed her eyes and said another prayer and let him sniff her wherever he chose. She was trembling so badly, her fingers started to slide inexorably from the tag axle.

He lunged, grabbing the biceps area of her prison shirt with his teeth. He tore the cotton into long faded-blue shreds and then spat them out.

Then he went for her face. Instinctively, her left hand came off the cross arm to protect her face. She managed to cover herself enough so that he couldn't rip into her cheek or forehead. But then her other hand started to slip and she had to grab both parts of the cross arms. Otherwise she'd fall to the street.

Meanwhile, Steve was grinding away on the ignition up above.

The dog, enraged, turned to the back of the truck now. He grabbed a piece of her pants leg and began to rip into her flesh. She kicked out at him, got him once on the nose. This only angered him more. When he lunged at her this time, he made sure to shred her flesh with his teeth.

She almost screamed but caught herself at the very last moment. The stab of those canine teeth blinded her with pain. But she couldn't scream, not without bringing Steve down to look under his truck.

She lashed out with her torn leg and caught the animal on the muzzle.

Now he was frenzied, growling and barking, and turning back to her face.

He had just started to attack her when the truck exploded into life.

She covered her face as best she could with her arm. She didn't try to hang on by one hand this time. She didn't have the strength.

The dog tried two or three times to get past her arm but couldn't get past the way she was deflecting him.

Then the truck reached the highway and started gaining speed and the dog was knocked over on his side. It scrambled fast enough to get most of his body out from underneath but an edge of his paw was run over by the left rear tire.

The dog began yipping frantically in pain. For a moment, Darcy was terrified that the dog's anger would only make him doubly dangerous.

But as the truck picked up more and more speed, the dog disappeared in the distance. Apparently, more than his pride had been damaged. Even though it had tried to hurt her, she felt sorry for the dog.

Darcy clung to the underbelly of the truck, the strength of her arms, hands and fingers waning even more with each passing mile.

The next stop, no matter what, she was getting off.

3

The trailer sat alone out on the edge of town. On the east side ran a dry creek bed and on the west ran a railroad track. In the rain, the trailer looked even more abused and sad. The newest thing about it was the propane gas tank on the side. It looked like a giant silver bullet, perfect for hunting giant werewolves.

The black man was named R.K. Greaves. He was a large, square man with a wide face that mixed anger and grief in equal parts. Next to him stood his wife, Verlene, and their two children, Mike and Diane. They were twins and they were seven years old. Verlene was a slender woman with astonishingly intelligent and tender brown eyes.

All of them had coats and hats on to protect them from the cold, steady rain. They were looking down the long mud road that led to their trailer. A white police car with a big whip antenna was making its way toward them.

When the car reached them, it stopped and the motor was turned off and the Chief of Police stepped out.

The town had had some trouble accepting Amy Foster as Chief. She was just too darned pretty to be Chief, too feminine. Why, she had coltish wrists and coltish ankles and a freckled face and a cute little nose and about the sweetest blue eyes you ever saw. And she couldn't have weighed more than one twenty-five, which wasn't much given her five-ten height. And she was a local gal. Born and raised right here, Homecoming Queen her senior year in high school, and an honor grad when she graduated from the University with an MA in Police Science. She *stayed* up-to-date, too. At least once a year, she and her officers took turns going to Des Moines for further training at the Academy.

'Morning,' she said, snugging on her plastic rain coat as she left the car.

'They did it again,' R.K. said.

'Can't you at least say hello to the lady?' Verlene said. 'Excuse his rudeness, Chief.'

'Don't worry about it, Verlene,' the Chief said. 'I don't blame him for being upset.'

'Does that gun shoot real bullets?' little Mike asked.

The Chief smiled. She had a great smile. 'Yes, it does, Mike. But it only shoots bad people. Not good little boys like you.'

Mike, flattered, smiled back at her.

'You can see it on this far side here,' R.K. said.

The kids started to walk along with their father and the Chief, but Verlene put gentle hands on their shoulders. 'No need for you two to take another look at it.'

'It says "nigger," doesn't it, Mom?'

'Yes, it does.' Tears glistened in Verlene's eyes.

'You know,' R.K. said as they walked around to the far side of the trailer. 'After I broke my back working out to the sand pits and had to move out of town to out there – I didn't have no insurance and we had to let our little house go, near broke Verlene's heart, the way she loved that house – figured the bigots'd leave us alone. I mean, it's one thing not to want us in town. But out here? Why would they care?'

It said NIGGER all right. In fact, it said NIGGER four times, black spray paint, a different angle for each use of the word.

The Chief went over and touched the paint and sighed. 'This'll taking some scrubbing to get off.'

'We got the other off,' R.K. said bitterly. 'We'll get this off, too.'

This was the third time in two weeks the Chief had come out here because of graffiti sprayed on their trailer house.

The Chief turned back to R.K. 'You didn't see anything?'

'Nope. Nothin'.'

'Hear anything?'

'Nope. Didn't *hear* nothin', either.'

The Chief's eyes scanned the grass and then raised to take in the entire small valley out here. Hardscrabble lives had always been lived out here. There were some shacks to the west where people still used outhouses. It could have been a hundred years ago. R.K. and his family fit right in. At least they had a flush toilet and electricity.

'I've got to ask you the same questions again. R.K. I know you're tired of hearing them but I don't have any choice.'

R.K. smiled sadly. 'Why don't we inside and have a cup of coffee?'

The Chief laughed. 'You didn't hear me say "no", did you? I'm getting real tired of this rain.'

A blue glass cream-pitcher was angled over the tan coffee cup. 'Say when.'

A stream of white cream trickled into the cup.

'When,' the Chief said. Then, 'Thanks, Verlene.' She looked around. 'You did a very nice job with this.'

'You mean it doesn't look like a trailer?' Verlene laughed. 'That's what the mail man said to me the other day. I guess he thought he was complimenting me.'

They'd brought their furniture from the house they'd had to give up. While it wasn't expensive stuff, it was nice enough, and it lent the trailer a very homey feel. The blue couch and matching blue wing chairs were especially elegant.

'So let's get it over with, Chief,' R.K. said. 'Ask me all those damn dumb questions of yours.'

'Now there's a nice attitude, R.K.,' Verlene said. 'Lady comes all the way out here to help us, and you insult her.'

'Wasn't insulting her,' R.K. said. 'It's just I answer the same questions every time. No, I didn't see nobody; no, I didn't hear nobody; no, no white folks have hassled me lately or anything; and no, there ain't nobody at work givin' me a hard time. I pretty much get along with everybody.'

'Well, don't forget Runyon,' Verlene said. 'He gave you some trouble last week.'

'Who's Runyon?' the Chief said. 'By the way, this is great coffee.'

'One of R.K.'s experiments,' Verlene said. 'He likes to mix different kinds of coffee together and see what he gets.'

'Runyon's this guy at work,' R.K. said. 'Last week somebody stole his billfold out of his locker. Broke right in and took it. He blamed me. He said it wasn't because I was black. Said it was because I had the locker right next to his. But I knew better and so did everybody else. He went to the boss and said he was gonna go to the police.'

'Then this kid said he did it,' Verlene said.

'Just started last week,' R.K. said. 'White kid. Says he'd got a bad crack problem and that's why he took Runyon's billfold. 'Cause he needed money so bad.'

21

'Runyon apologize?' the Chief said.

'Apologize?' R.K. said. 'You tell her, Verlene.'

'Next day we get this envelope in the mail and it's got a fifty-dollar bill in it and it says, 'I'm sorry about what happened, R.K. Runyon." '

'Well, he doesn't sound like anybody who'd spray your house,' the Chief said.

'He sure don't,' R.K. said.

'And there's nobody else who's been giving you a hard time?'

'Nobody,' R.K. said.

The Greaves were the only black family in Parkhurst. Others had been here for a time over the years but they always seemed to move away. A couple of times, the National Association For The Advancement of Colored People investigated complaints from some of Parkhurst's black citizens but nothing much ever came of it. There wasn't any evidence that pointed to anything. The harassment seemed to be random and unorganized, the most difficult kind of all to combat.

After the second incident with the Greaves, the local newspaper ran an editorial called 'Whither Hatred?', which claimed that each and every citizen of Parkhurst was responsible for the way the Greaves were being treated. This was not a universally loved editorial. In fact, the paper's letter column was filled with angry tirades denouncing the 'foolishness' of the editorial.

None of which, either way, did a whole hell of a lot for the Greaves, good intentions rarely being enough to solve a problem.

You had a black family that somebody kept harassing. The point of the harassment was unknown. Were these high-school kids just having some mean fun? Or was this something more sinister, evidence of a hate-group operating right here in town? Last year, the town's only Jewish family had been likewise harassed, a big swastika painted on their garage door and threatening phone calls coming all night. The family had finally moved away, the parents worried about the effects the ugly incidents were having on their kids.

'You know what they want, don't you?' the Chief said.

'What?' R.K. said.

'They want you to move away.'

'Well, that sure as hell ain't gonna happen.'

But Verlene didn't look so sure. She glanced to the back of the trailer, where the kids were playing in their room, and dropped her voice. 'I don't care to be around much more of this, R.K. I'd just as *soon* move if this keeps up.'

'You'll be giving in to them,' the Chief said.

'Sometimes, that's the only thing you *can* do,' Verlene said.

'Not me, I'm not goin' anywhere.'

'Even if it starts affecting your children, R.K.?' Verlene said softly.

R.K. made a frown then reached across the table and took her hand. 'You know I wouldn't to nothin' to hurt those kids of ours.'

'I'm going to find out who did this,' the Chief said, 'and make sure it doesn't happen again.'

'You've sure been a good friend to us, Chief,' Verlene said. Then, 'Kids, come out here and say goodbye to Chief Foster.'

'Oh, that's all right,' the Chief said. 'Let them play.'

'Teach them some manners,' Verlene said.

The two children appeared and stood formally and politely in front of the Chief. This was an in-service day so they didn't have to go to school.

'What do you say to the Chief, kids?'

'Thank you for coming here, Chief,' the little girl said, very shyly.

'Thank you for coming here, Chief,' the little boy said.

'Well, thank you both for being so nice and polite.'

Verlene said, 'Now, you two kids run along and play.'

The Chief stood up, the leather of her Sam Browne belt creaking as she did so. Everything sparkled and shined on the Chief, badge, ID bar, Sam Browne, bullets and shoes. She was a model of police decorum.

'Thanks again, Chief,' Verlene said.

'Yes, thank you very much,' R.K. said. Then, 'I'll walk you out to your car.'

When she put her hand on the car door, R.K. said, 'I wanted to tell you this without Verlene or the kids hearing.' Pause. They stood there in their rain coats and rain hats looking at each other. 'You know what I been thinkin' about doin'?'

'What?'

'Buyin' me a gun.'

She shook her head. 'Real bad idea, R.K. You're liable to shoot Verlene or one of the children rather than the bastard doing all this.'

'I got to do somethin'. I don't want my kids to grow up this way.

This's like livin' in the South when I was little.'

She put a hand on his shoulder. 'We're going to find him, R.K., and then we're going to throw his ass in prison for a long, long time.'

'I appreciate you working on this personally,' R.K. said.

'That's my job, R.K.' Then, after she had opened the door and started to slide beneath the steering wheel, 'Thanks again for the coffee.'

'My pleasure.'

She turned the Plymouth around in the grass in front of the trailer and then headed back down the mud road.

She looked at her fingers on the steering wheel. There were tiny splotches of black spray paint across three of her fingers. She would have painted NIGGER five times last night but the can had run out of paint.

4

The truck stopped.

Darcy dropped her head so she could get some sense of her surroundings. They were in town somewhere because she could see the wheels of parked cars and she could see curbings. Not too far away was a manhole cover.

She couldn't go on any further. Her strength was gone. She had to make her break right here. And she had to hurry. Steve was flooring the engine in neutral to keep it alive.

Her hands hurt from gripping the tag axle; her legs hurt from the dog's savage bites.

She took a deep breath and rolled out from under the truck.

She scrambled to her feet, surveying the street as she did so. A grade school covered most of the east block, residences covered all of the west side. She recognized where she was, Bancroft, a town she often traveled through, to and from Parkhurst.

Then she saw the two little girls coming down the sidewalk toward her. Pigtails; school books; curious expressions. She knew they'd seen her roll out from under the truck. They walked haltingly, as if they were afraid to come near her.

She had to get out of here. But the moment she put real weight on her left leg, the dog bite began to throb painfully.

She gritted her teeth and hurried down the block. She needed to find an alley.

Luckily, there were only two passing cars: one a van packed with youngsters, another a small delivery truck. Neither driver paid any attention to her.

She hobbled around the corner and limped as quickly as she could toward the alleys. She knew how to get out of Bancroft and start her way to Parkhurst. There was a train route that took her through steep hills. They'd be perfect cover. The thing was, she'd

25

need to get out of Bancroft first. The girls who'd just spotted her were bound to tell somebody. Her escape would soon be on the news – if it wasn't already.

Nightfall couldn't come quickly enough.

She reached the alley, looked both ways, and started down the narrow, graveled lane running between sagging garages.

She was soaked, and the rain was soaking her more; and she was in pain, and moving was putting her in even more pain. But what could she do? She had to reach Parkhurst sometime tonight. Tomorrow might be too late and, if it was, her only hope of proving herself innocent would be gone forever.

Ken McCain was out in the north pasture when he got the news. Thunderheads promised imminent rain so Ken decided to turn out all the horses he could early.

The McCain Stables made most of its money boarding horses. Ken's job was to feed the animals and clean their stalls and turn them out every day unless their owners were here to ride them. Turning them out meant letting them run in the grass pasture. The currying and the brushing he left to the owners themselves.

The stables made money buying and selling horses. A lot of people – especially kids – tired of their animals after a while and all but deserted them. Or sometimes families moved away. Ken bought the horses and then sold them, hopefully for a profit.

The stables also had three stallions that it made available for leasing fees; and every spring the brood mares birthed a few colts that would later be sold.

Ken wasn't in danger of becoming a tycoon but he enjoyed what he was doing. The only thing he loved more than his horses was his wife. Ironically, he was thinking of her when the call came.

He was out in the north pasture making sure that a certain colt was walking all right – the animal looked suspiciously stiff earlier today – when the flip phone in his back pocket went off.

'Ken?'

'Yes.'

'This is Dave Wingfield over to the supermarket.'

'Hi, Dave.'

'Just thought I'd tell you. I'm not even sure Amy knows yet. The dispatcher was looking for her, in fact. About Darcy.'

Ken felt a chill pass through him. Had something happened to Darcy?

'What about Darcy?'

'She escaped a while ago.'

'Escaped?'

'My cousin, Fred. The cop?'

'Right—'

'He called me and told me about it. He was at the station when the warden called.'

'Was anybody hurt?'

'No. They're not even sure how she got out yet. But she's gone.'

Ken thought about the past several months. How Darcy wouldn't answer his letters. How she wouldn't see him when he requested visits. The misery of these months. What was going on with her, anyway? In the weeks before her arrest for murder, they'd had some arguments about all the book touring she was doing. She'd been gone an awful lot suddenly. Ken's first wife had had an affair during their marriage – she'd fallen in love with her boss – and Ken had some problems with trusting women completely. The rational part of him knew that Darcy would never be unfaithful – just as he'd never be unfaithful to her. But the irrational part of his mind had started to pester him when she was gone to Chicago and New York and LA and . . . But they'd worked through it. Their marriage had never been better. And then she was arrested for murder.

'Thanks for telling me, Dave.'

'Just thought you'd like to know.'

He put the phone in his back pocket and then stood there as the first sprinkles pattered on his shoulders and the edge of his white Stetson.

He just kept thinking about all the danger Darcy had put herself in. Prison was hazardous enough – just last month one inmate had put a knife in another's eye – but being on the run from the law was even worse.

He wondered where she was. What she was doing.

He wondered if he'd hear from her.

Amy had just reached town when her cell phone buzzed.

'Chief?' asked the familiar voice of Connie Weymeyer, the day-time dispatcher.

'Yes.'

'Thought you'd want to know. Just received word that Darcy McCain escaped from prison this afternoon.'

27

'You're kidding. That's a very secure compound.'

'I know. They think she hid under a truck and got out that way.'

Judge Carmichael, Amy thought. Somebody must have got word to Darcy that Carmichael was dying, and she had to get out in time to talk to him.

Damn Carmichael, anyway. Why in God's name had he ever sent that letter to Darcy in prison? Because of the letter, enigmatic as it was, Darcy had tried to get a new trial. Thankfully, the appelate court had turned her down.

As she came into Parkhurst, Amy felt her usual proprietary pride in the place. She'd grown up here and come back here after spending her first two post-college years as a Chicago cop. The downtown was largely unchanged from when she'd been young. And she liked it that way. They were old-fashioned style stores, for the most part, built in the late forties and early fifties. Once there'd been a Woolworth's here and a Western Auto and an A&P, names unknown to the young generation. People stood on corners talking with each other and laughing; and in the small city park old men played checkers on benches in front of the Civil War memorial while a dozen pigeons perched on the edge of the bandstand roof watching them.

Amy loved the place and wanted to keep it just as quiet and peaceful as her father had. Dad had been police chief here for thirty-five years.

She passed a church and a public swimming pool and a full block of antique stores. She passed the public library with its ever-vigilant stone lions guarding both sides of the front steps. And she passed the city hall where she had just spent a good number of hours over the past two weeks making the case for an increased police budget. The city council's first reaction was, When the crime rate's this low, why do you need more money? She had to make them realize that *keeping* the crime rate low was a matter of expending the necessary dollars. Not an easy sell in a county where property taxes had just been hiked significantly. The citizens weren't in a particularly charitable mood.

But all the citizens had to do was think back ten years. Parkhurst was only five miles off the Interstate. Gamblers, hookers and drifters all veered off the Interstate and came to town. The place got a reputation quickly; a sleepy little neighborhood had been transformed into a sinful border-style town. Drugs appeared here for the first time in a serious way, quickly filtering down to the high school, and even junior high, level. And then a little girl, a six-year-old named Wendy Thompson, was sexually assaulted and murdered by a neighbor. The worst thing was, at the trial the Judge ruled that certain evidence had been obtained illegally. He threw the case out and the defendant walked free. Then, after a few months, the district began to change back the way it had been. It was as if the community as a whole had come to its senses. It wanted to be a sleepy respectable town again.

In the past eight years, only two murders had taken place, and those in the past sixty-five days. Two good friends of Amy's father, in fact, and members of The Thursday Night Poker Club.

But not even with these unsolved murders on their hands would the city council give her more money. They called the murders 'flukes' and insisted she had plenty of budget.

She reached the two-storey stucco building that was the police department on the first floor and a jail on the second, and swung into a PRIVATE PARKING space on the side. She hurried in a side door, exposed to the cold, slanting rain for only a few seconds.

The station smelled of floor wax. The place had beautiful hardwood flooring dating back to a time in the thirties when it had been a fancy restaurant and mini-hotel. Twice a year, the city council came up with the money to clean and wax the floors. The smell always reminded her of going back to school in autumn, when everything smelled new and clean.

'Bet you got soaked,' said the receptionist-secretary, JoEllen Hastings. She was a fiftyish woman who defiantly wore the same sort of bee-hive hairdo she'd been sporting the night she finally got a marriage proposal from one E. Jack Hastings, a legendary slow-dance man. He was legendary to JoEllen, anyway. This had been in 1963. Local wiseasses said JoEllen was related to Marge of 'The Simpsons'.

'Not too bad,' Amy said. Then, 'Any further word on Darcy?'

JoEllen shook the volcano on top of her head. 'Huh-uh. I just can't get over it.'

'That she escaped?'

'Yeah. I mean, she must weigh all of a hundred pounds.'

'They beef up. In prison.'

'I thought that was just men.'

Amy was looking through her mail as she talked. 'I'm sure a

woman's facility has weights and stuff like that, too.'

Amy finished with her mail and frowned.

'Nothing good, huh?' JoEllen said.

'No.'

Amy started walking to her office door.

'I'd be careful, Chief.'

'Careful?' Amy said from the doorway.

'You never know what she's going to do.'

'I'll be fine,' Amy said.

'They go psycho in prison sometimes. All that time on their hands, they brood about things and it makes them crazy.'

She might look like Marge Simpson, Amy thought, but she often sounded more like *Homer* Simpson. Amy wasn't physically afraid of Darcy – but she was afraid of what Darcy could stir up.

Amy went into her office and closed the door. She had purposely kept the decor simple. Something else she'd learned from her father: when you start treating yourself like somebody special that's when your officers start to resent you. The office contained a desk, chair, three khaki-green filing cabinets, a throw rug and an assortment of framed photos on the wall, most of times past in the department, dating back as far as the 1880s, when the cops had worn kepis as their official hats.

When she sat down, she picked up the only photo on her desk, a small gilt-framed shot of Ted, her husband. Dr Ted. The handsome boy she'd loved since second grade, the only true friend she'd ever had except for Darcy McCain and Cindy Carmichael. She'd done everything except kidnap Ted, even lied to Ted about being pregnant, so he'd marry her. And then look at how things turned out.

She put the photo back and then opened the center desk drawer for her roster of officers. She'd have to pull everybody in right away, even Sam Deeds, who was enjoying three days off on the Iowa River, fishing. She knew how to reach him.

The state boys and girls would be all over this town within the next few hours. If the paranoid local militia thought they'd seen a lot of helicopters in the sky before (along with a myriad UFOs), just wait a couple of hours. Helicopters would fill the sky. The countryside would be crawling with cops – and dogs. Hunting dogs from half the counties in the state would join the manhunt. Looking for Darcy McCain.

The phone buzzed. 'The Mayor's on line one, Chief.'

'Thanks.'

Amy sighed before she picked up. The Mayor was a real pain-in-the-ass. He'd done his postgraduate work in over-reacting.

'Amy.'

'Morning, Mayor.'

'You heard about Darcy McCain?'

'Yes, I did.'

'What're we going to do about it?'

'I'm not exactly expecting a crime wave, your honor.'

'She'll come back here.'

'I assume she will.'

'And she'll be armed.'

'Maybe. But I'd bet against it if I had to put money on it.'

'People are scared.'

You're scared, you mean, Amy thought. If anything goes wrong, the people won't re-elect you in the fall.

'The state people will be here to help us and so will the county folks. They're probably looking for her already, your honor.'

'Amy, we've got to get her.'

'I know we do. And we will.'

'I sure wish I had your self-confidence.'

'As I said, your honor, she's not a mad dog.'

'Prison changes people.'

'It doesn't change them *that* much.'

'Oh, God,' the Mayor whined. 'I sure wish this was all over with.'

And they said women were weak.

'I'll keep you posted,' Amy said and then, with a great deal of pleasure, hung up.

5

Dr Ted Foster, MD, was having himself a little nightcap. That it was 12:14 P.M. in the afternoon, and that he was in his office at the Parkhurst medical clinic and that he was already a wee bit tipsy – none of it mattered because, by God, he could handle his liquor. He was positively absolutely sure that almost nobody ever got even the slightest hint that he pretty much had something to drink three or four times a day during office hours.

Except Brad, of course. High and mighty Dr Brad Rayburn, one of the other three owners of the clinic.

Brad was a trouble-maker. Brad could never leave well enough alone.

A couple of times a month, Brad would get with the remaining two partners and start shrieking that they had to do something about fucking-Ted before it was too late. That was what he usually called Ted – fucking-Ted – behind his back. Ted knew this because he'd overheard him using the phrase many times. Just as he'd once heard Brad conducting one of his conspiracy seminars on just how they were going to get *rid* of fucking-Ted.

Screw Brad. Screw them all. He was just as good a doctor as any of them – and one hell of a lot better than Brad, who would have been happier being a CPA than a doctor. Money was his only interest.

A knock on his door. 'Yes?' he said.

Susan, his nurse, came in.

'I think you may have forgotten a patient, Doctor,' she said politely.

'Patient?'

'In Examining Room D. Mrs Peterson. Flu symptoms.'

'Oh,' he said. 'I'll be right in there.'

'Thank you, Doctor.' Then she walked over and held out two

pieces of paper. 'I did some more checking on that patient you saw. The one where the insurance form came back with two different names on it? Why don't I put it in your jacket?' Meaning that she knew he'd never look at it in this condition, but maybe when he'd gone home and slept it off, he could read it.

'Thanks, Susan.'

Brad was in the hall getting a drink of water when Ted came out of his office. Brad and Ted were contrasts in every way – Brad, thin, wiry, blond and contemptuous; Ted big, rangy, red-haired and hearty.

When he was finished with his drink, Brad stood up and said, 'That a new after-shave you're wearing, Ted?' Before Ted could answer, Brad said, 'Eau De Jim Beam?'

He stepped right up to Ted and stage-whispered. 'That fucking patient of yours, Mrs Peterson, has been in that fucking examining room for over half a fucking hour. Now you get your ass in there and handle her. And I mean right now.' Then, even angrier: 'Do I need to remind you of how important her husband is in this town?'

Then he stalked away.

He stood outside the door, preparing himself. Shoulders thrown back. Head held high. Hands steady. He even cleared his throat so that he'd be ready to speak the moment he crossed the threshold. He cleared it twice, actually, once for timbre, once to make sure he wouldn't slur any words.

Mrs Peterson was a plump older lady with tinted hair and a pair of huge eyeglasses. Her blues eyes looked sad and trapped behind the large lenses. She wore a white frilly blouse with an old-fashioned brooch at the neck. Her skirt was long and royal blue.

He saw her sniffing almost as soon as he came through the door into the small square room. Had he forgotten his Binanca? No, he *never* forgot his Binanca. Maybe he'd spilled a little on him. That happened sometimes, and that's when he noticed people sniffing the air.

'Afternoon, Wilma.'

'Afternoon, Doctor.'

He could see how she was watching him. Carefully, very carefully. Her small mouth was abloom with disapproval.

'How can I help you?'

'I have a terrible cough, a headache and a sick stomach.'

'We're seeing a lot of that today.'

And that was when he bumped into the tall, narrow, glass-fronted medical cabinet. It banged against the back wall.

He smiled. 'I always seem to be bumping into things.'

The disapproval grew on her mouth; now it could also be seen in her eyes.

'Let's listen to your chest a little bit here,' he said, unfurling the stethoscope on the small table to his right.

He started to raise the stethoscope to his ears then dropped it. He had to bend over to get it. He felt dizzy suddenly, as if he was going to pitch forward. He desperately grabbed the edge of the table with his right hand and the edge of the examination table with his left. He was safely propped up, at least for the time being.

'There I go again,' he said.

He'd stopped himself from falling but now he had to figure out how to bend down and pick up the stethoscope without pitching over. If he'd pitch over, she'd *know* he was drunk. He felt he was doing a pretty good job of keeping the truth from her.

'I've had enough, Doctor.'

'What?' he said.

'I was sure I smelled liquor on the breath the last few times I came here. Now I'm sure of it. You're drunk, Doctor. It's not even one in the afternoon and you're already drunk.'

'Listen, please, Mrs Peterson—'

She slid off the examination table, grabbed her purse and stalked to the door. He had to turn around to see this. He still felt dizzy and turning around just made him feel all the sicker.

He felt trapped, still clinging with one hand to the small table and with the other hand to the examination table. He was afraid to move, afraid he'd fall flat and not be able to get up.

He was muttering something but even *he* wasn't sure what he was saying. Something about Darcy. God, Amy would kill him if she knew that he still thought about Darcy. Absolutely kill him.

The door burst open. He squinted up at the high and mighty Dr Rayburn, the sanctimonious little prick.

'You're all done here, Foster,' Rayburn said. 'As soon as our partners hear what Mrs Peterson told Sandy at the front desk, you're done, pal. All fucking done.'

Foster was getting ready with this absolutely great defense of himself but before he could quite form any words, he collapsed, unconscious, on the floor.

Where was he?

Was he asleep?

Where was he?

'He's coming around.'

The voice was familiar. Greg's voice. Greg Holliman. One of his other partners in the health clinic. What was Greg doing in his bedroom? Did Amy know that Greg was here? She'd want to cover herself. What the hell was Greg doing here, anyway?

'Can you hear me, Ted?' Mark Dawson said. Mark was Ted's other clinic partner.

This was *very* strange indeed. Here he was in his bedroom at home and Greg and Mark were here. Must have broken in. Some kind of prank or something. Greg was the one with a beard who looked like a scientist in a Sci-Fi Channel movie. Mark was the balding one with the baseball-sized Adam's apple. He looked like a research scientist. He fooled everybody by having the best bedside manner in the state. His slight air of aloofness, even arrogance, vanished when he was with a patient. Both Mark and Greg looked crisp and professional in their white medical jackets.

Ted opened one eye.

His office in the clinic. What was he doing here? This must be part of a dream. Greg and Mark weren't actually in the bedroom. They were just in the dream.

He opened his other eye.

The office.

'How you doing, my friend?' Greg said.

'This is my office, right?'

'You got it, tiger,' Mark said. 'This is definitely your office.' Then he glanced at Mark and frowned.

A knock.

Greg went to open the door.

A familiar voice said, 'It's just made fresh. Good and hot and black.'

'Thanks, Julie.'

Julie the nurse. This really *was* the office.

Ted started to sit up in the chair. A laser beam of pain hit him directly above his left eye. He groaned. Then he tasted stale blood in his mouth.

'I take it I fucked up,' he said.

'You fucked up but good,' Greg said.

'With old lady Peterson yet,' Mark said.

'Just don't start yelling at me, all right?' Ted said.

'The yelling we'll leave to Brad,' Mark said.

'Good. I appreciate it.' He started to sit up. His head began throbbing again. 'Will it do any good to say I'm sorry?'

'Not much,' Greg said. 'I mean, you say it every time you fuck up like this.'

'Well, I guess I'll say it anyway,' Ted said, trying to sound amused. 'I'm sorry.'

'Drunken apologies don't have much influence any more, Ted,' Mark said.

'Drunken? Do I *sound* drunk?'

'You think you could stand up to a breathalyzer, my friend?' Greg said. 'You'd set an all-time record.' He handed Ted a cup of steaming coffee.

Ted accepted it with a nod of thanks. He blew on it, then set it down in front of a framed photograph of Amy and their oldest daughter Megan. He wanted to escape into the photograph, the nice sunny day along the Iowa river where the snapshot had been taken. He didn't want to be sitting in this small, blandly decorated office listening to two of his partners while they were pouring coffee down him.

'I'm sober,' Ted said.

'Good,' Mark said. 'Then you'll be able to remember what I'm about to tell you.'

The way his partners glanced at each other, Ted knew that what they were going to say was not something he wanted to hear.

'I'll be right up front with you,' Mark said. 'Brad wants to fire your ass.'

'He can't fire me. I'm a full partner.'

'Go back and read our contract, Ted. There's a clause that covers stuff like this.'

'Stuff like what?'

'Like what, Ted? Are you insane? Stuff like coming to the office drunk at least once a week. And today, passing out while a patient was still in the room.'

'I didn't pass out. I fell down.'

'Hey, great. There's a useful distinction.' Mark glared at Greg.

37

'You following this? He didn't pass out, he fell down.'

'Did somebody push you?' Greg said to Ted.

'No.'

'Was there a tornado that landed on the clinic I wasn't aware of?'

'You guys don't have to do this bullshit.'

'Oh? We don't?' Mark said. 'OK, we'll stop treating you like a child if you admit to us that you were drunk and passed out.'

'That isn't what happened.'

'No,' Mark said, 'then what happened?'

'I've been having bad sinuses and I took some Ceclor and it just made me woozy.'

'Not that Ceclor story again,' Greg said. 'God, at least come up with something new, all right?'

'I want to hear you say it,' Mark said.

'I wasn't drunk.'

'Of course, you were,' Mark said. 'That's why you passed out.'

'I didn't pass out. I fell down.'

'Oh, shit,' Mark said, 'I give up.' Then, 'Tell him, Greg.'

Greg said, 'We're going to put you on a ninety-day suspension with pay.'

'You don't have any right to—'

'You mind if I finish, Ted?'

'Listen to him very carefully here, Ted,' Mark said. 'He's laying it out all for you.'

'During the ninety days of your suspension, we want you to put yourself into a de-tox clinic and dry out. Then we want you to join one of the local Alcoholic Anonymous and start going to meetings at least twice a week. And if you do these things, we'll let you start practicing at the clinic again in ninety days.'

Ted sat and looked back and forth at their faces. 'You have any idea how arrogant this is?'

'Here we go,' Mark said.

'This is part of the game,' Greg said. 'We try and talk straight to you and you attack us. Well, this time, it won't work, Ted. We're not overstepping and whether you believe it or not, we really do have your best interests at heart.'

'This is final final?' Ted said.

'Final final,' Mark said.

'You should feel lucky we didn't give in to Brad. He had his way, you'd be history. Believe me.'

'So now I should be grateful, huh?'

'Right now, I don't give a shit what you are, Ted,' Mark said. He sounded weary suddenly. 'All I want is your word that you're going to clear out of here right now.'

'Right now?' Ted snapped. 'What the hell're you talking about? I've got patients to see this afternoon.'

'We're going to divide up your patients among the three of us,' Greg said.

'Well, isn't that sweet of you?'

'You want me to call Amy to come and pick you up?' Mark said.

'I'll get home the way I *want* to.'

Greg said, 'I don't want you to drive. That's the least we can do for this community.'

'You're so fucking sanctimonious,' Ted said. 'You make me sick.'

Three minutes later, Greg was helping him down the hallway to the back door.

Ted stood in the alley looking at a long line of brown dumpsters that belonged to the various businesses that officed in this small, professional park. Nothing was quite real, yet. Even the harsh words with Greg and Mark had softened somewhat now. This was all bluff, all bullshit. He'd show up tomorrow morning and everything would be fine. Brad would be a prick but when *wasn't* Brad a prick? Tell me something new.

Only now did he realize it was still raining. Not anywhere near as hard as it had been earlier. But he was definitely getting wet.

He looked longingly at his sleek little black Mazda sportster. He was half tempted to go drive it – but why push Greg and Mark any further?

He'd get a cab.

There was a bar just around the corner, a nice little mid-afternoon kind of bar where they had one of those satellite sports hookups, and a guy could go in there and have a few toddies and people would leave him alone.

He started walking unsteadily to the head of the alley.

6

By mid-afternoon, Darcy had managed to work her way – mostly through alleys and large storm sewers – out of the town of Bancroft and into a large railroad yard. The yard was busy, three different engines coupling up with boxcars. One of the tracks was headed east, which meant it would most likely pass through, if not stop in, Parkhurst.

She needed to get in one of the boxcars.

The railroad yard was in a small valley below. Heavy ground fog lent the yard an eerie, unreal look. To reach what appeared to be an empty car, Darcy needed to go down the hill, cross three empty tracks, and hop in one of the empties – plenty of opportunity for somebody to see her.

By this point in the afternoon, the rain had let up but was still coming down and the sky was almost as dark as night. Maybe she'd get lucky. Maybe nobody would see her.

She didn't have much of a choice, did she? She couldn't stay behind this tree much longer.

She started down the hill, which was largely mud by now. She had to dig her toes in to stay upright. The going was slow.

When she reached the flat, she saw the train engine backing up toward her. It was moving slowly but at this rate the engineer would see her within the next half minute or so.

She made the mistake of trying to run. She got across one set of tracks well enough but she tripped on the second set, sprawling face down across the rocky bed between the tracks. She cursed and scrambled to her feet. The engine was only seconds away.

She struggled to her feet, pain throbbing in her knee – either she'd landed on a sharp rock or broken glass – and staggered toward the empty boxcars one more set of tracks away.

Down here, the ground fog was worse. Now, she could barely see where she was going.

Straight ahead, she thought. Straight ahead and I'll run into the empty car.

Which was when she tripped a second time.

This time, she didn't hurt herself. She just sprawled across the rail bed.

'Hurry up!' a voice said somewhere behind the fog. 'They're gonna spot you any second now!'

The voice was that of an old man's. An excited old man. 'Hurry up!' he repeated.

She got to her feet and stumbled forward. She could see the outline of the boxcar and a figure moving around in the open door.

She moved as quickly as she could. But she didn't want to fall again so she didn't try running.

'Here,' the voice said. 'Take my hand.'

Through the swirling fog, she got her first good glimpse of him. A hobo in a weird long-billed cap, several layers of shirts and sweaters and trousers, and a stench she picked up even from here. He waggled his hands at her.

She took them and he pulled her up with startling strength. She stood inside the empty boxcar.

'Get out of the doorway,' the hobo said. Then he nodded toward the west end of the car. He moved so quickly it was hard to imagine that he was as old as he looked. She imagined he was well into his late sixties, if not older.

She went to the back of the car with him.

He had it all fixed up. Sleeping roll, three cans of pork and beans, three cans of sweet potatoes and a Coleman battery-operated lantern which he turned on.

The boxcar smelled cold and dank. She hadn't ever realized before that wood *could* smell dank.

'You want a Pepsi?' He looked like the last hippie, right down to his graying beard, hair tied in a pony-tail and the tie-dyed T-shirt he wore under his heavy pea coat.

'That sounds great.'

He looked right at her and smiled with little stubs of blackened teeth. 'You don't look like no 'bo to me.'

'Guess I'm not.'

He reached behind him in a paper sack and took out two cans of Pepsi. 'Ain't got no ice.'

'That's fine. I really appreciate you helping me like this.'

He handed her the Pepsi which she opened immediately. She needed the moisture *and* the caffeine.

As she started to drink, he said, 'Know what this is?'

He held up it up for her to see.

'Looks like a radio.'

'Yep, that's what it is all right.' It was a black transistor radio that an adult could fit in his hand.

She smiled nervously. 'Guess you've got all the comforts of home here.'

He smiled at her with those teeth again. 'Yep. Guess I do. And the rent's real cheap, too.'

'Thanks again.' Then, 'You headed any place special?'

His smile faded. 'I'm tryin' to find the man who killed my best friend, Yancey.'

'Oh. I'm sorry. About your friend, I mean. The police can't do anything about it?'

He shook his head. 'What do they care about one more 'bo? There's this whole gang of 'bos that ride the rails and kill people.'

'Why do they kill people?'

'Power. So the other 'bos'll be afraid of 'em. They get off on scarin' people. Seen one guy, they cut his head off and then nailed it down to the top of a boxcar.'

'Why'd they kill your friend?'

'He wouldn't give them his last pack of smokes.' He looked at her with sad, guilty eyes. 'I seen it comin' – what was gonna happen, I mean – and I got outta there. I shoulda stayed and helped him, I guess.' It was a guilt he'd never get rid of. 'So now all I can do is find the guy who killed him. Big guy with one good eye and a cheap blue glass eye. Reckon he won't be *too* hard to find.' He slipped a small hand gun from his pocket. 'Ain't gonna ask him no question or nothin'. Just gonna shoot him right on the spot.' Then he smiled again, sadly. 'Sounds like one of your mystery novels, don't it?'

Darcy said carefully, 'What makes you think I write mystery novels?'

He picked up the tiny radio he'd set on the floor.

'You're all over the news, young lady. A whole lot of people are looking for you.'

In the light of the Coleman lantern, she got her first good look at his hands. They were big, strong and filthy.

She thought about trying to dissuade him from his notion that she was who he thought she was. But what was the point?

'How'd you know?' she said, softly.

'Well, first, because they gave a pretty fair description of you on the radio. And then because of your prison get-up.'

She smiled. 'God, you know I *forgot* about my uniform there for a minute. I'm so – tired.'

'And wet.'

'Yes. *That* I didn't forget about. I'm pretty cold.'

'How about I give you a change of clothes?'

'Are you serious?'

'Yep. Stopped in the Salvation Army in Des Moines and bought myself some new duds. I ain't a whole lot bigger'n you, lady, so they should do all right.'

The clothes smelled of moth balls, and felt unclean against her skin, and she certainly wasn't going to be walking down any fashion catwalks in the near future. But they were warm and dry and that was all that mattered. She felt his eyes on her as she got out of her soaked prison clothes. But she didn't care. She just needed to get warm.

As she was balling up her prison uniform, the train began to move. She walked back to the Coleman lantern and sat down again.

She had to urinate but she didn't want to give him *that* much of a peep show. Seeing her in her bra and panties would have to suffice.

Then she didn't worry about it anymore.

She fell into a deep and dream-haunted sleep.

Amy got the call in the middle of the afternoon. She'd spent the previous hour working out plans to extradite a man who'd murdered his wife. He belonged in Florida where the crime had been committed. He'd come up here because he knew his sister would hide him but she hadn't done all that good a job. The man got himself caught by one of Amy's officers six hours after he hit town.

Her intercom buzzed. 'Sam Fulton on line one.'

The moment she heard Fulton's name, Amy knew there was trouble. And she knew who was involved in it and what kind of trouble it was. She felt sick and angry and sad all at the same time. She forced herself to say 'Thank you' and then to lift up the phone.

'Afternoon, Sam,' she said.

'I'm sorry about calling you at the station.'

'It's all right. He in there again?'

'Yeah. And he's in pretty bad shape. You know how he gets, arguing with everybody and everything.'

'I can't get over there for twenty minutes or so. Think you can handle him that long?'

'Oh, sure. I'll just put him in a back booth and give him his own bottle of Scotch. I'm sorry about this, Amy.'

'I'm the one who's sorry, Sam.'

'He's such a great guy when he's sober. Great doctor, too.'

'I just wish *he* realized that, Sam.'

'He ever think of joining AA?'

She laughed sadly. 'I always figured guys who owned bars would *hate* AA.'

'I'd rather lose a customer than see him destroy himself the way your husband is, Amy. And I really mean that.'

'Thanks, Sam. I appreciate it. See you in a little bit.'

After hanging up, Amy put her head down on her desk. She wanted to cry but knew she couldn't. Citizens didn't like cops who walked around with their eyes red from crying. There were some who didn't like the idea of a female police chief at all. Why give them ammunition?

But she did allow herself an enormous feeling of weariness. Sam was right about Ted destroying himself. She'd seen signs of it as far back as medical school. He had a genetic predisposition to alcohol abuse. His father and brother and two of his uncles were alcoholics. But he was the golden boy of Parkhurst, the golden boy of his family, and *he* was not going to let alcohol hobble him.

But he *was* letting it hobble him, and hobble him badly.

And now she'd have to go through the humiliating task of hauling him out of yet another bar.

The swaying of the boxcar scared Darcy at first. Soon as they'd gotten out into the country, the train really started picking up speed. She'd just have to get used to the rolling motion of the car.

'I didn't have no lunch,' said the hobo. Fletcher, he'd told her. 'How about you?'

'Sure. I mean, I could eat a little, I guess.'

'Maybe I better tell you.'

'Tell me?'

'Yeah. What it is. I surprised a guy once and just gave him some and he said it tasted real, real good. Then I told him what it was and he got pissed off. Started swingin' and everything. The sonofabitch. Didn't have no gratitude at all.'

'Well,' she said, starting to feel somewhat queasy herself. 'What was it you gave him?'

Fletcher reached in his pocket and brought up a large piece of aluminum foil. 'You got to eat them fast 'cause they spoil pretty quick without no refrigeration. I mean, I cook 'em before I eat 'em. They generally stay good for a couple of days. This here one I cooked up just last night.' Then he grinned at her with his horrible teeth. 'You a good guesser?'

'Sometimes, I guess.'

'Whyn't you see if you can guess this?'

'I'll try.' She was half expecting she'd get sick as soon as he drew back the aluminum foil.

'Chicken,' she said.

'That's what everybody guesses. Chicken.'

The meat had been cleaved into four two-inch-long pieces. Two pieces were dark meat; two light. None was especially substantial.

'I already ate the really good parts myself,' Fletcher said. 'But I'll let you have these if you want them.'

'I don't think so.'

His smile again. 'Now, if I'da told you that it *was* chicken, you woulda gone right ahead and eaten it, wouldn't you?'

'I guess.'

'Well, maybe if I don't tell you what it *really* is, it won't bother you.'

'It's too late for that, I'm afraid.'

'Law lookin' for you and all, seems kinda funny that you'd be so choosy about what you eat.'

'I've never had an especially strong stomach, Fletcher.'

'Old Chinese guy taught me how to nab 'em and clean 'em and wrap 'em up. An ole Chinaman 'bo I knew up near the Sierra Nevadas one afternoon.' He shrugged. 'Chinamen eat 'em all the time and don't think nothin' of it. Figure if a Chinaman can do it, why can't Fletcher?'

'You haven't told me what we're talking about yet.'

'You mean you haven't guessed?'

'No, I really haven't.'

'Is it rabbit?' she said, feeling like a foolish child.

'No, but you got the first letter right away. The "r." '

'Oh, God,' she said.

He grinned. 'The "r" gave it away, didn't it? You guessed it, didn't you?'

'You're eating rat meat, aren't you, Fletcher?'

The grin again. 'Sure am, ma'am. Sure am.'

7

This being personal business, Amy drove her own car. She pulled up in the alley in back of the bar, left the motor running and went inside the back door.

The place was long, narrow, shadowy. Two bumper pool tables and a jukebox took up most of the room in the rear. A line of six booths filled up the east wall, a long mahogany bar the west.

Sam the bartender saw her and then nodded to the front of the place where Ted was holding court with two men. He was an expert on everything when he drank.

The place smelled of cigarettes and alcohol. Amy didn't like either aroma.

She walked up to where Ted sat on the stool facing the front door and touched his elbow. 'Somebody tells me you're looking for a ride.'

At first, he didn't seem to recognize her, but then he grinned and winked at his beer buddies. 'I'll bet I'm under arrest.'

They laughed a little nervously. Cops made most people a little nervous.

'C'mon, Ted,' she said gently. 'Time to go.'

'Honey, I was just explainin' to them how they could make more money in CDs than they could in regular bank accounts.'

So today he was an expert on finance.

She slid her arm around him and that was when he shoved her away.

She was more embarrassed and hurt. Now Ted had guaranteed that everybody would be watching this sorry little scene.

'I'm havin' a few drinks with my buddies here, Amy. What the hell's wrong with that?'

Her cheeks were warm and crimson; her hands trembling. Sometimes, he went easy. Sometimes, he went hard. This was going

49

to be one of the hard ones. This would be one of the stories all the town gossips would lap up. Went in there to haul him out and then he wouldn't even go. Who wants a police chief like that?

'We're going, Ted.'

He glared at her. 'What the hell's wrong with you? I don't have the right to sit in here and enjoy myself?'

She glanced over the bar at Sam and nodded to him. Ted had been a brawler all his life. Sam wasn't as big as Ted but he was almost as strong and he had the advantage of being sober.

Sam came from around the bar. Ted was weaving, could barely stand up. Amy was ready to grab him.

The men playing pool cleared a path for him. They'd seen this particular routine before. The doc gets drunk and they help him out to his wife's car. Eight, nine times a year they see this routine.

She grabbed Ted by the arm. He had just passed out. Praise the Lord for small mercies.

Sam got the other arm and they began half walking, half dragging him out to her car.

They moved fast because of the rain. Practically threw him in the front seat. Closed the door. He was already snoring.

She and Sam stood under the overhang of the back roof. The temperature had dropped some more. This felt like late October.

'He mentioned something to me about getting suspended from the clinic,' Sam said.

Amy shook her head. 'Maybe that was just one of his boozed-up fantasies.'

'I don't think so, Amy. He said ninety days with pay. That doesn't sound made up.'

'Guess not.' She felt sad and alone and hopeless. It was hard not to cry standing here under this overhang listening to the rain drops from the edge of the roof go pock-pock-pock when they fell to the puddled floor of the alley.

'Guess you heard about Darcy,' Sam said.

'Yeah.'

'I still remember you two growin' up. You were inseparable.'

'Yeah, for a long time we were.'

He looked at the man in the car. The snoring man, the unconscious man. 'Then you got into it over him.'

'Yeah, I guess we did.'

'There's an old French saying I—'

She touched his arm. 'You told it to me about a year ago, Sam, and I still think about it almost every day.'

'Sometimes the only thing worse than losing your lover—'

'—is winning your lover.'

He glanced up and down the gray alley that was filled with garbage cans and the dirty backs of small buildings.

'That's what happened to me with my first marriage,' Sam said. 'Did everything I could to win her – stole her from my best friend, went into debt to keep her in gifts, even bought her a car – she was the prize, Amy. You should've seen her. You'd walk down the street with her on your arm and you could just feel the men watch you – not her. You. Because you'd won the prize and they wondered how the hell you'd done it. They wanted a little luck of their own like that. They wanted to win the prize, too, someday.'

Amy looked at Ted sleeping in the car. 'He was the prize, no doubt about that.'

'Best basketball player that ever came from this town, I'll tell you.'

'And maybe the handsomest, too.' Amy smiled. 'Even putting on all that booze fat, he's still the handsomest man in town.'

Sam smiled. 'Present company excepted, of course.'

She touched his arm. 'Thanks for the help, Sam. You're a good friend.'

She hurried around the car to get in on the driver's side.

'Good luck with him,' Sam said.

She waved and got into the car and closed the door.

She drove two blocks and started crying, at which point she dug in her purse and got out her sunglasses. Boy would that look phony, driving around with your shades on when it was raining like this. But she couldn't help crying. She was worn out with it all. Fifteen years of making excuses for him. Fifteen years of telling herself that he really was going to change one of these days. One of these days. Right.

A couple of drivers who recognized her gave her odd looks. The shades being the reason, of course. Or maybe it was because they recognized Ted slumped over, the back of his head against the car window, his face clear for everybody to see.

She'd overheard some of the cops making jokes about Ted one day. 'He was supposed to be the big hot-shot,' one of them said. 'He's just another fucking wino and if he wasn't married to the

51

Chief we'd be runnin' him in for public intoxication once a week.'
She'd felt sorry for Ted – even sorrier for their three daughters.

They lived in a Colonial-style house right at the bottom of the
hill among the rich folk.

She pulled in to the driveway and stopped next to the side door.
If she hurried, there'd still be time to get Ted into the house and
upstairs in bed before the girls got back from the movies. She knew
they didn't believe her lies but she couldn't tell them the truth. *Your
father's got the flu and he came home early. Let's just let him sleep through
the night. It's probably just a twenty-four-hour bug.*

Getting him out of the car was difficult. He seemed to weigh six
hundred pounds and have four arms.

She was just starting to drag him toward the door when a familiar-
looking van pulled up. Mrs Cummins from down the street. She'd
taken the two youngest girls and her own daughter to the Disney
movie out at the multi-plex this afternoon.

Mrs Cummins looked uncertain a moment but then gave her a
tiny, nervous wave.

Amy couldn't wave back. Not with her arms full of drunken
husband.

Just as the girls got in the door, and just as Amy was dragging her
husband inside, he suddenly lurched to his feet, and threw up over
the flowers by the door.

The timing was horrible.

At this same moment, Megan, their fourteen-year-old daughter,
was walking up the drive with her best friend, Lara.

'Oh, God,' Lara said. Like all of Megan's friends, Lara knew that
Dr Foster was a hopeless drunk. She'd just never seen its nasty reality
before. Vomiting outdoors. All this played out in Mrs Cummins'
headlights.

Amy got Ted inside and closed the door. Mrs Cummins backed
out of the drive.

Megan and Lara stood in the darkened driveway.

'Maybe you'd better go home,' Megan said softly, her voice and
eyes filled with tears.

'Yeah. Maybe I'd better.'

'I'm sorry—you know, about my dad and everything.'

'It's not your fault, Megan.'

But that's the way it *felt* sometimes. That it *was* her fault.

Lara touched Megan's arm tenderly. 'I'm sorry you have to

through all this, Megan. You're such a nice girl.'

'Thanks, Lara.' She looked warily at her house. When her dad was drunk like this – which was about half the time – then the house was like her prison. She wanted to escape and run far, far away. 'Well, I guess I'd better get in there.'

'Call me tonight.'

'I will.'

'Promise?' Lara obviously sensed that Megan would avoid her for a few days. She'd be too ashamed to even talk to her.

'Promise.'

Then Megan went inside.

Her two younger sisters were in the living room watching TV. They'd already willed the terrible scene in the driveway out their heads. Little kids could do that. *She* used to be able to do that sometimes. But not any more. You'd think that you'd get used to it after fourteen years, but now every incident cut deeper, hurt more, left her dazed and despondent.

She went silently upstairs to her room, passing her parents' room on the way. She could hear her mom in there trying to get Dad undressed and into bed. Her poor mom. She had it worst of all. Her mom was her best friend. They confided everything to each other. Megan even told her mom about letting Don Simpson put his hand on her breast at a movie two weeks ago. And one time Mom told her about how Dad had always been the most handsome boy in the whole class and how she'd had a crush on him ever since kindergarten when he'd stand on his bicycle seat while his bike was racing down the sidewalk. Megan ached for her mother, knowing how much she loved Dad – and yet couldn't stop him from drinking. Mom's dream had long since become a nightmare. Megan wished she could hate her father – or that *Mom* could hate Dad – but she couldn't. She felt sorry for him and loved him and that was the trap. Even when he humiliated her, as tonight, she couldn't hate him.

She thought of all these things as she sat on her bed in the darkness, her earphones on, blasting out the sad-sensual songs of Jewel. That was Megan's secret dream. To be a pretty rock star. To be twelve pounds lighter, to be a little bit prettier (her teeth a little straighter would do it), and to magically have Dad sober up once and for all. And then she'd be on this huge stage with all these people wildly applauding her and she'd see Dad and Mom out there and they'd be smiling proudly.

Mom startled her.

She hadn't turned on the light. Just come into the room and sat down next to Megan on the bed. Megan had had her eyes closed.

Megan took off the headphones.

Mom hugged her. 'I'm sorry you and Lara had to see that,' Mom said.

'I'm sorry *you* had to see it, Mom.' Then, 'This is a real bad one, isn't it?'

'Yeah.'

Sometimes his drunks weren't real bad ones but this one sure was.

'I'm sorry, honey.'

'It's not your fault, Mom.'

They embraced again.

Then Mom said, 'What's this?'

'Grandpa's gun. I thought I'd go shoot some rounds later on.'

Amy's dad, in addition to being Chief of Police, had also been an enthusiastic gun collector. He'd given Megan a Smith & Wesson .38, the kind policemen used to carry, and had also trained her to be an expert shot. Megan had taken second place in a competition last year up in Dubuque.

'It isn't loaded, is it?'

'No. I keep the bullets in my drawer. Just the way Grandpa and you taught me.'

'Good girl.' Then, 'Well, I'd better go start supper. You want to make the salads?'

'Sure.'

'I'm sorry, honey.'

'I know, Mom. I know.'

Megan got up from the bed quickly before she and her mom started crying again. Sometimes, Megan just got so sick of feeling sad all the time.

As night came on, not even the fire could warm Darcy. She huddled into her clothes, shivering. The train rattled and shook and swayed on into dusk.

Fletcher was just finishing up the last of his rat meat, seeming to savor every bite.

In the abstract, Darcy figured she could probably get used to it, eating rat meat. The trouble was the reality of it – actually putting it to your lips, actually ingesting it. All the time it was in her stomach, she'd have this image of a bloated silo rat with gleaming red eyes nestling inside of her like a mutant child.

'You headed any place in particular?' Fletcher said.

'Home.'

'Isn't that kind've dangerous?'

'Yes. But it's my only hope. There's a man who knows something that can help me.'

'A man.'

'A judge. The one who presided over my trial.'

'How d'ya know he'll talk to you?'

'He sent me a letter in prison. It was a kind of an apology and he said if he was sorry how everything had turned out.'

'How come he didn't go to the DA?'

Just the way Fletcher said 'DA,' she sensed that he'd had more than a passing acquaintance with the law. And probably on the wrong side of it.

'I don't know. That's what was so mysterious about the letter.'

'You show it to your lawyer?'

'Yeah.'

'What'd he make of it?'

'He was as confused as I was. *Why* the Judge would write it, and what he was really getting at.'

'So you're going home to talk to the Judge?'

'Yes. My lawyer tried but the Judge's family wouldn't let him in the house. The Judge is dying – he may be dead by the time I get there tonight. He wanted to die at home so they've set up a hospice for him there. He's had cancer the last year.'

'Where you from, anyway?'

'Parkhurst.'

'Parkhurst?' Fletcher said. 'You kidding?'

'No, why?'

'Parkhurst is one town 'bo's stay out of.'

'How come?'

'Rough town.'

'Parkhurst? You must be thinking of some place else. Parkhurst has the lowest crime rate per capita in the state. That's one of the bragging points when the Mayor tries to recruit new businesses.'

'Yeah, well, maybe if you live there it's a nice place. But if you're black or brown or like to smoke a little dope now and then, it ain't nowhere to be.'

She couldn't believe Fletcher and she were talking about the same town. Parkhurst was a neighborhood of gentle blue lakes, of stately old homes, of football games on nippy autumn nights. Parkhurst was a cliché of Americana: open, welcoming, warm.

She sat back. The last of the fire was guttering out.

He said, 'You still ain't told me.'

'About what?'

'About how you landed in prison.'

'You really want to hear?'

' 'Course, I do.'

She sighed. Maybe she'd keep warm by talking. Or at the very least, maybe by talking she would be able to ignore how cold she was.

So she told him.

He never did get Marietta Stoneman to fall in love with him. He'd been quite the rogue back in the thirties before World War II killed so many of his friends and left him with a permanent limp. Of course, he'd been one of the lucky ones, relatively speaking. A kid in his platoon, kid from downstate Illinois, he got his entire face burned off. Clean burned off. It was said that even the kid's doctors couldn't look at him for very long without getting sick.

Anyway, so he comes back from the war with two goals – to get into law school at the U of Iowa, and to start seriously courting Marietta Stoneman.

Plan one was no problem. He got into law school with no trouble.

Plan two *was* a problem.

Frank Carmichael, his humble self, came from one of the wealthiest families in Parkhurst. You marry a Carmichael, you married not only money but status and prestige, at least if you never ventured beyond the city limits of Parkhurst.

But he came back to find Marietta Stoneman knocked up. Saw her on the sunny street, in fact, just as he was cabbing home from the train depot. Didn't have his family meet him. Wanted to surprise them . . .

And then he saw Marietta walking down the street with this big belly and about the happiest expression he'd ever seen on anybody's face.

While he'd written her only occasionally, he'd just assumed that since he'd shown such an interest in her, she'd wait for him. What was really perplexing – he found out later – is that she married some mill hand. She could have had a genuine Carmichael, and yet she married a mill hand. Who the hell in her right mind would do something like that? And that was how he looked at the situation ever after – that she wasn't in her right mind. That she'd had a breakdown of some kind while Frank was overseas and that she'd lost her mind somehow. A mill hand, for God's sake. Marietta's father ran a tiny grocery store. Carmichael could have taken her away from such a hardscrabble existence. Didn't she understand that? Didn't she know anything about money and society?

Carmichael never got over her. He ended up marrying the Jennings girl down the street – her father owned half the coal in Iowa in those days, coal back then being a certified blue-chip investment. She was a nice-enough girl and all but he never loved her. Always, in his fantasy life, he and Marietta would get together someday. Somehow. Even when he became a district judge and when Marietta put on so much weight and her hair began graying, even then she remained (in *his* eye) the sweet, slender, shy girl of his youth.

Even lying here dying, he was thinking bitter thoughts of how fate had seen fit to deprive him of Marietta Stoneman.

He was *supposed* to be thinking positive thoughts.

He was *supposed* to be creating mental images of himself as a sturdy, strapping, *healthy* man.

Positive imaging or something, they called it. Some kind of touchy-feely bullshit they'd been force-feeding him along with two operations and several courses of chemotherapy.

But he was dying and they knew it and he knew it. Did not, in fact, have long to go. So he ordered them to take him home to his own bed.

Home . . . where he lay thinking not of his wife of thirty-seven years but of now-plump, now-gray Marietta Stoneman (he refused to think of her as Marietta Cramer, which was her married name).

He coughed. No, it wouldn't be long now. Not at all.

Mary, the maid, walked into the room in her usual brisk fashion. A thirtyish woman with a classically beautiful face, she was far more educated and aware than you would expect a servant to be. Or so Carmichael thought, anyway. One day he'd been watching one of the presidential debates and he wryly asked her which of the two idiots she was going to vote for.

'Neither,' she said. And then she told him about the Libertarian party and why she thought so highly of it.

Mary Ford was an impressive-looking woman. She'd been working for him for four months and his eyes hadn't tired of her yet. She had an apartment across town. She was usually gone in the evening but tonight was her night to order groceries and supplies for the next two weeks, so she'd spend a little extra time.

She got him to sit up and then plumped up his pillows.

'You're a lot better nurse than those nurses,' he said.

'I doubt that, Mr Carmichael.' She smiled at him. 'What you're really saying is that they won't put up with any of your crap and I will.'

'What kind of crap do I give people?'

She laughed. 'Nothing. You're a saint.'

'I don't think I'm a saint, that's for sure.'

She gave him a kiss on the forehead. 'Good. Because nobody else does, either.'

She was just turning away from his bed – looking trim and sexy in her black maid's uniform – when he took her wrist with surprising zeal.

'I wish I was twenty years younger, you know that, Mary? Because I'd show you a night you'd never forget.'

'I'll bet you would.'

He looked into her fine blue eyes. He liked the intelligence he saw here. He'd always been curious about how she'd ended up a maid. One day, he'd found her reading *The Great Gatsby* on her break. How many maids read Fitzgerald in their spare time?

'I ever ask you how you ever got to be a maid and such a damned good one?'

'You asked me once, Mr Carmichael.'

'And what did you tell me?'

'I said that was just the way things had worked out.'

He grinned. 'And I was satisfied with that answer?'

She grinned back. 'Not very much.'

He was tired, then. Death was a series of escalating bouts of tiredness. At some point, you got so tired that your entire system simply collapsed from exhaustion and you died.

No more witty repartee with Mary here. Not for now, anyway.

He was just closing his eyes when a familiar scent wafted on the air, preceding his daughter Cindy into the room.

Cindy Carmichael Todd had turned out much like her mother – lovely in an aloof and frosty way, a perfection that appealed more to the mind than the heart. Her husband, Gary, was nearly as wealthy as the Carmichaels so he was able to keep her in the designer clothes she was so fond of – she was forever dropping the names of the French fops who make billions out of rich American women – and she was a driving force at the Country Club. Carmichael had never much liked her and she'd never much liked him. She was here tonight out of duty – mother had died eight years ago, she had no brothers and sisters. Somebody besides the 24-hour nurses needed to be with him.

Cindy was too modern and sleek for the venerable old Victorian house with its Renaissance Revival furnishings. He loved the large scale and the dark woods and the claw feet but she'd been urging him since the death of her mother to have the place refurbished. That was the only serious disagreement she'd ever had with her mother, in fact. About the furnishings.

'Good evening, Mrs Todd.'

'Good evening, Mary.' Then, 'Why don't you leave us alone now, all right?'

His socially imperious daughter was in fine form tonight, Carmichael noted.

'I think he needs rest,' Mary said softly.

'I think I'm the proper judge of what he needs, Mary. You're excused now.'

'Yes, Mrs Todd.'

Mary walked softly from the bedroom.

'Hi, Dad.'

His eyes fluttered open. 'Hi, Cindy.'

'You're looking better.'

'Oh, yes, I'll be going to the dance marathon, after all.'

'You know what I mean.'

She was one of those people who could happily exchange banalities all night. You had to deflate her quick to stop her.

'How's my granddaughter?'

The granddaughter, Lisa, was another matter. The granddaughter, he was wild about. His deepest regret about dying was that he wouldn't see Lisa grow up. In fact, just this afternoon, he'd actually shed tears thinking about Lisa. Carmichael men were not given frivolously to sentiment or tears.

59

'She's fine. Says "Pampa" all the time.'

He smiled, and felt good, immortal for just this second. Pampa. That was her sort-of word for Grampa.

Yes, he felt absolutely immortal.

'How's Brian?'

'Oh, you know, he's – being Brian.'

Brian was five and the opposite of Lisa. He was in trouble a lot at school – he loved to fight – and had been caught stealing stuff from lockers on two different occasions. Why would a rich kid like Brian want to steal things from other children far below him on the social ladder?

'He still seeing the shrink?'

'Yes, though I'm not sure it's doing much good. You know how shrinks are.'

'He'll straighten out,' Carmichael said, mouthing the appropriate grandfatherly remark, reassuring and upbeat.

'I sure hope so. His father and I—' She shook her perfectly coiffed head. Then, 'I take it you heard about Darcy.'

'Oh, yes,' he said, nodding to the 32-inch TV set on a stand at the end of his bed. His bed was his world; he would want for nothing as long as he stayed in bed. 'They make her sound like John Dillinger or something. The reporting in this town has really gone to shit. It's all tabloid crap now.'

'Well, Dad, she may not be John Dillinger but she *did* murder somebody, don't forget.'

'That's what the jury said, anyway.'

She had started her usual job of straightening up his bed and the nightstand next to him. He was a Diet Pepsi freak. Even though liver cancer was killing him – wasting him away, actually – he insisted on drinking Diet Pepsi.

There were four empty cans on the nightstand. As she picked them up and put them in a small brown paper bag, 'You were the judge at the trial, Dad. If you didn't think she did it, you should have spoken up.'

'That's not exactly – or wasn't exactly – my prerogative when I was on the bench. I was there to guide the jury through the case, not prejudice them with my opinion. Anyway, at the time I was sure she was guilty.'

'Then what changed your mind?' she said, neatly stacking the Louis L'Amour paperbacks he had strewn all over the top of the nightstand. Louis L'Amour and Luke Short, the only two fiction writers she'd ever known him to read.

He looked at her. 'When members of The Committee started being murdered a few months ago. I guess I don't have to remind you about that, do I?'

Cindy returned his look. 'We *all* think about it, Dad. It's scary.' Cindy was dusting now. 'What do the nurses do all day? Sit in the TV room and stuff their faces. This room really needs to be cleaned.'

'They're nurses, not maids, Cindy. Mary does the cleaning and she's good at it. She didn't get any work done because I made her listen to me ramble all day. She kept trying to get up and do her work but I wouldn't let her. It's my fault.'

'Well, if Mary was busy being your audience, it wouldn't have hurt the nurses to get off their dead asses and do a little work.'

'They do fine work, Cindy. They keep me just about free of pain and they do it without knocking me out. I can still get through most of a Louie or a Luke in a day, or I can watch some old movie on cable and remember when I was a dashing young man.'

'You're too easy on people, Dad,' Cindy said. 'You always have been.'

Cindy had her mother's contempt for working people. She expected anybody who worked with her to make any sacrifice, bend any rule necessary, to keep her happy. He'd once seen her order a rather pretentious chef – who'd been brought in to cook the Fine Arts Festival meal at her home – to shovel snow off the back porch. The man had been enraged but he'd done it, anyway. Cindy was imperious enough to cow the Pope.

'I'll bet she's wet and scared, wherever she is,' the Judge said.

'Who?'

'Who? Who the hell do you *think* I mean? Darcy, of course.'

'Well, excuse me, Dad, for not being telepathic, and if you're going to get into one of your moods, I'll leave right now.'

'Calm down, for God's sake. Just because some cranky old bastard like me gets irritable once in a while doesn't mean a thing. You're like your mother. You take everything personally.' He looked at his daughter. He'd tried so hard to love her – liking her was even tougher.

'There you go again.'

'There I go again what?'

'Making a derogatory remark about my mother.'

61

'I didn't make a derogatory remark. I just stated a fact. Your mother took everything personally – and so do you.'

'Maybe if you hadn't criticized her all her life, she wouldn't have *taken* things so personally.'

She was starting to cry.

He wished he loved her. It would make moments like this easier.

'C'mere, Cindy.'

'For what?' she said, still crying.

'Because I want to hold your hand.'

'You do?'

'Hell, yes, I do. I'm your father, aren't I?'

'See, you can't even say something like that without being irritable. That's how you were with Mom all her life.'

Every once in a while he'd see evidence of the grief he'd inflicted on his wife and only daughter. And then he'd feel miserable. He hadn't cared for either one of them but they'd always been nice to him. And he should've reciprocated. Growing up, Cindy had always suspected that her father preferred the company of Darcy. Cindy had been very jealous of Darcy, as her mother had been, too. He doted on Darcy. Cindy told him this the night her mother died. She wanted him to know, she said, just how badly he'd treated both of them.

And how could he deny it? He'd been a shit, all right. And he knew it. Hence the lavish gifts; sending them off to Europe every few years; spoiling Cindy by sending her to Smith (something she'd never really taken advantage of other than to interminably drop the name with all her Country Club friends); and pretend to 'forgive' his wife when she had a weekend fling with an old beau in Chicago. There was nothing to forgive, really; he didn't really give a damn. He just hoped the sex was good for her. They hadn't had a good sex life in years.

'How come you wrote Darcy that letter in prison is what I want to know,' Cindy said.

'What?'

'You heard me. It still pisses me off.'

'Maybe I shouldn't have done it,' he said wearily.

'I woke up in the middle of the night. I'd had this dream that you wrote her that letter and she got out of prison and something terrible happened.'

'What?'

'That's the part I don't remember. The terrible part itself. But you know how you can wake up with this sense of dread sometimes and not even know what caused it – that's how that dream was. And it was because you wrote her that letter.'

The Judge tuned out her nagging. It was just as well she didn't know he'd written Darcy a second letter.

Now that she'd finished straightening and dusting, she said, 'I'm going to go have a talk with that nurse, Dad. She's sitting up in the TV room watching some damned soap opera.'

'If I pressed a button, she'd be here right away.'

'I still want to have a talk with her.' She made a clucking noise. 'The kind of money we're paying her and she sits on her damned rump and watches soap opera.'

'Maybe you can get her to go up on the roof and fix that TV antenna.'

'Very funny, Dad. Very funny.'

And with that, she left the master bedroom, unable to conceal the pleasure she was about to obtain from ragging on the night nurse.

'So who'd they say you murdered?' Fletcher said, talking above the jostling sounds of the train as it tore through the rainy prairie night.

He'd rolled himself a cigarette and was now sitting back and relaxing as Darcy did most of the talking.

'A young man named Rick Kenton.'

'Your boyfriend?'

'No, just somebody who claimed to be a painter. You know, portraits mostly.'

'He any good?'

'Not bad, not good. Just sort of mediocre. But he was handsome and charming. He knew just how to ingratiate himself into Parkhurst society. And the matrons kept him busy. A lot of young women fell in love with him.'

'You?'

'No way. I saw him for the phony he was.'

'How'd he die?'

'Somebody shot him. He was in his apartment – he had this flat over an old coach house – and the woman who rented to him fixed it up nicely. One of the first people the police interviewed was the woman's husband – he'd been jealous over the relationship Rick had apparently been having with his wife.'

'But they let him go?'

'Said they didn't have enough evidence.'

'But they had enough evidence to prosecute you?'

'They did when they found the murder weapon in my garage. Somebody was smart enough to put it there after killing Rick.'

'You want a little of this?'

She smiled at his offer of a cigarette. 'No, thanks. I gave up cigarettes shortly after I gave up rat meat.' Then, 'But I didn't tell you about the second letter.'

'From the Judge?'

'Uh-huh. I got it two days ago and all it said was "The Committee" and then it listed several names, including my father's.'

'You know what "The Committee" is?'

'It used to be a group of seven men who got together to play cards every Thursday night. They started out calling themselves The Thursday Night Poker Club. Then they came up with the name "The Committee" as a joke. This was back when I was a little girl.'

'Do they still play cards?'

'I think Judge Carmichael did until recently. And the father of an old friend of mine, too, Amy Foster. He was the police chief. But he's dead. And a minister named Reverend Selden. He was the youngest of The Committee and he still has his church. And a former mayor named Richard Hill. He's still alive.'

'Makes you wonder why the Judge wrote their names down.'

'It sure does.'

'You think it has anything to do with *your* case?'

'Why else would he write it down?'

'So now you've got to go back to Parkhurst and try and find out who killed Rick, huh?'

'There's something the Judge wants to tell me. That's what I sensed in his letter, anyway.'

'I forgot to ask you, why'd they think you killed this Rick?'

'Because he was tormenting my father. He was always calling him, always showing up at the door. My father had a heart condition. It was killing him.'

'You never found out what this Rick had on him?'

'No – and that's why I went over there that night. To tell him to leave my father alone. Then somebody killed him and I got blamed.

It killed my father. He died of a heart attack that night.'

She let her head press against the back wall. She was tired of talking, tired of being cold, tired of being tired.

As she had so many nights in prison, she wished that she could go to sleep and wake up and find that things had been magically taken care of. Released from prison to find herself able to write – and write well – again.

The anger was gone, that was the funny thing. The anger was gone two years into her prison term. She no longer hated the person who had done this to her – she simply wanted him or her to be honest and step forward.

They rode in silence for a long time. The sour smell on the air belonged to the roll-your-own that Fletcher was smoking.

'Put your hand out,' Fletcher said.

'My hand?'

'Yep.'

'How come?'

'Got a gift for ya.'

'Oh, God, Fletcher, that's all right.'

She wasn't being noble. She was just figuring he had some other deal like rat meat to offer her.

'C'mon. Put your hand out.'

What could she do? She put her hand out.

Something long, narrow and body-warm – he'd taken it from his filthy jacket – was laid across her palm.

'Pick it up and snick the button on the side,' Fletcher said.

She did as he told her to.

The switchblade opened with a real power.

'Twelve inches. You wouldn't have no trouble killin' anybody with that, let me tell ya.'

'I don't want to kill anybody, Fletcher. I just want to be set free.'

He closed his hand on hers. 'You take it and keep it, all right?'

She knew there was no point arguing. She was even a bit touched by him giving it to her.

'You may need it when you least expect it,' Fletcher said.

And maybe he was right.

As crazy as her life had become these past five years, who knew when she might need a switchblade?

'Thank you, Fletcher.'

'My pleasure, ma'am,' he said. 'My pleasure.'
The train roared on into the rainy night.

8

Waking up was the worst part.

It wasn't just the physical misery.

It was the terrible half-memories that played ghostly hints on your mind. Could you really have *said* that? Really have *done* that?

The office. Early afternoon. Falling down with one of his patients watching him.

God, had that really happened?

He lay in the darkness of the bedroom loathing himself with a disgust that was almost *physically* oppressive.

Such shame.

How could he ever face his partners again?

And then he remembered the bar that Amy had taken him out of. How many, many times he had humiliated her and the children.

He just wanted to die. Right here. Right now. An aneurysm would be so neat, so clean. There was still time for Amy to have another life for herself. New husband; sober husband; and happiness.

He swung his legs slowly off the bed. Moving was difficult. His entire body was pasty with sweat and trembling.

He sat up on the edge of the bed and reached out and felt for the table lamp. Turned it on.

Thunder. Rain.

Perfect complement to how he felt.

And then he saw his sport coat on the floor. He usually hung it on the back of the chair by the window. But he'd missed this time.

He staggered up and went over to it and picked it up. At least he could do *something* right.

Bending over, he almost blacked out. And then more images of falling down in front of his patient came to him.

My God, she would put the word all over town. What a fool he was. What a terrible, terrible fool.

He picked up the coat and carried it over to the chair. As he was doing this, he felt the papers in his inside coat pocket and wondered what they were.

He put the coat on the chair and carried the papers over to the table lamp.

Simply by scanning them, he saw how important they were.

He had his answer to who had killed the two Committee members in the past few months.

Following the murder of Dr Hamling, The Committee had needed a new doctor as county medical examiner. They'd been forced to take Ted, though only because Amy pushed the issue. She promised he'd behave soberly and properly and prove a good addition. He'd done none of these things. He'd let her and The Committee down. He'd shown up drunk at meetings – the first he'd been able to attend, that is.

But now he saw a way he could make it up to them – to Amy and The Committee, as well.

He was going to catch the killer all by himself.

Megan had just finished putting her two sisters to bed for the night. Now she was in the kitchen making herself some hot cocoa. She'd been too upset about her father throwing up to eat any dinner.

She was just taking the cup of cocoa out of the microwave when she heard her father in the hall closet. She wondered what he was doing up. Usually, when he was as drunk as he'd been this afternoon, he slept for many long hours.

He came into the kitchen. He looked pale, shaky. He had on a jacket to wear outside.

'I'll see you in a while, sweetheart.'

She sensed something was terribly wrong. And she was immediately afraid. As much as her father infuriated – and embarrassed – her sometimes, she loved him profoundly. And feared for him. He was like a child – so vulnerable – and sometimes she felt more like his mother or his sister than his daughter.

'Where're you going, Dad?'

'Just have something I have to do, hon. It won't take me long.'

'You want some coffee?'

'I'll pick some up at Wendy's.'

'You really think you should be going anywhere, Dad?'

'Honey, I'll be fine. I really will.'

But he looked shaky, as if he was about to collapse, as if his legs would just suddenly give out.

She set her cup of cocoa down on the breakfast-nook table and went over to him and took him gently by the arm. 'Why don't I fix you a sandwich or something?'

'Maybe later, sweetheart.'

He took her to him, hugged her. 'I'll be fine, sweetheart. I really will.'

'I just get scared for you, Dad.'

And then she couldn't help it. She started crying, standing there with her arms around him, just started crying the way she had when she was a little girl and she'd see him passed out on the floor and was terrified that he was dead. She worried about him all the time, just sitting in school sometimes, the other girls dreaming of boyfriends or cars or trips or stuff like that, she'd worry about her dad that he didn't die or get into any trouble — and she'd hope that someday he'd just quit drinking. Just like that. Just quit drinking. And then her mom and dad would be happy forever more. Like in one of the fairy stories Mom used to read to Megan when she was a little girl.

The phone rang.

'That'll probably be for you, sweetheart,' Dad said.

She didn't want to let go. She just had a terrible feeling about him leaving here now. She couldn't really explain it. Not even to herself.

The phone rang again.

'Better get it, hon.'

She reluctantly took her arms from his sides and walked over to the phone. She picked up. 'Hello.'

'Just wanted to see how you were doing.'

'Oh, hi, Lara.'

As soon as she said 'Lara,' Dad walked over to the back door. 'See you in a while, honey.'

Then he was gone.

A terrible sorrow came over Megan, then. She wanted to be up in her room, in the darkness, and never come out again. Not ever.

The Reverend Selden was sinning with his mind.

He would have been sinning with his hands but he didn't think that Mrs Sawyer was quite at that point yet.

Over the years, the Reverend had learned that the most vulnerable person of all – as seen from the perspective of a lay counselor like himself – was a woman whose marriage was in trouble.

You'd ease yourself over to her, slide your arm around her when she was sobbing, and with any luck at all you would soon find yourself embracing. And she would be grateful.

Of course, being a minister and all, one had to be discreet. There were three potential threats: one, the obvious, an angry husband. The Reverend Selden knew of a case in Wisconsin where a husband actually *killed* a minister with his hands. The other, and one few men in his position considered, was the woman falling in love. That presented all sorts of problems and lead, ultimately, to the relationship being exposed. There'd been an incident in Ohio in which a woman had talked to the press about the relationship she'd had with her upwardly mobile minister. That minister soon found himself at a mostly black church in Alabama. There was, of course, a third threat, that of being discovered by your wife.

A minister's wife in Delaware had secretly audio-taped her husband having sex with his lady friend from the church. The wife then played it over the loudspeakers the next Sunday at church. That minister ended up dishing out gruel at an inner-city soup kitchen in Chicago.

Because the night was so chilly, Kim Sawyer – age thirty-eight, the mother of two young boys, and a woman who had learned just last week that her accountant husband was having an affair at work – wore a tight emerald-green sweater, jeans and Reeboks. It was the sweater that was making Reverend Selden so dizzy. He could barely stop himself from leaping across the room and landing on her. In the meantime, he had to content himself with glancing at his own image imposed on the night-black study window. He himself was wearing a white turtleneck and black trousers. His long blond hair might be getting streaked with gray now – he was, after all, forty-four years old – but he knew that he still had it. His matinee idol looks were good for another twenty years minimum. In New Hampshire, a minister had gone on bopping his parishioners until well into his seventies.

'You know what I feel like doing?' the bountiful lady said.

'No, what?'

The woman flushed and waved away her words. 'Oh, I shouldn't have said that. I was just being juvenile and spiteful.'

'No, tell me,' Reverend Selden said. He felt the way he did the few times he'd tried out those phone sex hotlines – he wanted to get to the juicy parts as soon as possible.

'I was just going to say that I felt like going out and having an affair *myself.*' She looked around the snug little study, fire-crackling fireplace, book-lined walls, lovely mahogany desk complete with small Tiffany table lamp, thick gray carpeting. 'But two wrongs don't make a right, do they, Reverend?'

Was she teasing him? Did she sense what was on his mind? Was the same thing on *her* mind?

In this era of sexual-harassment law suits, you had to be very careful, or you'd find yourself facing your parishioner with a lesbian attorney on her arm.

'They don't, do they, Reverend?'

'Oh, I'm sorry. You said—'

'– that two wrongs never make a right.'

'Well, not necessarily.'

His erection was such that it was giving him the most exquisite grief of his life. Dear Lord, if he didn't jump her soon, he'd end up in a madhouse for sure. His erection was his salvation and his weapon – his means of revenge. He'd never been an especially manly man, at school he was never chosen for games and was constantly bullied by others who called him sissy and creampuff. But he'd learned early on that he had one way of paying back his male oppressors – his looks. He screwed their girlfriends, a far greater – and more pleasurable – form of revenge than simply punching in their faces.

'You mean two wrongs *can* make a right?'

'Not exactly,' he said. 'But you're presuming that having an affair would necessarily be wrong.'

'You mean, it wouldn't be?'

'Looked at from a strictly theological point of view – from Locke's point of view, say – one could make the case that God *wanted* you to have an affair.'

'Who's Locke?'

'A philosopher. Seventeenth century.' Or was it Eighteenth or Sixteenth?

'God, you're so smart, Reverend. That's why I love your sermons so much. Cassie, my eight-year-old, says you look like a rock star.'

He had the good grace to put on his best humble-pie mask.

Now, he was *sure* they were on the same wavelength.

This was going to be even easier than he'd imagined. Another ten, fifteen minutes of chatter, and she'd be his. He'd bought an extra-long couch two years ago. The best investment of his life.

He smiled. 'Well, *you* look like a rock star to *me*.'

'I do?' Obviously flattered.

'You're a very appealing woman.'

'Oh, thanks. I appreciate you saying that. I really need all the compliments I can get these days.' Then she shook her short dark hair. He could imagine how silky it would feel between his fingers. And she would be clean. Not all of them were. This pretty, this well-endowed, and clean – truly, he had been blessed.

His erection was becoming more insistent. This was like being fifteen again, when they had to handcuff you to the bed post to hold you back from the girls.

The phone rang.

Kim Sawyer looked at it.

'My wife will get it,' he said.

The rectory was old enough that certain parts of the flooring squeaked when weight was put on them. He heard the squeaking on the staircase, heard the squeaking come down the hall. The squeaking was his wife.

She knocked, just as he'd trained her to. Never, never break in on us, he'd always admonished her. You might cause permanent damage if we're at a particularly crucial stage. His wife had agreed. She wasn't the kind who'd care to inflict permanent damage on anybody. She was a sweet if somewhat bovine lady, a perfect piece of furniture for the rectory here.

'Donald, the Judge is on the phone.'

'The Judge?' he said. 'Judge Carmichael?'

'Yes.'

My God, Carmichael was in a hospice situation at home. They expected him to die any time now. And he was making phone calls?

'Excuse me,' he said. 'I'd better see what this is.' Then, to his wife, 'Thank you, honey.'

The floor began squeaking again as she walked away.

Reverend Selden had been sitting in an armchair across from Kim Sawyer. Now he got up and walked around to his desk, where the phone was.

'Hello, Judge.'

'Did I interrupt you screwing one of those sweet young things you always counsel?'

'That isn't funny, Judge.'

'No, but it's the truth. You should've been run out of town a long time ago, the way you've exploited those poor women.'

'Maybe they're exploiting me.'

'I never wanted you on The Committee, Selden. And you know it. It was the others who voted for you.'

'I'm really busy, Judge. Could we get to the point?'

'Very simple point, Selden. I have a funny feeling about tonight.'

Selden hoped it would be the night the Judge would do mankind a great favor and die.

'What kind of funny feeling?'

Then he told Selden about the two letters he'd written Darcy McCain.

On the other end of the phone, Judge Carmichael was thoroughly enjoying himself.

He'd always thought that Selden was a corrupt man and didn't belong on The Committee. Screwing his female parishioners was just one of his offenses. He lived the high life and the church paid for it.

He didn't have long to go, Carmichael knew, and he wanted to enjoy himself in the waning moments of his life. And what could possibly make him happier than hearing Selden panic?

'You sent her letters? But why?'

'I think we were wrong.'

'And so you took it upon yourself to tell her?'

'I didn't tell her anything specific, Selden. I just didn't want to go to my grave thinking she was in prison for something she didn't do.'

'But she *did* do it. We all agreed on that.'

'The more I look back, I don't think she did. I don't think she killed Kenton. Somebody else did. Because of what he knew about us. What we'd done and everything. Maybe it was even one of us who killed him. I didn't tell her anything specific. But she's a smart woman. She may figure this out.'

'You had no right to do this, Judge. No right at all.'

'Sleep tight, Selden.'

Judge Carmichael banged the phone down.

His erection had packed up and left him.

He sat in the terrible silence following Carmichael's call.

'Reverend?'

He raised his eyes, as if he'd just become aware of her.

'Are you all right?'

'Yes. Fine.'

So it was finally happening, everything coming down around him in smoke and ash.

'Would you like me to get your wife?'

'No, thanks.'

He looked at her sweater. He could appreciate her gorgeous breasts in the abstract – but at the moment they evoked no lust in him at all.

'Maybe you'd better go now, Kim,' he said in that same dead voice.

'That must've been real bad news, huh?'

'Yes,' he said woodenly. 'Yes, real bad news.'

She stopped up, taking her gorgeous breasts with her. 'I really appreciate everything you've done for me, Reverend.'

'Fine,' he said. 'Yes, that's fine. Fine.'

'And I hope I can see you again next week.'

'Just call me in a few days.'

He got up and walked over to the door. Opened it up.

'You're a wonderful man, thank you.'

As she reached the door, she leaned close and gave him a kiss on the cheeks. He could feel her breasts pushing against him. Why couldn't she have done this ten minutes ago? Why did that crusty old bastard Carmichael have to call now? And even more, why did that crusty old bastard Carmichael have to send Darcy McCain those letters?

The sonofabitch.

He let her pass in front of him and then he walked her down the carpeted hallway to the rectory's vestibule. He'd had stained-glass windows installed in the vestibule two years ago. Some church members had thought this was an extravagance. After all Jesus has given you, would you deny him some small-ticket item like this? the good Reverend had asked his church.

He always won the money arguments.

'Good night,' she said.

'Good night.'

He closed the door just as wind whipped rain drops inside the vestibule.

He needed to get to a phone quickly.

He needed to call Richard Hill and tell him what the Judge had done.

9

The train slowed considerably as it reached Parkhurst. Fletcher estimated the speed at ten miles per hour. He had spent the past twenty minutes telling Darcy how to jump and land without injuring herself. She thanked him for everything then walked unsteadily up to the open door.

Parkhurst was laid out before her, one of those sleepy little Midwestern towns that had seemed to resist all the modern temptations. Parkhurst people were always boasting how safe their town was – an oasis of safety and sanity in an ocean of trouble. City people didn't seem to understand this, but small towns had all the same problems – drugs, violence, gangs. The only difference being that these gang members were white.

As the train entered the city limits, she could see the downtown area. Strong sentiment overtook her. This was her town – or had been until a false charge of murder had turned her into a pariah. The cute young woman who'd been able to make her living writing mystery novels – and was therefore the pride of the town – had become the object of smirks and scowls. She admitted to the County Attorney that she'd had a terrible argument with Rick Kenton the same afternoon he was killed. The jury did the rest.

'So long, Fletcher.'

'So long, kiddo. Good luck.'

'Thanks.'

She jumped. Just decided to get it over with and jumped.

The landing wasn't as bad as she anticipated. She did what he told her to with her legs and found that he was right. If you can land running, you're in better shape.

She stumbled once, pitching face forward but staving off the worst of the fall by putting out her hand to slow her momentum.

The train rattled on past her. Fletcher waved and, as she stood up, she waved back.

Then there was just the dark rainy night again, and the lost lonely woman she'd become. Far ahead of her, near the next bend in the tracks, she saw a distant green railroad light. Maybe she should've stayed on board with Fletcher. Maybe flight was better than trying to find out why the Judge sent her those letters and what exactly he knew about the murder of Rick Kenton.

But, no, she was glad she'd come back. If nothing else, she'd have a few hours with her father.

The first place she'd go was the Judge's house.

She had started coughing from being so cold and wet earlier. She bundled tighter into the clothes Fletcher had given her, and set off.

Darcy had been something of a tomboy as a girl. Like her heroine, Nancy Drew, she was always up for adventure. And adventure meant – just as it meant to the boys – learning where all the secret, neat places were. Amy and Cindy, her best friends, almost always went along. They discovered an entire universe of storm sewers, abandoned buildings, alleys, empty houses and the cellars therein, where they could hide and play. And while sissy girls played with Barbies and all the other dorky doll characters, the three girls were mapping uncharted territory.

A lot of this knowledge came back to her as she made her way through the rain-dripping night. Here was a good alley to take; here was a storm sewer where you could walk three blocks without anybody seeing you; here was a park that would conceal you.

She smiled to herself, thinking of all the places her mother and father had warned her against playing – storm sewers chief among them. Her parents, what gentle and tender memories she had of them – well, *almost* all gentle and tender memories, anyway. She had resented them bitterly when they made their preference for her sister very clear. There were times when it seemed as if Darcy hadn't existed at all. But most of the time they were wonderful, upright, old-fashioned people, her mother a housewife, her father a school principal. They weren't rich like the Carmichaels, though they'd been good friends of the Judge and his group.

How she missed them sometimes . . .

She just kept walking, making her way through the shadows.

Soon, she'd know why the Judge had written her those letters, and why he'd listed the names of The Committee members, including the name of her father.

Soon.

It took her almost forty-five minutes to reach Judge Carmichael's house. By this time, she was soaked again. She desperately needed dry clothes.

The Judge lived in a beautifully refurbished Victorian on an estate grounds of two acres. Back at the turn of the century, President Teddy Roosevelt had often visited here, appearing in a spanking new coach, drawn by two fine black horses. The Judge's maternal grandfather was a man whose reputation and prestige was known around the world.

Now what she needed to do was figure out how she was going to get inside. A visitor had told her that the Judge was dying and had elected to live his last days in his own bed.

That's where she needed to go.

But how was she going to get inside?

This was a problem she hadn't planned for. She hadn't thought much beyond escaping from prison and working her way back to Parkhurst.

But now that she was here—

There was one police car parked along the curb and another in the drive. Amy knew about the letter the Judge had sent Darcy – and had dispatched cars here to watch for Darcy.

Just then a car came down the street and she stepped behind a rain-soaked tree to hide.

But it passed by without slowing at all. She was sure she hadn't been spotted.

She started staring at the house again.

She had to get in. But how?

10

Once she was sure that her father had dropped off to sleep again, Cindy went into the den and called Amy.

'How's it going with Ted?' she said. She'd talked to Amy earlier about Ted being suspended.

'He's sleeping it off. It generally takes him about four hours to be reasonably sober.'

'I'm sorry, Amy.'

She sighed. 'I guess I'm used to it by now.'

'You could always leave him, you know. I mean, it's not exactly unheard of in our society.'

'I've tried that before, remember? It didn't work so well. I took him back after three weeks.'

'Well, that's probably what he needs. To really hit rock bottom.'

'Now you sound like Alcoholics Anonymous.'

'Are they such a bad group?'

'I wouldn't say "bad," ' Amy said. 'But I don't think their approach works for everybody.'

This was getting nowhere. Cindy changed the subject. 'Any word on Darcy?'

'Not yet.'

'She hasn't been sighted anywhere?'

'A prison escapee like that, you get a lot of false calls and false claims. Nothing that sounds like much yet, anyway.'

'She could get killed.'

'Yes, she could.'

Cindy paused. 'And she could stir certain things up, too.'

'I've thought about that.'

'I asked my father if he'd sent her a second letter. He said no.'

'I just wish you could've stopped him from sending the first one.'

Cindy said, 'Is there a meeting tonight? There's supposed to be.'

'I think we need one.'

'So do I.'

'In case Darcy gets to them somehow and starts asking questions.'

'I'll call the others, then,' Cindy said. 'Same time as usual?'

'Yes.'

'See you then.'

On the way home, Amy stopped by Roundup Rick's convenience store to pick up a gallon of milk and a pound of Maxwell House Coffee. Tomorrow morning, her husband was going to need lots and lots of coffee.

She'd just picked up her items and was walking to the counter when she noticed the black woman chatting with the chubby young store clerk wearing the western-style straw hat with the Roundup Rick's motif.

Amy's first reaction was anger. She and the others worked so hard to keep the town pure. Nothing against blacks or Mexicans or Jews. It was just that she believed that people belonged with their own kind. Actually, Amy wasn't all that comfortable with Catholics. But there were so many of them hereabouts, there wasn't much she could do about them.

She stepped up closer to the woman and listened.

'You with me so far, ma'am?'

'Two blocks down.'

'Uh-huh.'

'And then a right turn.'

'Uh-huh.'

'Then about two miles straight west and I'll pick up the Interstate again.'

'Exactly.'

The woman was nicely dressed in a tan sweater and brown slacks. She was middle-aged, pretty. 'I really appreciate this.'

'No problem, ma'am.' Then he handed her a receipt. 'Here's your Visa receipt.'

'Thanks.'

She was lost, that was all. Wasn't stopping in Parkhurst. Had no plans to be here. Amy could relax. She paid for her items and left.

When Amy got home, the house was eerily quiet. She checked on her two youngest girls. Megan had tucked them into bed. Megan herself was asleep, too, in her own room.

Then she went to their own bedroom door. She thought she heard Ted snoring. Good. Then he hadn't gone through with it – whatever his mysterious phone call had been about. He was in there sleeping.

She took a deep breath. If Ted even rolled over, she was going to get him on his feet and march him down to the kitchen and tell him that things had to change. Now. And for ever. She just couldn't do this any more. And she just couldn't keep putting the girls through it, either.

She eased open their bedroom door. She could smell the booze and the sour whiskey-sweat of him in the darkness inside.

She tip-toed into the bedroom and closed the door behind her. She wanted to rouse him gently so he wouldn't start shouting and wake the girls. You had to be careful of him, he was liked a crazed animal sometimes. The smallest thing could set him off. It was a horrible way to live for all concerned. Even when the girls had their friends over, he'd sometimes go off. And what kind of life was that for the girls? They'd run in their rooms and bury their heads in their pillows and cry because they were so embarrassed by their father's behavior.

Their lives had to change. Had to.

She reached down through the shadows to touch his shoulder – and his shoulder wasn't there.

At first, because her eyes hadn't yet adjusted to the darkness, she couldn't see very well. He'd probably rolled over to her side of the bed.

She reached across the bed. Empty.

She felt an unreasoning panic.

Where was he?

She hurried out of the room to the second floor bathroom. Wasn't there either.

The kitchen. Coffee and a sandwich. His usual routine when fighting a hangover.

She went downstairs. Living room, empty. Den, empty. Kitchen, empty.

Ted was gone.

But where? And why?

She hurried back upstairs, to Megan's room.

'Where's Dad, honey?' she said, frantically shaking her eldest daughter.

'Oh, God, Mom,' Megan said, turning on the reading light above her bed. 'I fell asleep. I was going to wait up and tell you.'

'Tell me what?'

'He went someplace.'

'Someplace? He didn't say where?'

'No, he didn't. I'm sorry.'

And Megan started to cry.

Amy took her, then, and held her. Megan had borne the brunt of her father's alcoholism. It tore her apart inside. She was still obviously upset about tonight and the episode in the driveway. And now her father had mysteriously taken off.

It was kind've funny, the way things work out sometimes, Cindy thought, sitting by the phone in her father's den.

Three young girls – Amy, Cindy, Darcy – you'd expect one of them to end up happy, anyway.

Darcy had gone to prison.

Amy's reputation in town was being destroyed by her alcoholic husband (the most popular *boy* of '78).

And as for Cindy herself . . .

She smiled, thinking of how her father had always regarded her as this snotty, snobby and rather sterile beauty whose favorite activities centered upon the Country Club.

Maybe she'd have Evan snap a few Polaroids of her the next time she was doing her little striptease for him.

Evan was the tennis pro at the club. It was all a cliché, as she well knew: Country Club married woman, and handsome single tennis ace. The thing was, making love to her husband, Gary, was like making love to a gorilla – suitable punishment for marrying an all-state linebacker. She'd even bought one of those 'Art of Massage' videotapes for them to pick up pointers from. They had sat naked in front of the TV, the shifting colors of the picture tube painting their bodies psychedelics, and Gary had gotten so horny so quickly, he'd pushed her head down so she'd give him a blow job. So much for the fine art of slow, sensuous massage.

She'd met Evan swimming in the Country Club pool. It was kind of a stormy afternoon, with occasional bursts of summer rain, and they'd closed the pool. But Cindy had never shown a particular fondness for rules and she jumped in anyway. Evan came along and said, 'I thought the pool was closed.' Cindy laughed. 'Jump in. I led a revolution and now it's open.' Nothing much happened that afternoon – except one time when Evan got close enough to her to rub his erection against her right buttock – but they both knew as they were drying off that there would be consequences to the time in the pool. Evan was properly and sensibly scared: Gary was not only rich, he was powerful. He had friends all over the United States and his computer company was well known to everybody on the Fortune 500 list. If Gary wanted to destroy Evan's career, it would be easy to do.

That was part of the excitement, of course, that Gary was always around somewhere. Lurking. And that Evan was so damned good in bed.

Over the next six months, they made love in every conceivable way and in every conceivable place, including a century-and-a-half-old Catholic church out in the country. The place was empty when they got there and Evan thought it would be pretty cool (his exact words) to fuck each other in a confessional. So they opened one of the confessionals and went in and she dropped her walking shorts and he slid himself inside her and they fucked like porno-movie pros. The story would have been better if it'd ended with the priest discovering them and throwing a hissy fit. But that didn't happen. They just left the church, piled into Evan's red Triumph, and then headed back to town, where they fucked again in Evan's office at the Country Club.

Cindy wondered what her father would say about all this. Oh, moan to be sure – the scandal of it all! – but she was sure that he would be secretly amused, if not downright proud, to discover his only daughter wasn't a prig after all.

Then again, maybe not. You could never predict how her father was going to react to anything. That's what made him so scary. There was no internal logic to many of his reactions.

She stared down at the phone on the desk.

Jealousy was not part of the bargain, as Evan had told her many times. She had a family to take care of, and he had a number of ladies he saw in the evenings.

But, lately, she'd begun to feel possessive and this made her feel old and foolish, like a crone who hoped to win the heart of the handsome young prince.

She was a wealthy, middle-aged women with a nice pair of tits, an OK (but just OK) ass, and a beautiful, but deadly cold, face. For a guy like Evan, she was nothing special. They'd been drinking wine one afternoon and he'd let something slip that he most likely regretted later. 'These Country Club men think they're such hot shit. They treat me like a glorified caddy or something. Sometimes, I'd like to tell them that I'm screwing their wives – just to watch their faces.' Evan, who had gone to college on a sports scholarship, was from a working-class family and had a great deal of class anger. It was obvious that he had Gary in mind when he said that about husbands.

She lifted the receiver.

This was so juvenile, the kind of thing she and Darcy and Amy used to do back when they were in seventh grade.

Call a boy's home and then hang up as soon as he answered.

It used to terrify her to call boys she liked. She'd sweat and tremble and giggle uncontrollably, all of it a form of hyperventilation.

Now, all these years later, she was going through the same exquisite torture all over again.

One ringy-dingy.

Her heart was pounding.

Two ringy-dingies.

Her hands were soggy sponges of sweat.

Three ringy-dingies.

It was hard for her to catch her breath.

'Hello?'

His voice.

Oh, God, *his* voice.

There were so many things she wanted to tell him, among them that she'd slip over to his apartment tonight, to hell with the risks. She'd slip over and they'd have so much sex that they'd be exhausted by the time she left.

'Hello?'

Then, in the background, she heard a woman's voice, 'God, I hate that when some creep calls up.'

'Whoever you are,' Evan said, 'go fuck yourself.'

Then he slammed the phone down.

She wore the searing mask of humiliation.

Surely, he knew by now that it was she who called him like that, just to hear his voice.

But he was obviously showing off for the woman he'd blessed with his company tonight.

She felt older and more pathetic than ever, sitting there listening to his voice echo in her mind.

The lady he was with was probably in her early twenties and sexy by any standard one cared to apply. She'd seen him a few times at concerts with one of his 'friends.' He liked them fresh-scrubbed and healthy-looking – blonde (inevitably), trim, pretty, and spry. She doubted he cared much about their intellectual interests. Evan was not in danger of becoming smart.

She forced herself to think about Darcy again. She always felt better when she compared her problems with the problems of some of her friends. Terminal cancer was the best comparison of all. No matter how down she was, she always felt better when she thought of somebody with terminal cancer.

What Darcy had was almost as bad as terminal cancer. Life in prison, in fact, might be *worse* than terminal cancer.

She wondered if Darcy really would come back here and, if so, would she look up Amy and Cindy?

She wondered where Darcy was. Everybody just assumed that she'd show her face in Parkhurst, but Cindy wasn't so sure. Maybe Darcy would just keep on running. Maybe she'd write novels in Europe under a pen-name and nobody would ever learn her true identity. There was a writer her father liked – B. Traven, that was his name, he wrote *The Treasure Of Sierra Madre* among other books. But nobody had ever figured out who he was. There were all sorts of rumors but he went to his grave without anybody knowing for sure.

Maybe Darcy would do that.

She checked her watch.

In another half hour, the meeting would start.

She really didn't want to go home and the meeting was a perfect excuse to stay away.

She called Gary and told him about the meeting.

He was his usual nerdy self: 'That's all right, dear. I'm just working on my speech. Then I thought I'd make myself a bowl of popcorn.'

My God, who could believe this man was an actual tycoon, with strong ties to major politicians?

'Life in the fast lane,' she said.

'What?'

'Making popcorn,' she said, having to explain her humor as always. ' "Life in the fast lane" I said.'

'Oh, I get it.'

'I'll talk to you later.'

She hung up.

11

Now.

Darcy had been standing across the rain-shiny street for more than half an hour. Twice, she'd started across the street to the Judge's house but cars had come by. She kept watching the windows and the occasional silhouettes that appeared in the lighted ones. At least two different people were in there walking around.

Had to be very careful.

Finding the Judge inside wouldn't be easy. However, she'd spent a lot of time in the mansion during her youth and remembered the layout pretty well. The Judge was likely to be in the master bedroom on the second floor.

She walked down to the far end of the block and then moved quickly across the street. There were huge shadowy homes here. She would use their rear yards to come up behind the Judge's mansion.

The earth was soggy. She was beyond getting warm now but her circumstances made her forget the cold. All that mattered now was getting in to see the Judge. She moved skillfully across the wet ground until she had reached the hill behind the mansion.

She reached a section of brush that led on to the hill. She pushed through the foliage and stood in an open patch of grass, looking right down the slope. This had always been a great place for sleds, and Mrs Carmichael's special hot cocoa. It was still the best hot cocoa Darcy had ever tasted.

She crept down the hill, sticking to the deep pockets of shadow. Her shoes squished with water. Fletcher's switchblade thumped against her thigh as she walked.

A light went on upstairs and she stopped.

A silhouette in the window: Cindy.

God, what would Cindy do if she found Darcy in the house?

Cindy had been supportive during the trial – but maybe she'd changed her mind. Maybe she considered Darcy guilty now.

The light clicked off, then. Darkness once more.

Darcy moved. She hurried along the exterior of the long, screened-in back porch. On sunny afternoons, Cindy and her friends had sat on the porch playing records. Cher and the Beatles had been the big stars in those grade school days.

A noise – and she stopped again. Clung to the shadows on the side of the porch.

The man coming out the back door didn't look side-to-side. He was in too much of a hurry. At first, his tall, dark form didn't seem familiar at all. He just looked straight ahead. He hurried.

But as he crossed the porch and opened the door leading to the back yard, she saw him clearly for the first time. She was shocked to recognize Ted Foster. What was Ted doing here? She didn't know that he and the Judge were friends. In fact, the Judge had always been unhappy with Ted's drinking. So what was he doing here?

He did another thing that shocked her, too. He walked at an angle across the back yard, found an opening between the bushes, and disappeared. Apparently, he'd been sneaking in here, too.

But why?

Well, at least now she knew that she could get in the back door, the one Ted had just used.

She tiptoed up on the porch, opened and closed the door without a sound, and then tiptoed up to the inside back door.

The lights were off in the kitchen. The only illumination came from the spill light of a front room. The kitchen was big, with enough pots, pans, sinks, and freezers to please a real chef. In the old days, even a king or two had enjoyed a meal here.

She eased open the kitchen door and stepped inside. She closed the door behind her and then started through the house. She went room to room like an invading army, securing one position at a time. Kitchen, small dining room, large dining room, living room. No sounds on this floor. She remembered seeing two different female silhouettes against the window. The second woman was probably a maid. The Carmichaels had always had a maid. The Judge always picked them personally. He was not averse to surrounding himself with attractive women and his choice in maids was no exception.

Darcy tiptoed across the parquet floor of the vestibule just as a solemn grandfather clock intoned the quarter-hour.

She looked up the long, straight staircase. She could remember sliding down the banister when nobody was around to see. Back then, it had been a whole lot of fun.

This was the dangerous part. Getting up the stairs. Reaching the master bedroom. Having her conversation with the Judge without getting caught.

She was just about to start up the steps when she heard a door close softly on the second floor. And then heard footsteps coming toward the top of the stairs. A woman's cough. A pause in the walking. Another cough. The walking resumed, headed toward the top of the stairs.

There was a vestibule closet ten feet away. She quickly stepped in there amongst the coats. Closed the door. The darkness smelled of wet wool. Somebody had been in the rain. Probably Cindy, coming over from her house.

Steps on the stairs, coming down. She had no idea if this was Cindy or the maid. The steps were light, deft. Could easily be either one. She put her ear to the door, listened.

Heart pounding. Hot sweat now. Almost burning up. Fever?

The footsteps disappeared into the downstairs somewhere. She needed to know where. Distantly, then, she heard a sound from the back of the house. The kitchen? Had the person gone in the kitchen?

And that left one other person besides the Judge upstairs. She could wait until both Cindy and the maid were downstairs but that could be hours. Or all night. What if Cindy was here as part of a death watch?

She had to go upstairs now. She had no other choice.

She opened the closet door, peered out. She stepped out on to the parquet floor. She listened carefully. She heard the noise of a few pans being rattled. Whoever it was, was definitely in the kitchen. Probably heating something up for the Judge.

She crossed the floor to the staircase and began to ascend. She kept her head angled high so she could hear sounds from any part of the house.

She was halfway up when she heard somebody on the second floor. A door opening, then footsteps. A door closing. A long moment and then a stream of urine in a toilet bowl. Flushing. Water running. Footsteps again. The person returning to the room. Silence, again.

Darcy was at the top of the staircase now. The hallway was

decorated like a museum. Handsome oil paintings illuminated by small lights along the bottoms of their frames. Expensive artefacts – vases, especially – on small tables. A beautiful Persian rug ran the entire length of the hall, complementing perfectly the mahogany wainscoting on the walls.

The master bedroom was in the center of the hall. She was only three doors away.

She looked left and right. Listened. Nothing. Had to move now.

She tiptoed down the hall to the center door. Tried the door knob and pushed the door inward.

Peeking inside, she saw that all the lights were out. The Judge was probably groggy from drugs. Maybe he was asleep.

She tiptoed inside, closing the door behind her.

The room smelled like a funeral parlor. The overwhelming scent of fresh-cut flowers, a scent meant not to please but disguise.

As her eyes became accustomed to the darkness, she started walking toward the bed.

She could make out his shape now; the wide shoulders, the outsized head that had always reminded her of a Roman senator, the large hands folded across his flat stomach. Even lying down, he was an imposing man. He'd always scared her a little.

She bumped into the edge of a table and froze.

She imagined that the sound was large enough to alert people two, three blocks away. She cocked her head and listened – with dread – to see if anybody in the house had heard it. God, how could they have missed it?

But she didn't hear anybody scurrying about.

Her heart pounding, she started walking again. This time, she reached the bed without colliding with anything.

'Judge,' she whispered as she stood above him. 'Judge.'

No response. He simply lay there.

She touched his shoulder. She whispered, 'Judge.'

She wished there was at least some moonlight to help her see better. She was in almost total darkness.

This time when she touched his shoulder, she gave him a little shake.

'Judge. Please. Wake up.'

Still whispering. Still unable to see well.

And then she realized something, something she should have picked up immediately.

There was no sound of breathing. Nor any little twitch of movement. He lay there as if he were—

She put her head down close to his nose and mouth,

Nothing. No sound of breathing whatsoever. Then she put her hand on top of his chest and felt something moist there.

She turned around to the table she'd brushed against. She remembered seeing the shape of a flashlight there. She reached out and let her fingers grope across the surface of the table. There seemed to be dozens of medicine bottles there. Where was the flash? Then she found it. Picked it up. Snapped on the light.

She trained the beam on his face. Noble profile, no doubt about it.

Then she angled the beam down and saw the dark red slash across his throat and the blood soaking the top of his buff blue pajamas.

Somebody had cut his throat.

Darcy stood there trying to get control of herself again. What kind of person would cut the throat of a man who wasn't expected to live even two more days? Who could possibly hate somebody that much?

She was just standing there, trying to figure out what to do next, when the door burst open behind her.

In the long stream of hall light angling through the door, a woman in silhouette said, 'Who's there?'

The woman didn't wait for an answer. She turned on the overhead light.

'Darcy!' It was Cindy.

Before Darcy could respond, Cindy came into the room, moving toward her father's bed. She'd put on a few pounds in the two years that Darcy had been gone but otherwise was as imperiously beautiful as ever.

'What're you doing here, Darcy?'

'I came to talk to your father. I thought maybe he could help—'

Cindy looked at her father and said, 'Oh, shit.' No big melo-dramatic scream. Just a small, 'Oh, shit.'

She pressed a beeper that was pinned to her father's bed. He could summon a nurse day or night.

'I didn't do this,' Darcy said. 'That's what you've got to under-stand. He was like this when I came in here.'

'God, I never believed until this very moment that you killed Rick Kenton,' Cindy said. 'Now I believe it – and you killed my father, too. Look at the blood on your fingers.'

Darcy raised her hand. Her fingers were moist and red.

'Yes, Cindy?' said the maid from the open door.

'Call the police,' Cindy said.

'Is something wrong?'

'She just murdered my father.'

'What?'

'Just call the police. I'll explain it all to you later.'

The maid hurried off down the hall.

'I saw Ted Foster running from here about ten minutes ago,' Darcy said. 'Why don't you ask him what he was doing here?'

Cindy said, 'I don't want to hear any bullshit stories from you, Darcy. Save those for your mystery novels.'

Darcy had to admit that it probably did sound pretty lame, trying to blame this on Ted Foster.

She decided to try a different tack. 'Why would I kill him, Cindy? He knew something that would help me. That's why I came here. I'm the last person who wanted him dead. Now I'll *never* know what kind of information he had for me.'

But even as she spoke, Darcy could see that Cindy wasn't interested in anything she had to say. Just wait for the police, put Darcy back in jail and charge her with another murder. Then get on with life. That was Cindy.

Darcy bolted. Prison had toughened her up considerably and Cindy seemed to sense that. As Darcy ran toward the door, Cindy screamed for help but she didn't try to impede Darcy in any way. She knew she'd get hurt if she did.

Then Darcy was through the door and starting down the stairs. She flung the front door open and ran into the waiting night.

PART TWO

12

Ken McCain was closing the stable up for the night. He was glad to have this time with the horses. The bigger his riding stables got, the less time it seemed he got to spend with the animals themselves. There were employees to deal with, feed salesmen to listen to, brochure-writing and design to oversee (advertising people could come up with some pretty strange ideas sometimes) and important customers to keep happy.

He liked this time of night in the barn, when the horses were settling down in their stalls. There was a sweetness to most of these animals that lent him a real peace of mind.

He went over and checked on the colt. Life was so precarious for some of these little guys. But this one, a beautiful chestnut, was coming along just fine. Mother and baby looked sublimely happy; and that made Ken happy, too.

He stood there in his black western shirt with the white piping and his jeans and his Texas boots and thought of how much more happy he'd be if Darcy were with him. He wondered if she was all right – and where she was now. With the police looking for her, she was in great danger, whether she knew it or not. He still didn't know why she'd cut him off so abruptly. No letters. No visits.

He said goodnight to mother and colt and left the barn for the ranch house.

The small, brick convenience store was an oasis in the dark night. There was a pay phone on the outside wall.

The rain had abated again. Everything smelled cold, fresh. Darcy stood in the shadows a quarter block down from the store. She wanted to use the two quarters she had to call Ken. He was her only hope now.

She decided to try it, leaving the dark street for the lighted drive of the store. A teenage girl was pumping gas into her rusted-out Ford. Two other teenage girls were standing off to the side smoking cigarettes and laughing.

Darcy kept her head down and walked quickly over to the phone. Or started to. But she paused abruptly when she saw the police car swing into the parking lot.

She knew better than to run; but that was all she could think to do. She glanced a second time at the police. The cop riding shotgun was watching her. Not with any great suspicion, it seemed, probably just checking her out physically. Then she remembered that she was wearing Fletcher's clothes. My God, no wonder the cop was staring at her.

Then the police car swung into a parking space to the right of the store. The driver didn't shut off the car, just jerked on the hand brake and got out. 'I thought you wanted a Snickers. When'd you switch to Mars bars?'

The shotgun cop laughed. 'Living dangerously, man.'

The driver walked into the store, giving Darcy only the quickest of glances.

She had a paranoid thought: what if this was a ploy? What if the cop inside was going out the back door so he could circle around and get her, while the cop in the car came at her from the other direction?

She looked over at the phone and then angled her head toward the cop in the car. He was watching her.

She had to get out of here. She had no choice.

She slowly turned and started walking back toward the darkness. She was trembling.

She wanted to look back, to see if he was still watching her, but she knew not to. Just keep walking, not too fast, not too slow. Just walking. Just an innocent citizen doing an innocent citizen's business.

She was half a block away when she saw the police car go by her. The shotgun cop was still watching her.

Could this be another ploy?

No, she didn't think so. He apparently had been looking her over sexually. Maybe he dug women in raggedy clothes. Every person had his or her own kink. Cops weren't any different.

Then, when the cop car was about a quarter of a block ahead of her, she saw the brakes light bloody in the night – and heard the whine of a massive car moving fast in reverse.

They'd decided she was worth checking out, after all.

Her only choice now was to run.

She ran between two small houses, tripped over a coiled garden hose, banging her shoulder painfully against the edge of a house, and then hobbled on toward a dark, cindered alleyway.

Sometimes Ken talked to her. She was in prison, and yet he talked to her as he walked through the rooms that once bloomed with her presence.

He talked to her and she responded by telling him that somehow, someday they'd be together again.

He was thinking of this as he made himself dinner after coming in from the stables. Turkey sandwiches and wheat bread with crisp leaves of spinach and lots of mayo.

Ken finished off his meal and then wandered, restless, into the living room. He wondered again where she was, how she was doing. What she was doing was dangerous. Very dangerous. Any time a manhunt was conducted, there were always a few people who wanted to be heroes, a few people who wanted a real good story to tell their grandchildren. Yep, the night I shot that escaped convict, I was scared as hell, and I don't mind admittin' it. But when I seen her, I just opened fire, and damned if she didn't fall down dead right in front of me.

At lunch this afternoon, he'd taken out the photo album she'd left behind. He'd looked through the fifteen years of their courtship and marriage. She got better looking the older she got. He just looked like more of cowhand, skinnier than ever. She always told him that he was one of those men who didn't grow into their faces – big nose and a shelf of brow – until they were in their thirties. He guessed he'd grown into his face by now.

So many memories . . . football games in Iowa City . . . the rodeo in Cheyenne, Wyoming (rodeo being the only western event she really liked) . . . skiing in Colorado (which they both loved) . . . hang gliding near Malibu with one of her editors . . . her family reunions . . . his family reunions . . . so many memories.

He sat in the silence now and said a silent prayer for her. Things had gotten so crazy with the trial and all.

If she was in town, he just hoped she had sense enough to turn to him . . .

Running. Stumbling. Wet grass. Mud puddles. The cop car hurtling through the alley. Distant sirens exploding into sound. People looking out their back windows.

Darcy was still limping from the knee injury she'd gotten from stumbling over the coiled hose. The cop car was now parked down in the middle of the alley. The two officers were out of their car, guns in one hand, big flashlights in the other. Their two-way rasped constantly, the voice of the dispatcher almost inhuman.

They were working their way back toward her. She had to decide on a plan quickly.

She scouted the two houses she stood between. One showed a light in the living room. The other looked completely dark. It also had one of those old cellars that you entered from the outside by laying back a wide door. This was her only hope.

She moved across the wet grass, trying to ignore the pain in her knee, and reached the cellar door.

She reached down to pull the door up toward her but something was holding the hasp lock together.

She could hear the policemen not far behind her. One of their flashlights beams played across the back wall of the house next to her. They were only seconds away.

A ten-inch piece of white plastic clothesline had been knotted to hold the door in place. She undid the knot and pulled the door back quickly, scampering into the dark cellar and easing the door closed as she went down the steps.

She almost tripped again, tumbling down the stairs. She put both hands out and grabbed the cellar walls. She was able to right herself.

The smell was of rotted earth. She didn't know how else to describe it. The rotted earth of a crypt, perhaps. Of a tomb.

There was no light at all and she moved by half inches. She had to find some place to hide. The cops were bound to look in here.

She groped her way through the darkness until she started to get some sense of the layout. The cellar was a squared-off room with plaster walls and a wooden plank floor. Between the ceiling and the wall there was a space of perhaps three feet. Originally, back at the turn of the century, these had been root cellars, used for storing fruits and vegetables. They were rarely finished off completely. The walls often did not touch the ceiling. This was the only place she could find to hide.

She spent the next few minutes searching for something to stand on. She managed to find a stool. She stood on it, her knee throbbing, dug her hands into the top of the wall and then began the torturous process of pulling herself up into the free space between wall and ceiling.

She felt drained, angry, sorry for herself but she kept pulling her way up. Twice, she slid back down. She wasn't exactly a world-class gymnast. But she knew she didn't have any choice. It was either this or turn herself over to the police.

She heard them outside, then, right on cue.

'Hey, look at this,' one of them said.

'What?'

'This cellar door.'

'Yeah. You want to check it out? I'm gonna ask the people next door if they saw anything.'

'Right.'

This time, she jumped as high as she could before reaching for the top of the wall. She brought her feet against the wall, too, for more purchase. And then she scrambled up the wall and rolled back toward the even deeper darkness beneath the front of the house.

Moments later, she heard the cellar door creak open. Saw the beam of the cop's flashlight play across the ceiling.

Then the cop came all the way down into the cellar. He didn't spend much time. Apparently, it didn't occur to him that anybody might hide between the ceiling and the top of the wall. Or maybe he was spooked by the fetid death smell of the place. A cellar like this really brought home what awaited the human body after it died.

He got out of there fast. His flashlight beam went away, his footsteps grew silent, and the cellar door creaked closed again.

For the moment, she was safe.

Ken spent some time going over some rough drawings he'd been making for expanding the stables. He wouldn't do it right away, of course. Couldn't afford to. But if business held steady, he'd be able to double his capacity for boarding horses, and that would increase his cash flow, making it less necessary to borrow from the bank. Some smart businessmen he knew felt that borrowing money was a good thing. You always had the cash flow you needed. But borrowing scared Ken. What happened if he got sick? Or there was a downturn in the general economy and people didn't have money for horses anymore? He'd seen too many businesses similar to his go down because of outstanding debt. Wherever possible, he was a pay-as-you-go man.

The phone rang once and he snapped it off its cradle on the wall.

'Hello?'

Silence.

'Hello?'

It was her, Darcy, he was sure of it.

Then, 'Bob?'

An old man's voice.

'No. You have the wrong number.'

'Oh, I'm sorry.'

'It's all right.'

He hung up and went back to his drawings. It was nice to dream. Without the hindrance of an actual budget, you could design the mother of all stables and not have to worry about the tab.

The phone rang again.

After the woman introduced herself, he said, 'I figured I'd hear from you.'

'She's back in town,' Police Chief Amy Foster said.

'Is that what people say?'

'She was at the Carmichael estate just a few minutes ago. I'm on my way there now. Cindy said that she saw Darcy in the Judge's bedroom. Somebody'd cut his throat.'

'My God.' Then, 'Darcy wouldn't do anything like that.'

'Prison can change you.'

'Not that much.'

'She's already killed one person that we know of, Ken. That's why she was in prison, remember?'

'You grew up with her, Amy. You know what kind of woman she is. She's not a killer.'

Amy sighed. 'No, I didn't think so, either, Ken. But the evidence was pretty overwhelming.' Then, 'You're going to hear from her.'

'I hope I do.'

'Then it'll be your legal obligation to call me and turn her over.'

He didn't say anything.

'Ken? Did you hear what I said?'

'Yes.'

'Your legal obligation, Ken.'

'I know.'

'Cindy saw Darcy with blood on her hand.'

'Meaning what, exactly?'

'You didn't listen very well, Ken. A woman with bloody fingers is standing over a dead man who has just had his throat cut. That doesn't suggest anything to you?'

'She didn't have any reason to kill him.'

'Maybe she did. I guess the Judge wrote her some letter and got her all excited about asking for a new trial. Maybe she was disappointed when she learned that the Judge didn't really have anything for her, after all. He was just trying to make her feel better before he died.'

'That doesn't sound like Judge Carmichael.'

'You'd be surprised,' Amy said. 'He really liked Darcy. In fact, when we were teenagers, I think the Judge had a little crush on her.' Then, 'As soon as you hear from her, I expect a phone call, Ken.'

'All right.'

'All right, you'll do it? Or all right, just get off the phone?'

He laughed. 'Man, you're a real tough hombre these days, Amy.'

'Goes with the territory.' Then, 'I expect that call, Ken.'

'Hard to believe we all used to be friends, Amy.'

'I'm just doin' my job, Ken. That's all. Same as my father used to do.'

Ken sighed. 'Yeah, I s'pose that's true. Sure wouldn't be a job I'd want, though.'

'Just remember to call me.'

She hung up.

Darcy waited until all the noise had died down outside, cops and neighbors alike moving on. Presumably, the cops had concluded that she had somehow made it off this block and was now in another part of the town. The neighbors were probably a bit chilly by now and wanted to head back to their houses and their TV sets.

She crawled out of her hiding place, eased herself down the cellar wall, and stood on her feet. She'd long ago adjusted her vision to this particular darkness and could now see things pretty well.

But she didn't go longer than a few moments without a paranoid thought: what if all this was a set-up? She could picture it. The cops hiding in the alley, waiting for her to come up out of the cellar. Easy for them. They wouldn't have to take chances in the dank shadows of the cellar, confined spaces always being a bad place for a confrontation that might eventually involve guns. And, at this point, they might assume she was armed.

She could see herself easing open the cellar door to find a semicircle of armed cops standing above her.

But what choice did she have? There was only one way she was going to find out if there were cops waiting for her. She certainly couldn't stay down here all night. She needed clothes and warmth and food. Only one person could possibly provide all that: Ken. She just wasn't sure how he'd react to a call from her.

She walked carefully across the cellar floor, past a three-shelf case that held dusty old Mason jars, a holdover from the root-cellar days. She pictured a nice, warm autumn afternoon, doing some canning and baking some pies. Right now, that sounded very nice.

She tiptoed up the steps, still imagining the cops and the shot guns out there waiting for her. Then touched her fingers to the door.

She took a deep breath, held it momentarily, and then let it out.

Might as well get it over with, she thought.

She pushed open the door. All she saw at first was a patch of night sky. A few rain drops hit her face.

She walked up the remaining steps.

The first thing she noticed about the woman was the Remington rifle; the second thing was the man's battered fedora. Somehow, it looked just as right and imposing on her as it would have on a man. The rest of the woman was dressed in flannel shirt, brown corduroy trousers, and brown suede ankle-length boots.

'You got a gun, Darcy?' the woman said.

'No, I don't.'

'Then get in the house.'

'What?'

'I said to get in the house. There's a side door.'

There was something vaguely familiar about the woman. At least, it seemed so in the turmoil of this moment, anyway. From the little Darcy could see of the woman's face, she put her age somewhere in the late sixties. But she didn't move like an older person. She was dead steady with that rifle of hers.

'You want me to put my hands up?' Darcy said.

'Huh?'

'My hands up in the air. Like this. You know, how they do it in the movies.' She raised her hands over her head.

'You being a smart ass?'

'No. I just wondered if you wanted my hands up.'

'You want 'em up, put 'em up, I don't care.'
'Then I'll leave them down.'
'Fine by me. Now get in the house.'

13

The prompt man is a lonely man, a poet once said, and the good Reverend Selden certainly knew this to be true. He was neurotic about being on time. In fact, he set his wristwatch and all of the household clocks to run fast so he'd be sure to give himself a ten-minute lead time.

He arrived at the cabin fifteen minutes before the meeting was scheduled to start. He drove up the narrow road deep in several acres of timberland. The place was perfectly isolated.

The cabin was a long stone-and-wood structure that the Carmichael family had built back in the thirties sometime. It had beds enough for six, in case anybody was really hot about staying overnight, a modern kitchen and a great leather-padded poker table. Ostensibly, that was why the men had met out here the past nine years – to play poker. But there were other reasons, reasons that might someday be exposed to the scrutiny of the press and public. And then the Reverend's life – along with several others – would be destroyed.

That was what the meeting tonight was about: damage control. A lot of curious reporters would soon be swarming all over Parkhurst. The combination of the Judge's murder and Darcy's escape was a great news story. But The Committee had to be very careful exactly where the press went, and how far.

There were parking spaces to the left of the cabin. He pulled into one of them and killed the motor. He could go inside but the truth was, being alone in the cabin spooked him for some reason. He always waited for the others.

He started thinking about Kim Sawyer, the woman who'd been in his office earlier tonight. She practically made him weep with lust. If only that call hadn't interrupted him—

That's when he happened to glance in the rear view and saw a shadow-shape moving behind his car.

105

For the second time that evening, his erection quit on him. Somebody was creeping around the cabin tonight.

He hit the auto-lock. He was now sealed safely in his car.

He turned around and looked at some bushes to his left. That's where the shadow-shape had disappeared. Into those bushes. He shuddered.

Then he felt as glad as a little boy who had not seen his father in a long, long time. Coming up the dirt road were two cars, the Pontiac that Chief Amy drove, and the silver Jag favored by Cindy.

He got out of the car, taking a last suspicious look at the bushes where the shadow-shape had vanished.

Or had he simply imagined the shadow-shape? Let his fears play tricks on him?

Maybe it was just God paying him back for sitting in his car and having carnal thoughts of a woman not his wife. God was like that sometimes – pissy. No doubt about it. Pissy pissy pissy. A guy tries to have a little fun and then look what happens.

Just then the ladies pulled up and he turned his eyes from the bushes.

He just missed seeing the shadow-shape peering out at him.

'You mean you're not going to turn me in?'

'Did you kill Rick Kenton?'

'No.'

'Did you kill Judge Carmichael?'

'No.'

'Honest?'

'Honest.'

'On your father's grave?'

'How do you know my father?'

'Answer my question. You swear on your father's grave?'

'I swear on my father's grave.'

'That's what I figured, that you're telling the truth, and that's why I'm not turning you in.'

The kitchen was a museum. There was a white refrigerator in the corner with its motor on top. The floor was ancient linoleum. And the sink was big enough for a small person to take a bath in. The kitchen of the future was here – in 1931. The strange thing was, it was a very pleasant room. And the woman, now without her fedora, looked at home in these surroundings. She had soft, appealing features, pure white hair, and a body that still looked sound and straight.

'You want some coffee?'

'God, are you kidding? I'd *love* some coffee.'

The woman went across the small kitchen and turned off the heat under an old-fashioned metal coffee pot. It was easy to imagine her in one of the movies of the thirties and forties. A good woman, a smart woman, an industrious woman, the kind who joined the war effort during World War II. Darcy had always admired self-possessed women like this one. She secretly suspected that many women in her generation – including herself until she ended up in prison – were too soft.

'You like some sugar?'

'A little sugar'd be great.'

'You're shaking.'

'I'm cold. It's been a long day.'

The woman brought Darcy a cup of coffee. 'It's real hot, so watch it.'

Darcy thanked the woman. She took the cup. She was trembling with anticipation of the heat that would soon be inside her. She sipped at the coffee then blew on it. The woman hadn't been kidding. This was very hot coffee.

The woman sat down next to her at the small wooden kitchen table. 'You go right down that hall there and you'll find a bathroom. Have yourself a warm bath. Plus I laid out some clothes for you. Nothing fancy. But they're clean and warm. I even found a pair of old oxfords and some socks. What size shoe do you wear?'

'Seven and a half, usually.'

'These're eights. Should fit you fine with socks on.'

Darcy watched her a long moment. 'I just wish I knew why you were doing all this for me.'

'Think it's some kind of trap?'

'I guess it'd crossed my mind.'

'I'm repaying a debt.'

'Oh?'

The woman said, 'My name's Bernice Donlon, by the way. I don't expect you'd remember it.'

'Then I used to know you?'

'Not in the sense that we were friends. I used to clean your father's office at the bank. I still do a little cleaning part-time. You know, whenever the maintenance service needs a substitute.'

Darcy smiled. ' "Bernice Donlon." That's why the name is so familiar. "Fudge from Bernice Donlon." You used to make us this great big box of fudge when I was a little girl.'

'Right.'

'My father loved you. Said you were the best employee he ever had.'

Bernice looked solemn. 'He must've loved me. I had a son born with a bad foot. He couldn't walk very well. My husband died when the boy was six and we didn't have any insurance for the operation. Your father paid for it. I've never forgotten.'

'How's your boy doing now?'

Bernice's eyes glistened. 'Died over in Vietnam. 1967. Stupid war. Stupid men and stupid war.'

'I'm sorry.'

Bernice watched her closely. 'All the time your trial was going on, I just kept trying to figure out how such a sweet little girl like the one I'd made fudge for could turn into a murderer. I guess I always figured you were innocent.' She blew on her own coffee. 'Now I've finally got a chance to pay your father back. When I heard the cellar door open, I wondered if it might not be you. I get a hobo every once in a while down there but not very often. Then when the police showed up, I knew it was you. What'd you do, hide up there between the wall and the ceiling?'

'Uh-huh.'

She smiled. 'Smart girl.'

They sat there for a time sipping their coffee. Then Bernice said, 'I read all your books. You're the only author I ever knew. I always show 'em to people and say I used to make fudge for this girl.'

'That's sweet. Thank you.'

'You're a good writer.'

'Well, I try.'

'I never could figure out how a person could write a whole book. I could barely finish my school papers. But I've always been a big reader, though. My husband was, too. He read western magazines.' She smiled, her eyes sweet with sentiment. 'He always said he wanted to be buried with one, in case they let him read up there.'

'He sounds like a nice man.'

'The best. I guess that's why I never remarried.'

'You're very pretty. You must've had offers.'

'Oh, every once in a while somebody'd ask me out but I just never found anybody that interested me all that much. Too hard to please, I suppose.' Then, 'You're married to Ken McCain, right?'

'Yes.'

'Boy, his operation out there is growin' bigger every month.' She sipped her coffee. 'He's a nice guy, Ken.'

'Yes, he is.'

'I was so embarrassed to see him when he visited me in prison, I was afraid I'd drive him away.'

'He's still in love with you.'

'Maybe. Or maybe he just feels sorry for me. I don't want him to be around just because he pities me.'

'Somehow, I don't think that's the case.'

Darcy was steeling herself for later when she had to call him. She didn't have any choice but to turn to him now.

'I'll go start the water for you. There's a linen closet in the hall. Grab yourself a towel and a washcloth.'

'I really do appreciate this.'

'My pleasure. Least I can do for your father.'

A few minutes later, Darcy stood in a small bathroom with a claw-footed tub and a toilet that had a chain flusher hanging from above.

The water was running – took a while for a tub this big to fill up – but the steam from the water felt good. She finally started to feel warm.

Bernice had even left some bubble bath out for her. Darcy picked up the plastic bottle and squirted a ribbon of fluid into the water. This was going to feel so good.

She allowed herself to forget completely about the manhunt. She slipped into the water. It was actually a little hot but she didn't want to turn the cold water on to balance out the temperature. She'd been heat-starved for so long, she was willing to put up with a few minutes of discomfort.

She even managed to doze off a bit, her head laid against the back of the tub. Bernice was such a nice woman. Made Darcy sentimental about her father, too. He was a good and wise man. Everybody had respected his judgment and sense of fairness. He'd been the model citizen, husband and father, in fact. And somehow, for a man of such decency, he'd also been an *interesting* man. She loved to sit on his lap when she was little and have him read to her.

He liked the Edgar Rice Burroughs books of his youth – though her mother wished that he would read her something more 'feminine' – and later he introduced her to Sherlock Holmes. Two Holmes–Watson stories and she was hooked. She not only wanted to spend the rest of her life *reading* mystery stories. She wanted to *write* them as well.

It was so nice to lie here, warm and safe, and think about her father.

So nice.

14

Bernice sat in the kitchen, thinking things over for fifteen, twenty minutes. Then she got up and went into the small living room – she'd put doilies on every piece of furniture that was appropriate and a few that weren't – and picked up phone and phone book. The number was easy to find.

Two, three, rings.

By this time, Bernice was expecting to hear one of those telephone answering machines. She knew she was old-fashioned but she absolutely *hated* those things. She'd rather get no answer at all than talk to a machine.

Maybe she shouldn't be doing this, anyway.

Maybe she was going to get herself in trouble with the police.

Maybe they'd arrest her and put her in jail.

Wouldn't that be a story they'd be talking about at St Patrick's Catholic Church for years? Quiet little Bernice Donlon, going to prison.

Four rings now. And still no answer.

But even if she *did* get in trouble, she wanted to help Darcy because of all the things Darcy's father had done for Bernice over the years.

Five rings.

'Hello?'

'Mr McCain?'

'Yes.'

'My name is Bernice Donlon. I'm at Four Three Five River Street. Do you know where that is?'

'Roughly, yes. What can I help you with?' He sounded impatient. Probably thought she was one of those telephone solicitors.

'Oh, a friend of yours just got back in town and I thought maybe you'd like to see her.'

'A friend of mine?' Then, 'Oh. Yes.'

'We're just having some nice coffee and talking up a storm and wondering if you'd like to come over.'

'What was the address again?'

'Four Three Five River Street.'

'Well, thank you, Bernice.'

'My pleasure.'

As she hung up, she realized that she was having a good time. A good church-going woman like herself helping an escaped convict and having herself a good time. She wondered if this was a venal or a mortal sin?

'Was that Ken?' a voice said from behind her.

She turned around.

Darcy actually looked like a human being now. She wore a long-sleeved white shirt, a blue sleeveless pull-over sweater and a pair of tan corduroy trousers. The white socks and black Oxfords weren't exactly high fashion but they'd do.

'Was that Ken you were talking to?'

'I probably shouldn't have done it, Darcy. I'm sorry.'

'What'd he say?'

'I think he's coming over. He sounded that way.' Then, 'You mad at me?'

Darcy smiled. 'No, I was going to call him, anyway. You just beat me to the punch.'

Darcy came in and sat down. The living room was another relic. There was even an ancient console-model Philco radio in one corner. Darcy was sure that if she turned it on she'd hear some wonderful old radio show from the forties.

'You're a great friend, Bernice. I really appreciate all this.'

'Now I've had two chances to pay your father back.'

'Oh?'

'Yeah, one night at the office – your father worked a lot of nights, as you know – one of his friends went a little crazy. Maybe he was drunk or something.'

'One of his friends?'

'Yes, Judge Carmichael.'

'That's hard to imagine. Judge Carmichael, I mean, acting crazy.'

'That's what I thought, too. But he was really angry and loud. He just kept saying, "He was innocent! He was innocent! And look what we did to him!" I could hear them arguing and then I heard things being smashed inside your father's office. So I went in there and Judge Carmichael was just about to hit your father with a vase. I told you he was crazy. I jumped up and grabbed the vase from him and then your father grabbed Judge Carmichael and slapped him very hard and then threw him down into this chair.' She smiled. 'I figured I saved your Dad a few stitches in the head.'

'Did you ever figure out what they were arguing about?'

'No. Just what I overheard that one time, about the man being innocent.'

'Did you have any sense of who the man was they were talking about?'

'No.'

'Did you just go home and leave them there?'

'Your father called Chief Foster. He came over right away. He was always real nice to me, too. He told me that I should just finish up for the evening and go home. I remember that your father and Judge Carmichael started to yell at each other again but Chief Foster went in and told them to be quiet until I left. I figured there was something secret going on there.'

'You remember when this was?'

'Oh, let's see. Say, five years ago or so. They still had The Committee meetings all the time. Your father, Chief Foster, Judge Carmichael and Reverend Selden, I mean. In fact, just as I was leaving, I saw Reverend Selden pull up.'

'Did you see my father the next evening when you were cleaning?'

'Oh, yes. He was hard at work as usual.'

'Did he act any different?'

'Different?'

'You know, as if something was really troubling him.'

'He acted pretty serious. He'd always tell me little jokes and things – before, I mean.'

'Did you ever hear him arguing with anybody else as he had with Judge Carmichael?'

'Not really. He'd get irritated with his secretary once in a while – she lost a lot of stuff for him – but never another blow-up like the one he had with the Judge.' Then, 'How about some tea?'

'That sounds great.'

'You sure you're not mad at me?'

'Of course not, Bernice.'

As Bernice started to leave the room, Darcy said, 'Did my father ever say anything to you about the argument with the Judge?'

'No. He just thanked me for helping him out.' She thought a moment and then said, 'He didn't *say* anything more. But I did hear him the next night talking on the phone about somebody getting killed.'

'But you don't know *who* got killed?'

'No. I heard him talking to a couple of different people on the phone about it. The only reason I remember it was because he sounded so angry – the way Judge Carmichael had.' Then, 'You sit there. I've got some herbal tea that's just great.'

While Bernice worked in the kitchen, Darcy thought about what she'd just heard. Why would her father have gotten so upset over somebody's death? Grief, yes – but rage? And why would one of his best friends, Judge Carmichael, try to hit him?

Even though she was sure Bernice was reporting it accurately, the story made no sense. No sense at all.

Then Bernice was back with the tea and it was every bit as good as she'd promised.

15

Five minutes after finishing his conversation with Bernice, Ken McCain tugged on his cowboy boots, his denim jacket and his western hat. He glanced at a note he'd written himself and thumbtacked to the back door: CAR READY TO PICK UP AT SANDERSON'S. Ed Sanderson ran the DX station and worked on all of Ken's vehicles. Ken had dropped his Pontiac Firebird off this morning for a tuneup. Sanderson hadn't been sure he could get to it today. But then late this afternoon, he'd left a message on the phone machine saying the Pontiac was all ready to go and that he'd leave it outside in the back.

Ken said goodbye to Socrates, the male tabby that he and Darcy had found at the animal pound right after getting married. Socrates was the only feline Ken had ever really liked, probably because he was such an ornery old cuss who pretty much ran the house as he saw fit. This amused Ken greatly.

Ken walked out the door. The front door of the house opened on a hill that gave people a good look at the valley below. The driveway swept eastward, down to a gravel road that ran north-south.

There was a timber road that cut deep into the hardwoods. Right now, parked outside the PRIVATE PROPERTY signs, was one of those unmarked police cars that gave themselves away by their very plainness.

Amy was watching him. Not her personally, but there'd be one or two of her men in the car, staking him out in case he decided to meet up with his wife somewhere.

He decided to try to cut across the pasture land and exit by the far gate. Leave those boys down there just sitting the rest of the night.

He backed up the sleek black Ranger and then headed across bumpy earth toward the far gate. The rain was little more than mist

115

now. Behind him, the ranch house looked dark and foreboding – the way it had looked to him since Darcy had left him.

He climbed two large hills in the Ranger and then came down-slope at thirty miles per hour. There was a meadow of buffalo grass stretching out to the east of the far gate. When he reached the gate, he jumped out of the truck, opened up the padlock, then swung the gate open. Then he had to repeat the process in reverse after he got out on the road.

He looked around. This was more heavily timbered than the land in front of the ranch house. There were also more hiding places. Though there wasn't a road, there were wide enough avenues between some of the trees to hold a police car. He saw none. Either they were very good at hiding or his eyes weren't what they once had been.

He got back in the Ranger and took off down the gravel road. He'd gone a mile, maybe a mile-and-a-half and, damn, there was another unmarked police cruiser.

They'd managed to stash themselves in the woods without him spotting them.

Now what?

There was no way he was going to lead them to Bernice's house and Darcy.

He drove the speed limit all the way into town and then made a big deal of stopping off at the Dairy Queen for a cone. They sat across the street watching him. Two of them. He could see them from here. One of them had a daughter Ken had given riding lessons to.

There was an exit in the rear off the drive. That was his only hope of losing them.

Knowing he was being watched, he backed out of his stall and turned the Ranger so it was facing them, as if he was going to drive out into the street and turn right or left.

But he surprised them. Just before he got to the street, he turned abruptly and started to drive around the Dairy Queen building itself. Then he raced for the exit.

When he reached the dark back street, he turned right and raced down the street.

What stunned him was that they were only half a block behind him suddenly. The driver knew what he was doing.

Ken gave them a run for about three blocks and then got an

116

idea. He stopped at the next red light, the way any law-abiding citizen would do.

Now, in the aftermath of the rain, Parkhurst looked clean and snug. He wished he was sitting home tonight with Darcy.

He had to be quick, or his plan wouldn't work.

The cop car was right behind him. He imagined the guys inside were pissed. Cops didn't like high-speed chases and he couldn't really say he blamed them.

But he was about to put them through another one.

He peeled out so fast, the Ranger fishtailed. He shot across the intersection and disappeared into a dark section of the city along the riverfront. This was a stretch that the urban renewal folks hadn't gotten to yet.

It was very important that he get a two- or three-block lead on them. He floored it. There was no traffic on this stretch of asphalt so he didn't feel he was endangering anybody but himself.

By now, he was doing seventy-five mile per hour.

The next left turn was crucial. Could he slow down enough to make it?

He got down to sixty and wrenched the wheel to the left. The block he'd turned on to was a stretch of small, deserted stores, some of which had been built as long ago as the 1920s. They were weather-grayed, boarded-up, and all marked NO TRESPASSING.

He kept looking for a good spot. He also kept checking the rear view mirror.

One block, two blocks. He still didn't see anything that would suit his purposes.

Then he saw the dark side street and decided that this was his best hope.

He whipped the car to the right, cut lights and engine, and hopped down. He made sure to keep the truck near enough to the street light so that they couldn't miss it.

He took off running down an alley that ran behind the deserted stores. Through openings between the buildings, he saw the unmarked vehicle hurtle down the street. Then the sound of brakes screaming. They'd obviously spotted the truck. Now they'd have to spend several minutes approaching the Ranger, making sure it wasn't a trap of some kind. By the time they'd radioed for help, and got inside the Ranger to take a look, he would be long gone.

The running started to get to him so he slowed to a jog. By now,

Darcy was probably thinking that he wasn't going to show up.

He could imagine her in his arms again. He could imagine himself saying he was sorry for all the petty jealousy that had driven them apart; that he was sorry he hadn't trusted her; that, if he had another chance, he'd trust her this time.

Sirens. Help was on the way. They'd really give the Ranger a going through. He wondered if they'd put an All Points Bulletin out for him, as they had with Darcy. He didn't care. He wanted to help her. Whatever she wanted to do, he'd be with her.

It took him nearly fifteen minutes to walk out of the deserted section of the city and back into an area with lights, traffic, and people.

He kept to the shadows, walking the sidewalk with his hands in his pockets, and his head down.

A car load of smart-ass teenagers hollered something at him. A cop car cruising past slowed for him and then drove on. No APB apparently – not yet, anyway.

And then he saw it, a large DX gas station closed for the night, three bays for working on cars and a large drive. Ken Sanderson would be damned if he'd turn it into a little shopping market. 'I work on cars,' he always said, 'I leave milk to the grocery stores.'

Wind skittered papers across the rain-slick drive; puddles shimmered.

Ken took his keys out of his pocket and started to walk around to the back of the station.

That was when he heard a car slow in the street. He turned to see a patrol car sitting at the curb.

'Hold on there a minute,' the cop behind the wheel said.

He brought up a flashlight. The beam was powerful enough to reach Ken.

A quick decision. On the one hand, the cop probably didn't know who he was. He was most likely suspicious of a burglary of some kind. But if he called Ken's name into the station, Ken would be taken in for sure.

Ken bolted.

'Hey!' the cop shouted. 'Stop right there!'

There were three large, empty oil barrels pushed against the wall of the gas station. Ken veered into them before he got his footing in the mud.

In the back were three cars sitting in the center of a large area of concrete. One of the cars was his Firebird.

He could hear a lone cop running toward him, the other cop was wheeling the patrol car on to the drive.

He couldn't get the key in straight. Stress – nerves. Calm. Had to be calm.

He jammed the key in. This time, it worked. He jerked open the door and slid inside.

'Stop!' the cop shouted as he reached the back of the station.

Ken floored the car. Hurtling back to the alley.

The cop fired a warning shot into the air and then crouched and neatly put a bullet in the right rear tire.

Though steering became difficult, with the car pulling so much because of the ruptured tire, Ken didn't slow down. He kept on heading straight out of the alley.

River Street was six blocks from here. He turned his lights on and drove the speed limit. He'd have time to reach River Street without attracting attention – if he drove sensibly.

He was amazed at how different Parkhurst looked now. The town he'd grown up in was a place of shadows and strangers, of enemies with guns who wanted to keep him from the woman he loved – and who would do harm to her if they had half a chance.

He'd always been curious about the criminal mentality. Now he had a sense of it. How the danger fed you like a drug, and how it altered your perception of things.

The cop car was half a block behind him when its siren screamed to life. He couldn't outdrive them. Not with a flat tire. He slammed on the brakes, killed the engine, and jumped from the car. He started running . . . and found the address on River Street.

Directly behind Bernice's house was a very old two-stall garage. He ran inside there and hid. One stall was filled with a dusty twenty-year old Plymouth. The other stall was empty.

Headlights; the squawk of a two-way radio. A patrol car was coming in the alley. Bernice had two large silver garbage cans sitting next to the gravel of the alleyway.

After the car had disappeared at the opposite end of the alley, Ken stood up and started walking to the back of Bernice's house. She'd probably been expecting him to show up at the front door. He needed to get out of the garage right away. The cops would come back soon and search the alley on foot.

There was no back porch, just three steps leading to a back door. A cellar door was nearby.

He knocked and then waited. The kitchen was dark. He'd been hoping to get a glimpse of Darcy. It had been a long, long time.

Of course, what if Bernice had called on her own? What if Darcy didn't *want* him here?

After a few moments, a small woman silhouetted against a light from the living room came to the back door and peered out.

Bernice had a sweet face.

'I'm Ken.'

'Yes, I know,' she said, opening the door.

He came inside. 'You want me to take my boots off? They're probably muddy.'

'If you wouldn't mind, I'd appreciate it.'

He leaned against the doorframe in the kitchen shadows, taking his boots off one at a time.

'Never could see why people wore those things,' Bernice said. 'They really comfortable?'

'After a while, they are.' Then, 'Darcy here?'

Bernice smiled. 'You mean you'd rather see her than stand here and listen to an old lady ramble on about cowboy boots?'

She took him by the arm and led him in all his sock-footed glory to the living room. There sat Darcy. And, as if he needed any reminder, he certainly got it now: he had never loved a person as deeply and truly as he loved her.

Then she was up off the chair and in his arms, and he made a sound that was either a laugh or cry, or maybe a little of each.

Wise lady that she was, Bernice said, 'I'll just go into the kitchen and attend to the tea.'

16

There were four of them sitting around the poker table in the Carmichael cabin.

Amy wore her khaki police uniform; Cindy was dressed in a starched white button-down shirt, blue V-neck sweater and jeans; and Reverend Selden preened in a black turtleneck and Miami Beach tan slacks.

Cindy had a small bottle of medicine sitting in front of her on the table. She was sipping from a glass of bourbon that Amy had brought her.

'What kind of medication are you taking?' Reverend Selden said.

'Don't worry about me,' Cindy said. 'I'm not one of your flock.' Like many young women in Selden's church, Cindy had once had a passionate teenage crush on the good Reverend. She was used to having her way and when she didn't get it, she turned against Selden. She'd never gotten over her dislike of the man. Cindy's selfishness precluded her from seeing Selden's dilemma. It was one thing to occasionally bed a married woman he was counseling. It was quite another to hit on the teenage daughter of a Someone as important as Judge Carmichael.

'I was just trying to be nice,' Selden said.

'We don't need any more stress than we have already,' Amy said. 'We're here to work through everything, not snap at each other.'

'I was just trying to be nice,' Selden said again.

'I heard you the first time,' Amy said.

'Any further word on Darcy?'

Amy shook her head. 'No, but we now think that Ken's helping her.'

'Ken?' Cindy said.

'Yes, he seems to be giving her a hand. I put a couple of cars on him and he managed to elude them. I'm assuming he met her someplace.'

121

Cindy started crying, then. She'd been doing that ever since the three of them had sat down. 'God, I loved my father so much. And I was so shitty to him most of the time.'

Reverend Selden looked as if he was about to go over and comfort her. Amy shook her head. She simply put her hand out and laid it gently upon Cindy's.

'He despised me,' Cindy sobbed. 'And I don't blame him. I was such a bitch. He always liked Darcy. She was his favorite, not me. I should be back there taking care of the funeral arrangements. I can't even do that right.'

'Of course he loved you, Cindy. He loved you very much.' But even as she spoke the words, Amy knew they were lies. The only one of the three girls Judge Carmichael had ever liked was Darcy.

'You really think he loved me?' Cindy asked, sounding uncharacteristically helpless.

'Yes, I know he did.' Another lie: 'He told me that a few months ago.'

'He did?'

'Yes. He told me how proud he was of how you'd taken over running his house and everything.'

'Oh, God,' Cindy said, taking Amy's hand this time. 'I'm so glad you told me that.'

Reverend Selden said, 'We need to talk about The Committee. I mean, that's why we're here. I'm sorry if I sound insensitive, Cindy.'

'Oh, yes,' Cindy said, 'you're such an exemplary man of God, Reverend. I remember the night you tried to feel me up when we sat next to each other at a football game a few years ago. I think that's just what Jesus would have done, don't you? I should've said something to my husband.'

'God, you two,' Amy said. 'Please knock off the bullshit, all right?'

Cindy and the Reverend looked like chastened children.

'Cindy,' Amy said, 'do you know if your father sent Darcy a second letter?'

'No, I don't.'

'So she may know something about The Committee?'

'I'd say there's good chance that she *does* know something about The Committee.'

'I still don't understand,' Amy said. 'Why he'd write to at all.'

Cindy brought a Kleenex to her tear-red nose. 'Because I think he saw The Committee as wrong.'

'But he was the one who started it,' Selden said.

'I think he thought it was a good thing up until—' Cindy shrugged. 'Well, I don't have to remind you what happened, do I?'

'So you're saying, maybe he wanted the whole thing exposed?' Amy said.

'I'm not sure it was that conscious. But let's just say I don't think he would've *minded* if it had all been exposed.'

'Great,' Amy said.

'And he takes the rest of us – and our families – down with him,' Selden said.

'You going to give us one of your "family value" sermons, are you, Reverend?' Cindy said.

'C'mon now,' Amy said. Then, 'So it sounds as if she really *may* know something. Darcy, I mean.'

'That's just ducky,' the Reverend said.

Cindy looked around the table. 'You know the funny thing? She should be here tonight, sitting at this table. I took over *my* father's chair, and *you* took over your father's chair, Amy – and she should be sitting here in *her* father's chair.'

'Yes, she should,' Amy said. 'But we knew better than to ask her. She wouldn't want anything to do with The Committee. She'd turn us all in.'

'I thought she was such a good friend of yours,' Selden said.

'She was,' Amy said. 'But she has a real rigid sense of right and wrong. She'd never understand that we were acting on the best of motives.'

' "The best of motives," ' Selden said. 'That sounds very nice.'

'I think you should kill her, Amy,' Cindy said simply.

'Good Lord, Cindy,' Selden said.

'You mean that hadn't crossed your mind, you hypocritical bastard?' Cindy said. 'That's why we're here, isn't it? To figure out how to take care of Darcy. Because if Darcy knows as much as we think she might, then everything that happened will be exposed. And our families will be ruined.'

'Look!' Selden said suddenly.

'What?' Amy said.

'The window over there. Next to the couch.'

'What about it?'

'I saw somebody there just now,' Selden said.

Amy touched her chest. 'Well, that sure got my heart started. Are you sure you saw somebody?'

'Yes, and I saw somebody earlier, too, when I was waiting for you.'

'What did they look like?' Amy said.

'I didn't see either time. It was just like a shadow or something.'

'Or a ghost maybe?' Cindy said. 'Maybe this is a haunted cabin.'

'You can make fun of me if you want,' Selden said. 'But I saw somebody just now – and I did earlier, too.'

Amy looked at Cindy. 'I suppose I should check it out.'

'He's just imagining things.'

'Maybe not,' Amy said. 'I'll just take a flashlight and look around out there.'

'Well, I'm not staying in here with him, that's for sure,' Cindy said. 'I'll go with you.'

'I'll just hold the fort,' Selden said.

'What a hero,' Cindy said.

She didn't want it to feel this good – this warm, this reassuring, this *protected* – but that was exactly how it felt to be in Ken's embrace, and Darcy couldn't deny it.

Years fell away within moments as they stood in Bernice's small living room holding each other. Just holding each other.

'Been a long time,' Darcy said.

'Too long.'

She tilted her head back so she could see his face. 'I was thinking the same thing.'

'You didn't answer my letters.'

'I didn't want you to get involved, Ken. That's why.'

'But I *am* involved. You know that. You're my wife, remember?'

He held her close again and kissed her on the lips. Her sensory memories of him – his smell, the angle of his bones, the texture of his skin – overwhelmed her.

'God, I'm glad to see you again.'

'Me, too.'

'You've got a lot of people looking for you,' Ken said. 'And now, so do I.'

He told her what happened in the past forty-five minutes, being trailed by the police cars, finally eluding them.

'Oh, Ken. Now you're in trouble, too. That's why I haven't

answered your letters. I didn't want you to get involved.'

'But I *am* involved,' he said again. 'So you've got a partner whether you like it or not.'

'Knock, knock,' Bernice said as she approached the living room. 'I've got some tea here.'

Darcy leaned forward and kissed him gently on the lips. 'What a way to see you again.'

'Better than seeing you in prison.'

'Guess I couldn't argue with that.'

Bernice was there, then. Ken and Darcy sat next to each other on the couch while Bernice laid out more tea and food.

Darcy said, 'I'm going to gain twenty pounds tonight.'

'You're skin and bones,' Bernice said.

Darcy grinned. 'Something tells me I've found myself a new Mom.'

'It'd be an honor to be your mother, hon. Celebrated mystery author like yourself.'

'Don't forget to add "escaped convict" to my list of accomplishments,' Darcy said.

They ate and drank and made small talk.

Then Ken said, 'The last time I wrote you, I mentioned that Rick Kenton had a girlfriend. She's back in town, in fact, working as a stripper out at a roadhouse on the edge of town. We need to talk to her. Tonight's her night off. I've been keeping an eye on her. She usually stays home her nights off.'

'You know where she lives?'

'Over by the old railroad roundhouse.'

'We also need to look up Ted Foster,' Darcy said.

'Amy's husband?'

'Right.'

'Is he involved in this?'

She told him about Ted fleeing the Carmichael house that night.

'Did he see you?' Ken said.

'I don't think so.'

'You actually think he killed the Judge?'

'He was inside the house,' Darcy said. 'That at least makes him a strong suspect.' Then, 'I wish I could get in the Judge's office. There was something he wanted me to know.'

'How about asking Cindy?' Ken said.

'She'd just turn me in.'

125

Bernice said, 'The cleaning crew I work for? Remember I mentioned them?'

'Yes,' Darcy said.

'Well, they'll be cleaning the Judge's office pretty soon. There's a chance you could sneak in the front door. It's open sometimes.' Then she added, 'You're going to need a car.'

Ken nodded. 'We are if we're going to talk to the stripper.'

'I've got one in the garage. I'm assuming it'll start.' Bernice smiled. 'I only drive it a couple of times a month and sometimes the battery runs down.'

'They could still spot us,' Darcy said.

'We can stick to the side streets pretty much,' Ken said. 'At least for most of the time.' He checked his watch.

Darcy nodded. 'The girl's probably our best bet for finding out what Rick Kenton had on my father. I'm sure he would've discussed it with her.'

Darcy felt that she needed only a few minutes alone with the stripper and she'd be able to find out what the woman knew. Darcy was desperate and – as she'd learned inside – desperate people were dangerous people. Darcy had had to scrap her way through a couple of fights in prison. She had a lot more confidence in her physical strength than ever before.

Bernice excused herself and went to a closet. She came back with a gray fedora. 'Belonged to my husband,' she said, handing it to Ken. 'They'll be looking for a guy in a cowboy hat. Not a fedora.'

He thanked her and put it on.

Bernice reached into her pocket and handed him a single key. 'The car key.'

Darcy said, 'Thanks again for everything, Bernice.'

'Don't start thanking me again. Good Lord, it'll go to my head.'

Ken stood up. Went to the front window. Parted the drapes and looked out.

'No sign of any cops,' he said.

'I'll check the back,' Darcy said.

She walked to the dark kitchen and peered out the window. The backyard and alley looked cool and clean after the rain.

Ken and Bernice came into the kitchen.

'How's it look?' Ken said.

'Don't see anything.'

'Just be patient with her,' Bernice said. 'My old jalopy, I mean.

She always sounds like she *doesn't* want to start but most of the time she comes through.'

They said their goodbyes, put on their jackets, and started out the back door. The night was even chilly and autumnal. The fresh air invigorated Darcy. There was a lot to do and she needed all the energy and focus she could summon.

Ken raised the garage door on Bernice's old car. Then they got in the front seat and Ken began the process of getting the engine to actually fire and start.

'She said we'd need patience,' Darcy said.

'She wasn't kidding.'

Ken turned the ignition key again.

The engine sounded as if it was about to turn over – and then stalled again.

17

The woods around the Carmichael cabin were damp and dark, the only illumination being the beam of Amy's flashlight. Amy remembered these woods because this was where, her first year as a cop serving underneath her father, she saw her first-ever corpse, an old man who'd suffered a heart attack while looking for mushrooms. The medical examiner said that he'd lived a while before dying. Amy and another rookie had been searching the woods for a missing girl – later found at a friend's house – and had inadvertently discovered the old man. A number of animals had had their way with the corpse, making it a sight Amy would never forget.

'I don't know why they ever made him a member of The Committee,' Cindy was saying, still angry with Reverend Selden.

'Because at the time, he was new in town and they didn't know what he was really like.' Amy could remember how Selden had become an almost instant celebrity. He was well-read, handsome, and eager for the spotlight. In addition to stirring sermons on Sunday, he could be counted on to introduce the symphony orchestra, greet VIPs when they came to town, and even to performing dramatic readings of Dylan Thomas at library events. To middle-aged women he was a matinee idol; and he knew enough about hunting and fishing to pass himself off as a regular guy.

'He must've looked awfully good on paper.'

'He did,' Amy said. 'At least, that's what my Dad told me. But he said that as soon as they found out that Selden was sampling all the ladies, they wanted to get rid of him.'

'How could they?'

'That was the problem,' Amy said. 'They couldn't. He knew everything they knew and so they couldn't have him just floating around.'

'This is probably a wild-goose chase,' Cindy said. 'He probably just *imagined* he saw somebody. He's such a twit.'

'I wouldn't disagree with you there,' Amy said.

They came to a clearing on a hill overlooking the cabin. They'd been out here maybe fifteen minutes now. The full moon was just starting to appear between ragged drifting rain clouds. It was a nice night to sit in front of a cozy fire.

They crossed a section of grassland that had two large glacial erratics – field stones left from the time eons ago when ice had covered all this land – bold and jagged rocks that looked like alien symbols.

Empty beer cans, crumpled cigarette packs and red Trojan wrappers were evidence of civilization even out here in the boonies. This was prime country for summer keggers. Amy'd had to break up any number of out-of-control underage beer parties out here during the warm months. One night, the damned thing had turned into a near-riot, with one of her officers getting decked by a football player. The cop got his jaw broken; a smart lawyer managed to get the punk off with probation.

'Wait,' Amy whispered, and held her arm out to stop Cindy behind her.

'What is it?' Cindy whispered back.

'Sssh.'

The wind soughing the budding trees; a nearby stream rolling over rocks; a distant and lonely dog barking – these were the sounds of the night. And yet Amy thought she heard another sound, too, a noise just on the edge of hearing, a faint movement in the undergrowth.

Or was she getting spooked, like the Reverend Selden? Hearing things that weren't there?

'I don't hear anything,' Cindy whispered.

'And you won't, either, if you keep talking.'

'Great, that's all I need. Some of your Girl Scout bullshit. My father was just murdered by a friend, so if I'm a little fucked up, I guess you'll just have to live with it.'

They spoke these words in harsh, angry whispers.

And then Amy saw it, or thought she did.

'There!'

'Where.'

'There!'

Amy shone her light on a small path that wound between three

large pin oaks. The undergrowth here was tangled and ran to
gooseberry and Virginia creeper and dogwood.

'I don't see anything.'

'I think *I* did.'

'You *think* you did?'

'Yes, Cindy, I think. I'm sorry if I can't be absolutely sure. All
right?'

Amy took out her service revolver and started walking toward
the path leading into the deepest part of the woods. It was getting
downright cold out here now. Her knuckles stung from holding
the flashlight, the way they stung when she used to make
snowballs without wearing gloves. She'd had such an innocent
childhood; how had she ever become a part of The Committee,
anyway?

'Where're you going?'

'Into the woods.'

'That's crazy, Amy. I mean, if you really think you saw something,
shouldn't you call somebody?'

'Who would I call, Cindy? I'm the police chief, remember?'

'That's why I'd hate to be in charge of anything. I always want to
have somebody to call.' Cindy nodded to Amy's service revolver. 'I
wish *I* had a gun.'

'Oh, right. So you can walk behind me with a loaded weapon.
No thanks.'

With that, Amy started walking ahead. Cindy followed behind
with mincing little steps.

The path was also littered with beer cans and condom wrappers,
the two universal passions of teenagers everywhere. Amy remembered when she and Ted were young – when he was still sober. Like
rabbits, they used to be. Everywhere, all the time. Hump hump
hump. They hadn't had good sex in several years now. Couple nights
a week, when he was passed out in their bed and the kids were
asleep in theirs, Amy would go into the bathroom, lock the door
and try to run down the batteries in her vibrator. It was a good
thing it wasn't an *electric* vibrator. There'd be power outages all over
Parkhurst.

Amy kept shifting the beam of the light from left to right. So far,
there'd been no sign of anything more menacing than the face of a
raccoon watching them from inside a haven of foliage.

Amy was beginning to have her doubts. Maybe she really *hadn't*

131

seen anything. Maybe she was just caught up in the events of the night, as Selden clearly was.

She'd give it a few more minutes and then, if they didn't sight anything, she'd turn back.

She could hear the river now to the west. Indian Peak was a favorite diving spot for teenagers, too. God knows she'd dived off it into the river many times. Of course, she'd ground either one of her girls if *they* ever did it. It was a damned dangerous thing to do, and over the years at least five teenagers had perished from diving into the rapidly moving water.

Only after a time did Amy sense that Cindy wasn't behind her. The sense came gradually.

'Cindy?' Amy whispered over her shoulder.

Nothing.

'Cindy?'

Then she stopped and turned around.

Amy shone the light around on the path behind her. They had just come around a long curve that was obscured by thick underbrush on either side of the path.

'Cindy?' she whispered again. 'Cindy?'

That was when she heard Cindy scream. She wasn't far away.

Gripping the flashlight, Amy started walking quickly back toward the head of the path. Cindy must be somewhere nearby.

Nearby – and apparently in real trouble.

But where was she? 'Cindy! Cindy!' she called out, shining her light in the undergrowth to the left of the path.

No sign of Cindy. No sign of her at all.

So Selden hadn't been overreacting. There really had been somebody lurking around the cabin.

Amy waded into the thick undergrowth in search of her friend.

Reverend Selden was looking through the cupboards of the cabin – he was a natural snoop – when the lights went out.

His first reaction was that a fuse had blown. This presented two problems, one being that he had no idea where the fuse box was, the second being that he had no idea where he'd find a flashlight.

His second reaction was that it wasn't a blown fuse at all. The shadow-shape he'd seen earlier had come back for him.

The cabin looked suddenly different to him. In the inky stillness anybody – or anything – could be hiding.

There was a telephone on the end table next to the couch. He had to make sure it was still working. Just in case he had to call 911 or something.

He banged into a chair crossing the room and scared the hell out of himself. He hadn't seen the chair in front of him at all. It had been a shock.

Oh, my God, he thought, heart pounding, he was sure glad the girls weren't here to see just what a chickenshit he was. He was able to believably portray himself as a hunter and a fisherman but when it came to actual physical courage—

He was a lover not a fighter. Hadn't Jesus said that once somewhere?

His heart was still racing as he leaned down and picked up the receiver.

He put the phone to his ear and listened.

Then he began frantically trying to raise a dial tone.

Dead. The phone line was dead.

His first impulse was to run from the house, shouting for help. But what if the shadow-shape was right outside the door, waiting for him?

On the other hand, maybe the shadow-shape was right inside the cabin here, getting ready to spring at him.

Then going outside would make sense. Going outside would make a *lot* of sense.

He thought: what I really need is a weapon.

The silverware drawer. Surely there'd be a knife of some kind in there.

He glanced around the cabin, making certain that the shadow-shape hadn't emerged from the cloak of darkness. No sign of him. Or her. Or it.

He really needed to get control of himself. He really did.

He edged his way across the cabin to the drawer, opened it as quietly as possible, and then groped around inside for the feel of a carving knife. All he could find was a collection of dinner knives, dull and useless.

He closed the drawer, trembling.

He thought his eyes would have adjusted better to the gloom but they hadn't. The interior of the cabin was almost completely dark. On overcast nights like this, little light came inside.

He looked across the length of the cabin to the front door.

133

He could just kind of amble in that direction – as if he wasn't going any place in particular, just in case the shadow-shape was in the cabin watching him – and then he could fling the door back and dive outside.

And then trap the shadow-shape inside.

He took a couple of deep breaths. He was moist with sticky sweat. He felt cold and hot at the same time. His bowels felt as if they might explode at any time.

If he could just start ambling . . .

He moved at an angle to the front door, so that anyone observing him couldn't tell for sure just *where* he was going.

He was halfway there when the thing jumped him.

It was the same texture and color as the dark itself and, when it swooped down on him so soundlessly, he was totally shocked because there had been no warning. It was as if a piece of the night had landed on him.

The thing was strong and quick and held something silver in its dark gloved hand. Its ski mask and black jacket and pants made it virtually invisible.

The thing pounced on Selden's back and slammed him into the edge of the poker table. Selden's weight and motion pushed the table all the way across the room into the wall.

This close to the window, and the feeble light of outdoors, Selden glimpsed the silver instrument in the gloved hand, a straight razor with a bone handle.

But he barely had time to recognize what it was before the gleaming edge of the razor was slashing downward, right toward his throat.

He tucked his chin down so that the razor's blade could not find the soft flesh and vulnerable veins of the throat itself.

Instead, the blade ripped through the Reverend's cheek and even in this moment of panic and horror, he thought, I'll need a good plastic surgeon to fix that up for me.

Then the thing dropped to the floor and grabbed Selden's hair, grabbed it so hard that Selden could feel clumps being ripped out at the roots.

Too late, he realized that would throw his head back and his neck would be exposed to the blade.

The razor came slashing down again but Selden was able to jerk away. He even shot an elbow deep into the thing's mid-section,

134

hard enough to knock the killer back a few inches.

But Selden's triumph didn't last long. Just as he turned to dash to the front door, the thing jumped on him once more. It no longer cared about the neck. It just wanted to inflict damage.

Slash – a large wound was opened up on the side of Selden's neck. Slash – a piece of Selden's ear was cut clean away. Slash – a deep gash was torn into Selden's shoulder. Slash – the blade cut wide across his ribs.

The shock of the wounds slowed Selden. He was no longer sure where he was or what was happening. Was this a dream?

But somehow, he still managed to keep the thing from getting to his throat. He knew instinctively that if the blade ever touched his throat—

Then he surprised himself.

The shadow-shape was right in front of him and he threw a punch.

The last time he'd thrown a punch was back in 1968 when David Wyman told Suzie Cross that Selden wanted her to be his girlfriend. While this was absolutely true, Selden didn't appreciate Wyman mentioning it to Suzie. Selden hit David directly on the nose and it felt pretty darned good, actually.

He hit the thing on the nose much as he'd done with David all those years ago.

A good, strong, clean punch, one solid enough to rattle the thing sufficiently that it dropped the straight razor to the floor.

For an almost comic moment, Selden and the thing stood there glaring at each other. Then they both moved at the same time. Selden pushed the thing by the shoulder, knocking it off balance momentarily. Then the shadow-shape returned the favor by kicking Selden in the groin. Selden cried out, and slowly sank to the floor, knowing that if he didn't find the stamina to move, the shadow-shape would grab the straight razor and kill him.

The thing bent over, swept up the blade in its black-gloved hand. Selden managed to get himself worked up into a crouch, and then he charged forward, his head slamming into the stomach of the shadow-shape. Selden kept on driving, pushing the thing all the way back to the wall. Then Selden, his groin still radiating pain, stomped on the instep of the dark intruder. The thing made a noise deep in its throat, and then Selden grabbed for its wrist.

The shadow-shape was strong and quick and immediately seized

135

Selden's throat with its free hand. It would not let go of the knife no matter how hard Selden twisted its wrist.

Selden decided to try turning the wrist back on the intruder. He got the blade close enough to do damage and then pushed inward suddenly, slashing a wound across the intruder's belly.

Even wounded, the intruder was capable of surprise. With its free hand, it snatched the razor from its other hand, startling Selden. Then it brought the razor down across Selden's chest in a deep, painful slash.

Selden staggered back into the wall, clutching the chest wound, the blood already flowing.

The shadow-shape moved toward him, the razor whipping and cutting the air with mortal precision. Soon, it would be cutting up Selden in just the same way.

Selden grabbed a broom that was leaning against the wall. It was his last, best hope. He used it like a ball bat, swinging wildly, making the shadow-shape duck and weave.

The intruder lunged a few times but Selden handled it easily.

The thing tried to feint left then right. But Selden was ready. Every time it made a move, Selden swatted it.

The shadow-shape picked up a whiskey bottle from the kitchen counter and hurled it at Selden. He ducked. The bottle broke against the cupboard.

Then the intruder ran.

With no warning, it simply turned and raced out the door.

Selden had never felt so macho. in his life.

Was it possible that a man of God could be both a lover *and* a fighter?

His shirt soaked with his own blood, Selden slowly sank to the floor, thinking of how impressed Kim Sawyer was going to be when she heard about her brave pastor. A beautiful image of her breasts filled his mind as he knelt there in the middle of the dark cabin, bleeding his macho blood.

'God,' Cindy said, 'look at these shoes.'

'That's what you were screaming about?' Amy said. 'Dog shit?'

'It may not be a big deal to you but these're new shoes. They're suede.'

'My God, I thought somebody was killing you.'

'I'm sorry. I just got pissed off and started screaming, I guess.'

'Shut up a minute.'

'What?'

'I said shut up a minute.'

They were still on the trail deep in the woods and Amy had her flashlight moving quickly about.

She went off-trail, wading into the undergrowth.

'What is it?'

Right now, she was sick of Cindy and didn't want to answer her.

'Can't you even answer me?'

'Just shut the fuck up, Cindy.'

'My father just died, or did you happen to forget that?'

What could Amy possibly say?

She followed the beam of her light several more yards into the undergrowth, spent a couple of minutes looking around a small clearing, and then shook her head. There were so many things going on – Darcy's escape, the Judge's murder, the disappearance of her husband, Ted. Had he left the house so he could keep on drinking – or was there another reason? She'd left her kids with a baby-sitter and they were fine – but how about Ted?

'Selden may have seen something,' she said, turning around and walking back to Cindy, 'but whatever he saw isn't here any more. We may as well go back.'

'It really pisses me off how you treat me sometimes. You treat me like a child.'

'Good. Let's head back to the cabin.'

'Did you hear what I said?'

'I heard you.'

'That you treat me like a child?'

'Cindy, you *are* a child, and a spoilt one at that. Now will you please shut up, or I'll make you walk back to the cabin in the dark by yourself.'

Amy went on ahead, hurrying.

Cindy soon caught up.

18

Bernice's car kept stalling.

It had died twice now as it sat idling at stoplights. But there was no way Ken was going to get out to look under the hood. Somebody might recognize him.

The streets were busy again after the rain. Teenagers were out cruising, and even some of the oldsters were lining up at the Dairy Queen despite the chill.

'Maybe this stripper won't know anything,' Darcy said.

'She knew Rick very well,' Ken said, referring to the blackmailer. 'She must know something.'

He looked over at her. 'We're going to figure this thing out. We really are.'

She looked out at the rain-streaked streets. Even though it felt great to be out of prison, it also felt odd – she wasn't quite used to it yet. She kept waiting for a huge female prison guard to appear – fifty foot high, like in that dorky movie of the fifties about the giant woman.

'You OK?'

She shrugged. 'Maybe I didn't do the right thing.'

'Of course you did.'

'What if I can't prove I was innocent? Escaping prison adds another five-to-ten years to my sentence. Thirty years was bad enough.'

'Hey, you're forgetting.'

'Forgetting?'

'I'm the pessimist, remember? You're the optimist.'

She smiled sadly. 'I wish that was true. Right now I'm starting to get a little overwhelmed by it all.' She looked out the window at the strange town. Her home town. It looked alien somehow. 'I could never understand what ex-cons meant when they said that they felt

139

safer in prison. Now I do. It's all kind of confusing out here.'

'Culture shock,' Ken said. 'That's all you're going through. You've lived in a cage too long.'

'I'm feeling sorry for myself, I guess. Going to prison and all.'

He reached over again and took her hand. He looked handsome in the battered fedora Bernice had given him. 'That's why we've got to fight back, hon. So you won't *have* to go back to prison.'

She laughed. 'I've got to kick a little ass is what I've got to do, huh?'

'No.'

'No?'

'You've got to kick a *lot* of ass. And we're going to start with Kenton's girlfriend.' Then he laughed, too. 'Hold on now. I'm gonna take this puppy all the way up to forty miles an hour.'

She leaned over and kissed him on the cheek.

They tried to look like nice, normal people paying a call on a nice, normal person of their acquaintance. Sure, they were fugitives from justice and she made her living exposing parts of her body to beer-besotted hicks, but they had to keep up appearances otherwise somebody might recognize them for who they were and call the police.

Jamee Killane lived in one of those apartment houses that needed new doors, screens, windows and walkways. It was the sort of place where the oldest inhabitant was twenty-eight (she was white and had three children and lived on welfare) and where at least a fourth of the residents had extensive police records. You could argue that they were doing the public a favor by all living in the same place. Whenever there were muggings, burglaries or drug deals gone awry, the local gendarmes need look no further than this dreary place or its clones (three of them) on the opposite side of the street.

Ken parked in back amidst a parking lot filled with sad junkheaps that bespoke the griefs of their owners. They passed a couple of dumpsters with FUCK and FUCK YOU painted on them as they reached the steps leading to the walk that would take them to the front.

The front porch tilted at a forty-degree angle and the vestibule smelled as if a dozen cats had used it as a sandbox for a couple of nights.

The battered gold mailboxes revealed that Ms Jamee Killane lived on the second floor in B-12. They climbed the sloping stairs, breathing air that was a mixture of fried food, marijuana and hopelessness. The last was the most depressing smell of all.

Country-western music whined behind several doors as they walked down the narrow hallway.

When they reached B-12, Darcy knocked. Ken's little talk had done her some good. She was angry again, resentful that her life had been twisted into such a dark and intolerable state.

She wanted to find the real killer, and turn him or her over to her old friend Amy.

Darcy knocked again.

The door opened inward with such force that Darcy and Ken were almost sucked inside.

Ms Jamee Killane was a goddess of a woman. She was not especially pretty – and her blonde hair needed another soaking to get rid of the pesky black roots – but she was so tall, so well-proportioned that she was almost a fantasy. She wore a pink tube top and black shorts, no shoes, no makeup, no jewelry of any kind. If you liked them outsize, here was the woman for you.

'Yeah?'

'You're Ms Killane?'

'No. I'm Hillary Clinton. Who the hell you think I am?'

'I'd like to talk to you.'

'Now it's my turn.'

'For what?' Darcy said.

'To find out—' Then she stopped. 'Hey, shit, you're that writer they're looking for.'

'It's very important that we talk.'

'No way. Get the hell out of here.'

Darcy figured this was her test. Before the bigger woman could stop her, Darcy pushed into the apartment past her.

'What the hell you think you're doing?'

'Get in here,' Darcy said.

'This is my apartment.'

'Right now I don't give a shit whose apartment it is,' Darcy said. 'Get in here.'

Still angry – though perhaps a little intimidated by the smaller woman's icy rage – Jamee Killane turned around and walked back into the apartment. Ken quietly closed the door behind her. They'd already agreed that he'd stand guard in the hall, in case somebody tried to get in.

'Anybody else here?' Darcy said.

'Maybe.'

Darcy walked room to room. Nobody else. 'Sit down.'

'Hey, knock off the bullshit, all right? This is *my* place, remember?'

'I want to talk about your old boyfriend, Rick Kenton.'

'What boyfriend? And before I answer that, I want to get my glass of wine.'

'Where's that?'

'In the kitchen.'

The apartment was decent-sized but filled with kitsch, from the two velvet paintings – The Pope and Elvis – to the looming poster of a rock star who had recently been arrested for sleeping with a fifteen-year-old girl. The rock star was fifty-seven.

The rest of the furnishings spanned several decades, from the blond coffee table of the fifties to the lime green bean-bag chair of the seventies. Kind of a hymn to bad taste through the ages. Maybe she gave tours.

'I'll be right back,' Jamee said.

'Hurry up.'

'Yessir, your high-nass.' Jamee smirked and flounced as she delivered the rather juvenile put-down.

Darcy sat on the arm of the frayed green couch.

She'd been sitting there no longer than ten seconds when she heard an unmistakable sound: a button being depressed on a telephone.

Darcy flew off the couch and ran into the kitchen.

Jamee had the phone up to her ear and was pressing a second or third button when Darcy got her around the neck and dragged her away.

She shoved Jamee through the arch leading to the living room and then she returned and hung up the phone.

'Now you sit in that god-awful bean-bag chair and you answer every one of my questions? You understand, Jamee, because right now I'm ready to be a really bad girl. You know what I mean?'

'Yeah, you're really scary.'

'Want to stand up and see how far you get?'

For the first time, a trace of fear gleamed in Jamee's eyes. She was just starting to feel some of Darcy's desperation and it was a little bit spooky.

'Tell me about Rick.'

'He was an asshole.'

'That's not an answer.'

'It is to me. You asked me to tell you about him and so I told you.' She had started to tug nervously on her tube top.

'A lot of people are assholes.'

'Not like him. He was *really* an asshole.'

'In what way?'

Jamee shrugged wide, beautiful shoulders. 'Just about any way you care to name.'

'You knew he was blackmailing people?'

'I knew he had to be supporting himself some way. I mean, he had a nice apartment and nice clothes and he always seemed to have a lot of money.'

'You didn't have any idea how he got these things?'

She tugged at her top again. 'I didn't until I figured out who he was seeing on the side.'

'You mean in addition to you?'

Jamee smirked. 'In addition to me and a few others. Rick wasn't exactly what you'd call faithful.'

'So who was he seeing?'

'Cindy Carmichael.'

'God, are you sure?'

'Is walking in on them while they were humping good enough for you?'

'Where was this?'

She shrugged her creamy shoulders again. 'His apartment. He forgot he'd given me a key. So one rainy afternoon I decided to surprise him with a bottle of wine. I took a shower and put on some sexy panties and went over there to cheer him up. He had these terrible mood swings and he'd been going through one of them. Anyway, I let myself in and I heard laughing from the bedroom and I tiptoed up and there they were.'

'How'd he react?'

'Well, he always wanted you to think you were the only one. He'd even talked about us getting married and everything. The stupid thing was, I sort of believed him. Until I saw good old Cindy in his bed, anyway. At least he had the decency to be embarrassed. He got kind of hysterical and I got kind of hysterical, I guess.'

'How about Cindy?' Darcy was still numb from Cindy's entrance into all this. Fancy Country Club Cindy seeing somebody like Rick.

143

Cindy was the one who always worried if Ken was a good enough 'catch' for Darcy. 'Did Cindy get upset?'

'Oh, no. She just stayed in character – you know, a real ice queen. She just kind of gave the impression that she'd let the riff-raff worry about it. Me and Rick being the riff-raff, of course. She just put her clothes on, lit a cigarette, and walked out. Didn't say goodbye to Rick or anything.'

'What did Rick say to you?'

Jamee tamped a new Winston out of a pack, fired it up and blew out the match with elegant lips. 'Oh, you know, he gave me the usual bullshit. How he'd met her at this art exhibit and how one thing had led to another and how he didn't really care about her at all. He'd just seen her a couple of times and he wouldn't do it any more. Later on, after we made up and we were drinking the wine, he told me that he'd gotten her drunk one night and she'd told him something about her father and some other men that he'd been able to really cash in on.'

'My father being one of those men?'

Jamee looked uncomfortable. 'Yeah.'

'But he didn't say what it was?'

'No.'

'Sounds like a real sweetheart.' Darcy could still remember the stricken look on her father's face when she'd walked into the den and seen him there with Rick. He'd looked so old and beaten and miserable. Rick, on the other hand, had looked so young and cocky and sure of himself. She *had* wanted to kill him, no doubt of that. She didn't know the nature of his relationship with her father – she just knew that Rick somehow had the power to destroy him.

Jamee said, 'He taught me to read.'

'To read?'

'Yeah. I was a drop-out, Seventh grade. Started doing a little hooking in Des Moines and then moved to Davenport. I always looked a lot older than I was. Anyway, I couldn't read worth a damn. And he taught me to read. I mean, he really made a point of it, like it wasn't just *my* goal to learn, it was his goal to *teach* me. You know what I mean?' She pointed to a small bookcase packed with paperbacks. 'Steinbeck and Hemingway and Fitzgerald. He got me reading all those guys.'

'Who do you think killed him?'

She smirked. 'I thought the jury said you did.'

144

'I didn't.'

She took another deep drag. 'And I'm supposed to believe you?'

'Maybe *you* killed him.'

'Maybe I did.'

'Or maybe Cindy did.'

'You know,' Jamee said. 'I actually thought of that.'

'You did?'

'Yeah. Because she kept calling him all the time. I mean, she was obviously hooked. Ole Rick was great in the sack. Never had anybody half as good and believe me, I've had quite a few.'

'They ever have a fight or anything?'

'All the time. She'd want to see him when her husband wasn't around and sometimes it wasn't convenient. You know how that goes.'

'Her husband didn't know about it, I suppose.'

'Hell, no. The guy might be rich but he's stupid. He bored her ass off. From what Rick told me, she wasn't what she seemed to be at all.'

'How so?'

'He said, get her in the sack and the ice queen melts. Underneath she's a real hot lady.'

In all the years that Darcy had known Cindy – which was most of her life – she'd never seen the ice queen melt. Even when Cindy was sad and vulnerable because of something that had happened, she always retained that slight air of superiority.

'She kept on bothering him?'

'Sure. She struck me as somebody who was used to getting her way. She got pretty reckless, Rick said. Started dropping in during the day time when people could see her and everything. Then we had our little thing.'

'What was that?'

'Oh, I had to get up early one morning – I forget why now – so I decided to sleep at my own place. Anyway, I was leaving Rick's real late and who do I see coming up the walk? Her. I figured she'd just walk on past me. But she didn't. When we got abreast of each other, she reached out and slapped me and said, "Rick deserves a lot better than you. I want you to leave him alone." I couldn't believe it. I mean, this bitch is not only *sleeping* with my boyfriend, now she wants him all to herself.'

'That was it?'

'No, I threatened her. I told her that if I saw her hanging around any more I'd call her husband and tell him what was going on.'

'What'd she say to that?'

'Nothing. But she tried to slap me again. That's when I grabbed her wrist. I damned near snapped the thing in two. She started crying. She was like a little girl. She made me sick.'

'That was your only run in with her?'

'Umm-hmm.'

'Did she keep coming around Rick?'

'Not for long. Somebody killed him two nights later.'

'Did you ever see her again?'

'Just around town. You know, at the mall every once in a while. Saw her at the cine-plex a couple of months ago.'

'How'd she act?'

'Like I don't exist. You know what ice queens are like. As far as they're concerned, you don't exist.'

'And you never found out what Rick had on my father and the others?'

Jamee stubbed out her cigarette. 'It had something to do with their meetings. They met out at this cabin once a week, right?'

'For poker.'

'Well, maybe it was for more than poker.'

'Did Rick tell you that?'

'No. But I followed him one night. And that's where he went.'

'To the Carmichael cabin?'

'Yeah.'

'And who was there?'

'The Judge and your father and the Reverend and Amy's father.'

'Did Rick go inside?'

'Yes.'

'Did you hear what he said to them?'

'No. But they sure didn't look happy.'

Suddenly, there was a knock on the door.

Jamee started to get up but Darcy said, 'I'll get it.'

She went to the door.

Ken said, 'I saw a cop car cruising past here. Twice, now. Maybe we'd better get going.'

Darcy nodded. 'Yeah.'

She turned back to Jamee. 'This has been very helpful. Thanks.'

Jamee stood up and came to the door. 'You really didn't kill him?'

'No, I really didn't.'

Jamee studied her. 'Then I guess I won't call the cops and tell them you were here.'

Darcy touched her elbow. 'I appreciate that.'

Then they were gone, back into the night.

19

As soon as they reached the hill above the cabin, Amy noticed that all the lights were out.

They stood downslope. In the moonlight, the cabin looked dark and ominous. The wind was clean and cold.

'Wait here.'

'What's wrong?' Cindy said, still a few steps behind her.

'The cabin. No lights.'

'God, you're right.'

'Just stay up here. I'm going down there.'

'You think something happened to Selden?'

'I don't know yet. That's why I want you to wait here. All right?'

'I'll be nervous.'

'You'll survive.'

'Are you still pissed off at me?'

Amy sighed. 'Why don't we talk about this later, Cindy?'

'I was only acting that way because my father was killed tonight.'

What a bitch, Amy thought. Cindy had acted this way all her life. But it was only recently that Amy had lost patience with her old friend. Probably because of all the stress from Ted's drinking.

'If everything's all right,' Amy said, 'I'll call out for you.'

'What if you don't?'

'Then you take the long way around and get in the car and head back to town.'

'In the police car?'

Amy sighed again. 'It drives like any other car, Cindy.' She dug in her pocket. 'Here are the keys.'

'Maybe I'll accidentally set off the siren or something.'

She grabbed Cindy's hand and planted the keys in the middle of her palm. 'Just take the fucking keys, all right?'

'No need to get mad at me.'

No, of course not, Amy thought. Who could possibly get mad at *you*?

Then she drew her gun and went down to the cabin.

'Where to now?' Ken said, once they were in Bernice's old car.

'I'd like to get into Judge Carmichael's office.'

'You're really hot about that.'

'He was the one who started The Committee, I remember that. Maybe we'll find something there.'

She looked down the empty streets. The red and blue neon of a convenience store played on the rain-wet macadam. With the chill wind blowing the way it was, rocking a yellow stoplight, everything looked lonely and melancholy to her. She wanted this to be finished. She wanted to go back to the house where she'd lived with Ken and start all over again.

She was afraid that before dawn she'd find herself back in prison. It was a relatively short ride in the back seat of a police vehicle. She knew this for a fact. She'd made the ride herself.

'I'm not any good at picking locks,' Ken said.

'I may be.'

'Really?'

'Uh-huh. My first roomie was a burglar. She was always telling me about locks. I got the feeling she wasn't being what you call rehabilitated. I think she'll go right back to it the day she gets out.'

'You really think you can pick a lock?'

'I can sure give it a try.'

Judge Carmichael still had the same private law office he'd had for years before taking the bench. His office was housed in a bank building that had been built in 1903, back when the downtown area still had hitching posts, a blacksmith shop and saloons with real batwing doors. Darcy had set her second novel, *Night of Shadows*, in that era and in the course of writing it had learned a lot of fascinating town history. She hoped it was fascinating, anyway. She'd put a lot of it in her novel.

By this time of night, the downtown area was rolled up for the night. All the storefronts were dark with the exception of a video store with Sylvester Stallone posters plastered all over the windows.

Ken drove into a side alley. The backs of aged brick buildings formed high walls whose edges shone with silver moonlight. Being the writer she was, Darcy took a moment to note that this alley would be a perfect setting for a murder. If she ever broke her block. If she ever got out of prison.

A lone parking place next to a dumpster presented itself.

'This is real risky, you know,' Ken said. 'Cop car checks out the alley and finds this car here, they'll come looking for us.'

'Then why don't you go someplace and park where it isn't risky? I'll meet you back here in twenty minutes.'

'Are you serious?'

'I'll be fine.'

Ken shook his head. 'I may not see you again. I mean if they catch you—'

She leaned over in the seat and took his face tenderly in her hands and kissed him gently on the mouth. 'Not even the cops can fight destiny.'

He smiled. 'So that's what this is, huh, destiny?'

'That and the fact that you're a much better cook than I am and you always come up with better endings for my novels than I do.' She slid her arm around his shoulder and just held him. 'No matter what happens, Ken, I'm sure glad I got to see you tonight.'

'I thought you just said the cops couldn't fight destiny.'

She laughed. 'It sounded like the right thing to say at the time.' She gave him another quick kiss. 'Wish me luck.'

She eased herself out of the car and quickly walked to the head of the alley, stepping around the puddles that reflected moonlight.

Any minute, a cop car could come along.

She had to hurry. Hurry.

Amy kept thinking about the night she'd almost been killed by a burglar when she was still a rookie. She and her partner had gotten a call that a flickering light could be seen in the back end of a furniture store, where the offices, and the safe, were located.

Amy, gun drawn, went in first.

She was no more than three steps across the threshold when the burglar opened fire on her. She could still remember the panic and the helpless feeling that overcame her. What happened to all her training?

She dropped to one knee and returned fire. She had a semi-automatic pistol and squeezed off more than a dozen rounds. The burglar screamed and then started crying. She assumed she'd hit him.

Just then her partner came through the back door. For just a brief moment, he was silhouetted in the doorway. The burglar, who'd been faking his wound, opened fire, catching Amy's partner in the shoulder. Amy returned the favor, emptying her semi-automatic pistol into the approximate area where the gunfire had come from.

This time when he screamed, the burglar sounded deeply sincere.

She wondered if she was walking into a similar situation now. No lights. No sound. Selden's car still sitting where it had been parked.

She slowed slightly as she reached the back of the cabin. Hefted her weapon. Hefted her flashlight. Took several deep breaths. Listened carefully. The soughing of the wind. A distant truck on a distant highway.

She walked around to the front. The cabin door was open. The faint moonlight exposed the shape of the furniture inside. The kitchen area and the poker table were sketched in. But the poker table had been shoved into a different position. The chairs were overturned. One of them looked broken. There must have been a hell of a struggle.

On the front step, she saw six drops of blood. She aimed her flashlight closer. Inspected the blood more closely.

'Selden?' she said. She tried to make her voice sound confident, strong. 'Selden, are you in there?'

No response.

She put a booted foot on the lowest of the three steps. Might as well go in and get it over with. Maybe Selden was alive but wounded. Maybe there was still time to help him.

She walked up the next couple steps and inside the cabin. She played the light around the interior. Chairs, bottles, a small bookcase, a table lamp were overturned. There was considerably more blood over by the kitchen area.

She found a wall switch and tried to flip the lights on. Nothing. She walked over and set down her flashlight and picked up the phone. Dead.

Then she heard the moaning.

The sound dappled her arms with goosebumps and she felt a chill ice her entire body. The moaning was faint, almost ethereal. She wasn't much for the supernatural but maybe she'd have to reconsider.

She picked up the flashlight and started walking around inside the cabin. In several places, she found considerable pools of blood on the tiled floor. On one wall, she found bloody handprints, as if someone had tried to keep from sliding down to the floor.

The moaning sound again. She worked her light quickly in the direction of the sound.

She found nothing. Then she played her light on the bathroom door. The doorknob was wet and sticky and red. A sliding handprint was right below the doorknob.

On the other side of the door, in the bathroom, was where the moaning was coming from.

She probably wasn't going to like what she found. She still had problems with certain kinds of accidents. The things she'd seen in some car wrecks, for instance, she would never be able to forget.

'Selden?' she said.

Then, barely a whisper: 'Help me.'

'Selden?'

'Help me. Please.'

She opened the bathroom door with the toe of her boot, flung it backwards enough to get the beam of her light inside.

The bathroom was nicely appointed. Shower, double sink, linen closet, even a small area to sit in the warmth of a heat lamp. Not exactly roughing it.

Selden was slumped between the toilet and the wall. The sink was a mess, blood everywhere, even streaked on the mirror.

She knelt down next to Selden.

'I kicked the shit out of him,' Selden said. And he had this eerie smile on his blanched and haunted face. 'All my life people've said I was a pussy. I kicked the shit out of him, Amy. I really did.'

Just like something Jesus would say, Amy thought.

She checked his wounds as well as she could with her flashlight.

'Did you see who it was?'

'No, not really. Ski mask. But believe me, I kicked the shit out of him.'

I Kicked The Shit Out of Satan, Amy thought. Maybe that could be the title of Selden's next sermon.

But she shouldn't be sarcastic. His wounds looked serious. She stood and took her flip phone out of her back pocket. The light was on the edge of the sink, trained on Selden. He sat there blinking, looking lost. He kept babbling about how people thought he was a pussy but that he'd showed them, hadn't he?

'This is Amy,' she said to the dispatcher. 'I need an ambulance right away at the Carmichael cabin. Reverend Selden got cut up pretty badly. A lot of blood lost.'

'Tell 'em,' Selden said, waving his arm in Amy's direction. 'Tell 'em what I did.'

'He kicked the hell out of the guy,' Amy said.

'Huh?' the dispatcher said.

'Reverend Selden just wants you to know he's not a pussy.'

'You feeling all right, Amy?'

'Never mind. Just get the ambulance out here right away.'

Then she attended to Selden as well as she could, giving him a drink of water, washing some of the blood off his face.

'I'm not any cream puff, let me tell you,' he said.

'Right,' she said. 'I just wish you had some idea of who did this to you.'

And she also wished he would knock off the macho stuff. He was plenty pathetic already.

Puking always did it for him, made him feel better.

He had puked two different times tonight, in fact. Once after running from the Carmichael house – and seeing Darcy – and a second time after reaching his car.

He kept thinking about what he'd seen at the Carmichael house. The Judge with his throat cut.

Now, Ted Foster was sitting in Pizza Hut forcing himself to eat at least two slices of onion-and-hamburger pizza, and to drink a minimum of two cups of coffee. The place smelled of various kinds of cheeses.

People were looking at him and whispering. Oh, not everybody. Not the majority, in fact, they were taken up with their girlfriends or boyfriends or children. There were a lot of moms and dads with very young kids in here tonight. God, what time did these people put their kids to bed, anyway?

In a town like Parkhurst, a doctor who was a drunk quickly got noticed. Some people felt sorry for you, some thought you were an offense to the profession, some just welcomed the opportunity to feel superior to somebody who made more money than they did.

You never quite got used to the smirks and knowing glances – not quite. You felt shame and humiliation and a self-loathing that was impossible to describe to anybody else.

There was a rap song on the jukebox. He was probably a middle-aged racist but he just couldn't understand the appeal of rap. He'd grown up listening to black artists like the Supremes and the Temptations. How the hell did you get from such exquisite pop music as that to Snoop Doggy Dog and all that bullshit?

Dr Ted Foster, MD – and music critic.

Right now, he was thoroughly sick of himself. He didn't want to hear any more of his own opinions or excuses.

He was a drunk and he'd driven away his family – and now he'd been suspended from his own medical clinic.

He was even sick of blaming Bob Coleman, the next-door neighbor who had molested him when he was eight. The abuse had left Foster deeply troubled with his own sexual identity. He'd gone through a long period in high school and college when he feared he was gay. That's how the drinking had started. When he was a few drinks in for the evening, he felt very much male. But over the years the few drinks became many and now he had two problems – the aftermath of being molested (the depression, the nightmares, the free-floating anxiety) and now alcoholism. The funny thing was, he no longer worried about his sexuality. He was hetero (though this didn't make him unsympathetic to gays; he'd come close enough that he had a real sympathy for them). But now he was a drunk. He'd gone to three different de-tox clinics over the past ten years. But sobriety had never lasted longer than six months. The downward spiral continued – until today, and the suspension.

But something else had happened today – Susan, his nurse, who also handled all the medical insurance and the other billing, accidentally stumbled on something and turned it over to him – something that was going to help redeem him in the eyes of Amy. The thing with the insurance company started when a patient's billfold had fallen to the floor one day. Foster saw a piece of ID. It was not the same name the patient was using. Right now, he didn't give a damn about what his partners or the town in general thought of him. All he cared about was Amy.

'More coffee, Doctor?'

He looked up to see a cute teenage girl standing there with a coffee pot. She smiled. 'Remember me?'

'I remember your face.'

'Trudy Smythe. I had the measles last year.'

'Say, that's right.'

'You were real nice.'

'Well, thank you.'

'So would you like more coffee?'

'Please.'

She'd made him feel wonderful. It was pathetic, he thought, how eager we all are for just a little flattery.

After she left, he reached inside his sport coat pocket and took out the paper that Susan had given him this morning.

The paper was from an insurance company noting that this particular policy had originally been issued to a person with a different name. Susan had brought it to Foster and he realized right away – even though he'd already had a few drinks – what he was looking at.

He tamped the paper against his thumb.

This paper was going to help him show Amy that he was serious this time about straightening himself out. He'd not only go back to AA, he'd also start seeing a shrink once a week. This time, he was really going to do it.

He wanted to share all this with her.

He stood up, checked his pocket for change, and walked back to the telephone which was located in an area right next to the bathrooms. The traffic – and the noise – was very heavy.

He called the police department and asked to be put through to Amy.

'She's pretty busy right now,' the dispatcher said. 'Somebody just attacked Reverend Selden.'

'That's why I'm calling,' Foster said. 'I've got information Amy needs. Please put me through to her.'

'Hang on a sec, Ted.'

'Thanks.'

During the next sixty seconds, Ted listened to a pair of teenage girls giggling about their dates tonight.

'God, why doesn't he just rape me right in public?'

'Mine keeps rubbing my boobs "accidentally" with his elbows.'

'Wow. That's seventh grade.'

Then, they were giggling again.

'Ted, where are you?' Amy said.

'I should've left a note.'

'I can't talk right now. But I can call you back in about ten minutes.'

'I just wanted you to know two things – one, that I'm going back

156

to AA and that I'm going to see a shrink – and, two, that I'm pretty sure I know who killed Judge Carmichael and attacked Reverend Selden.'

'Who?'

'I just want to make sure I'm right. I'll call you in a little while.'

'Ted,' Amy said, sounding frantic. 'I don't know what you've got in mind but this sounds crazy.'

'I want to start a new life for us, Amy,' Foster said. 'And I want to start it with a bang. I'll let you know what I find out. I love you, honey, and I'm really sorry for how I've messed up our lives.'

He hung up before she had a chance to say anything else.

20

This was a night of learning for Darcy. She learned very quickly that if she ever turned to burglary for a living, she would soon be living on welfare.

The bank building had one entrance, a double-door with its hours posted on it. Next to the bank was an unassuming wooden door with a glass top that led up a dark flight of stairs. This led to Judge Carmichael's office. The bank probably had every sort of alarm imaginable. But Carmichael's door should be relatively easy.

She spent five frustrating minutes trying to remember everything she'd learned about burglary in prison. Apparently, she hadn't been paying sufficient attention. Nothing she tried worked. All the time she worked, she had to watch for police cruisers. Actually, she had to watch out for *every* vehicle. Anybody could see her, anybody could report her. She was in a vulnerable spot, right out on a well-lit street. She had the sense she was standing on a movie set.

She tried one more time, inserting the tip of Fletcher's knife. And that was when the car came around the corner.

Cream-colored, new and expensive, it was an Oldsmobile or a Buick, GM – she wasn't sure. It paused at the corner and then proceeded to turn on a red light. A respectable looking couple sat in the front seat. She recognized them: the Ambersons. They'd known her family well. They'd know who she was for sure.

She hurried down the street, looking for a doorway to duck into. The first three were too shallow. If they happened to be scanning the street, they'd see her.

She found a deep, shadowy entrance at the flower shop. She vanished into the gloom, standing absolutely still as she waited for the cream-colored car to appear.

Where was it? Had it turned left, after all?

But no. Then it was there. Cruising past. Mr and Mrs Amberson having a nice, civilized conversation in the cosy security of their big new car and paying absolutely no attention to the passing scenery.

She gave them a full two minutes to disappear. Then she walked up to the edge of the shadowy entrance and looked out on the street. It was rain-slick and empty, the wind still tossing around the tops of trees. Then she saw the white panel truck pull up in front of the bank. It said A-I CLEANERS on the side.

The truck stopped and two men in dark-blue jumpsuits got out. They were carrying vacuum cleaners and buckets and mops. But they weren't headed into the bank. They were headed into Judge Carmichael's law offices.

One of the cleaners took a long row of keys and opened the downstairs door. He held it open as the other man began lugging some of the cleaning equipment up the steps.

The man with the keys took a wooden wedge from his pocket and shoved it between door and frame. He put his keys back in his pocket. Then he went over to the truck and climbed inside. Apparently, he'd gone to get the rest of the equipment.

She had to move quickly.

She rushed to the door and slipped up the shadowy stairs. She had to be careful when she reached the top. She didn't want the other cleaner to see her.

She came out in a reception area with a large desk, two leather couches and an overstuffed leather chair. There were framed photos of all six partners including a theatrical shot of Judge Carmichael. No sign of the cleaner.

Darcy had never been in these offices before and had no idea where she was going. She walked down a narrow hallway that opened directly off the reception area. Two doors on each side of the hallway. Four names, none of them Carmichael's.

There was one office to her right, another to her left. The left had the name Carmichael on the door.

The cleaners started talking and that startled her a moment. She froze, her hand on the doorknob.

The rattling of waste-paperbins and the familiar sound of a vacuum-cleaner calmed her. The men were just going about their business. Nothing to get upset about. The thing was to hurry. She had to meet Ken soon.

She turned the knob and walked into the office. Streetlight shone on handsome, elegant office furnishings. She saw an antique rolltop

desk, beautifully preserved, a large, neat secretarial desk and a line
of filing cabinets.

A mahogany door led to an inner office. She went inside. This
was stamped with Judge Carmichael's taste: a large framed photo
of President Kennedy, whom he'd known in World War II, a small
bust of Socrates and a Norman Rockwell painting of Will Rogers.
And one single filing cabinet.

She set to work, having absolutely no idea what she was looking
for. She'd been so desperate to get up here she'd forgotten to ask
herself the fundamental question – would it be worth the trouble?

After two drawers of files, the answer was no.

All she'd found were the Judge's notes on various legal matters
he'd handled. He seemed to keep voluminous notes on all his trials.
Maybe he'd planned to write a book someday.

The next two drawers offered nothing any different. More notes
on more trials.

She was wasting time; she had only minutes before she was to
meet Ken.

Then a light came on in the outer office.

She closed the file drawer and crawled beneath the desk.

'I'll just set this stuff in here and we can get to this office later,'
one man called to another. 'I'll come down and help you with that
drain now. Are they too cheap to call a plumber? They expect *us* to
do it?'

'Yeah, but they give nice Christmas bonuses,' his co-worker said.

'I hate to tell ya this but we got a long way to go till Christmas.'

The light clicked off. The door closed. Their voices were muffled
now as they walked back down the hallway to the other side of the
office.

As she crawled out from the desk, Darcy thought that she might
as well look through the desk drawers while she was here. As much
as she *wanted* to find something incriminating, she realized that she
was afraid to find anything that implicated her father. From the
way Jamee talked, Darcy's father had been right in the middle of
whatever had been going on.

She started going through the drawers. The filing-cabinet drawers
contained case-notes; these drawers held personal items. He must
have had two hundred photos of his grandchildren; and numerous
plaques and awards from groups as various as the Iowa Bar
Association, the American Legion, the Veterans of Foreign Wars,

the Iowa Chamber of Commerce, the Hawkeyes Booster Club – God, why wasn't this stuff up on his walls? She found pipe tobacco, pipe cleaners, peppermint candy, a couple of unused handkerchiefs, a Luke Short novel, vacation photos of the Judge and his wife at an ancient Greek temple.

And then she found the clippings.

They were in the bottom drawer, pushed way to the back, beneath a package of cough drops.

She carried the clippings over to the window so she could get a better look.

They were all from the local paper and they all detailed the death of a local person. Somebody had written the dates in in blue ballpoint – 1/2/96; 4/17/94/; 5/11/92 – and several more, making nine for a total.

Since they were the only thing of any interest she'd found, she stuffed them into the pocket of the corduroys Bernice had loaned her.

Ken was probably going crazy. He probably thought somebody had already nabbed her. Or maybe Ken himself had been nabbed. Maybe a cop car had recognized him and pulled him over and arrested him. Maybe the cops were waiting for her now downstairs.

But there wasn't time to worry about any of it. All she could do was keep going and hope that everything would somehow work out. Somehow.

She moved swiftly through the gloom of the outer office and into the lighted hallway. She paused, listening for voices.

From what she could hear, the cleaners were still on the far side of the reception area.

She rushed down the hallway, to the front of the offices.

Now there were three of them.

The two she'd seen before – and this one, a redheaded kid no older than twenty or so. He wore the same uniform as the others.

She looked at him and he looked at her. At first he looked surprised, then suspicious.

'Who're you?'

'I was going to ask you the same thing.' Maybe she could brazen her way out of this.

'I'm with A-1 Cleaning.'

'Well, I'm a secretary here.'

'Oh, yeah?' he said, taking in her clothes. 'We're s'posed to report anybody we see around here. Maybe I should get Al up here.' He turned then and shouted, 'Hey, Al!'

No time to think. She did the only thing she could. Bolted for the stairs leading to the street.

Then, 'Hey! You're that writer chick the cops're lookin' for!'

The redhead grabbed for her but she eluded him by inches, slamming into the door, pushing it open, and jumping two steps down to increase her lead.

'Al! Al!' the kid was shouting behind her.

She continued taking the steps two at a time.

She tripped once, grabbed the narrow wooden rail for support, and bounded down the stairs.

She crashed through the front door, the redhead growing ever closer, saw Ken sitting in the old clunker right at the curb.

Ken saw what was happening and opened the door for her.

She dove inside and, before she could even close the door, Ken was flooring the old heap and tearing down the street, leaving the redhead to stand there giving them the finger.

21

The town had started to sprawl, was in fact in the process of becoming a small city. On the outskirts there were apartment houses that hadn't been there even two years ago. The interlocking streets and driveways were like towns-within-towns. And small strip malls had sprung up to serve them – grocery stores and bars and laundromats and even (glory be) a few churches.

Somewhere in this maze, Ted Foster knew, was the killer.

He had the address written down but the streets were short and the street signs hard to read without adequate light. He saw a man out walking a schnauzer and pulled over to ask him the address.

The man looked wary at first. That was another sign that the small town was giving in to city ways. Suspicion like this.

'You want to go down a block and take a right,' he said. He was bald and frail-looking. He wouldn't come near Foster's car.

'Thanks. I appreciate it.'

Just then, the schnauzer took an outsize dump on the grass. The flies would declare tomorrow a national holiday.

Foster drove off. A few minutes later, he came to a dead-end street and found the GWENDOLYN ARMS. It was a good bet that the owner – or her daughter or granddaughter – was named Evelyn.

He pulled into a half-empty parking lot. To understand the sociology of an apartment house like this, all you had to do was glance at the cars. The people who lived here hadn't arrived yet but they were clearly on their way up. Sure, the cars ran to Chevvies and Plymouths and Fords but they were *new* Chevvies and Plymouths and Fords. These were white-collar people, probably sales-types who got commissions as well as draws. An old doctor he'd worked with during his internship said that the easiest way to read a person was to look at his shoes. If they looked new and well-kept, he was probably a good bet for paying his bill. If they were old and scuffed, the doctor said, the sonofabitch'd probably pay you off in chickens. Foster reckoned that if you substituted 'car' for 'shoes' the doc was probably right. Not that he'd ever taken the old man *too* seriously, though. Guy was a chain smoker – Chesterfields – and died of lung cancer. Not a real good thing for a doc to do.

Foster pulled into the lot. He stood outside his car taking in the clean, cool air. The moon was vivid. He felt steady, in control. No cobwebs; no shakes. He'd need all his strength and focus for what he was about to do.

He went up the walk. There were three doors. He wanted C unit. C-14.

He went inside. The vestibule was carpeted and well taken care of. Upwardly mobile for sure.

There was very little noise. This was a sign that the apartments were well built. It wasn't that late. A lot of people should still be up. But the sounds they made didn't travel beyond their own walls.

C-14 had a rubber rug that said WELCOME on it. It sat outside the door. A pair of muddy black rubber boots were perched on the edge of it. The mud was brown and still wet.

Foster knocked. He heard nothing from inside. He looked down at the muddy boots again. Very fresh mud. He thought of what Amy had just told him, about somebody stabbing Reverend Selden. He knocked again. This time, he heard a faint stirring deep within the apartment. Then the sound of a shower running – and suddenly being shut off. Hard to hear somebody knocking when you were in the shower.

He heard voices in the vestibule. A young couple came up. They were blond and thin and Midwestern and looked happy. They nodded to him and smiled and then hefted their grocery bags and walked on passed him to a door at the end of the hall. They didn't look back at him again. Very polite people.

After the couple got into their apartment, he knocked a third time.

'Just a minute,' said a voice from inside.

He could feel her eye on him through the spyhole in the door. The door opened immediately.

'Why, Dr Foster,' Mary Ford said. 'I'm surprised to see you.'

He had to give old Judge Carmichael one thing, he sure picked beautiful maids. Mary Ford was an elegant and lovely woman, even in a white terrycloth robe with her blonde hair damp.

He smiled. 'I guess this is kind of a house call. Mind if I come in?'

For the first time, a hint of suspicion appeared in both her eyes and her voice. 'Come in? You mean now?'

'Please. There's something I'd like to talk to you about.'

'But it's late and—'

'This won't take long. Really.'

It's a good thing that medical doctors are such exalted figures in our society, he thought. Otherwise, we'd never get away with half the things we do.

He stepped inside.

The decor was spare. Modern chrome-and-glass furnishings, an amber and slightly severe-looking couch, and some well-framed lithographs of modern artists. The only one he recognized for sure was Chagall. An FM station played classical music. Oh, yes, old Judge Carmichael had liked them classy.

She sat on the edge of the couch. He followed her and sat a foot away on the same couch.

'I'm surprised to see you, Doctor.'

'I'm sorry for the intrusion. But I want to show you something.'

He noticed that she kept pulling her robe together at the top. Didn't want him to see her wonderful breasts. And she did have wonderful breasts. He'd paid them particular attention when she was in the other day.

He reached in his pocket and took out a plain white number ten envelope. He put his fingers inside and extracted a Xerox copy of a news story. He handed it to her.

'What's this?'

'Just read it, please.'

She scanned it. 'This is about a man from Parkhurst who committed suicide three years ago.'

'Right. What was his name?'

'Richie – uh, Richard Kelly.'

'And he was from where?'

'From Parkhurst.'

'No, I mean originally. It's in the story there.'

She looked at him, clearly angry. 'I guess I don't understand the point of this, Doctor. It's late. As you know, Judge Carmichael was murdered tonight. I'd just like to go to bed. So if you don't mind—'

'Please. Just read where he was from originally.'

167

She sighed, looked down at the story again. 'From, Falls Church, Virginia. It says here.'

'I noticed you called him "Richie." '

'What?'

'When you first glanced at the story. You said "Richie" even though the name given there is Richard.'

'Is that supposed to mean something? Calling him "Richie"? I'd really appreciate it if you'd leave, Doctor.'

'Just one more thing.'

'I insist that you—'

He opened the envelope again and this time he took out the billing the nurse had done for her visit. He put it in her lap.

'You changed your name when you came out here, Mary. From Mary Kelly to Mary Ford. But when the print-out came back it listed both names *and* it listed Falls Church. I'd seen your brother a few times as a patient. I remember him telling me he was from Falls Church. He was killed, wasn't he?'

She just sat there and looked at him.

'Over the past two months, two members of The Committee have been murdered, Mary. You're the one who killed them. And you killed Judge Carmichael tonight.'

She smirked at him. 'I'm surprised to find you sober at this time of night, Doctor. I'm actually quite impressed.'

'Your brother was innocent, wasn't he, Mary?'

'I need to get a drink,' she said.

As she started to stand up, he said, 'I imagine you would even have got around to killing me, wouldn't you, Mary?'

She was still in the process of rising from the couch when she turned back toward him suddenly, bringing something from the pocket of her terrycloth robe as she did so.

The ivory-handled straight razor was still bloody from earlier use. But there wasn't time to worry about that now.

She moved before the good doctor quite had time to gather himself, the blade coming down in a swift, sure arc, ripping open his throat before he could do much more than squeak out a faint noise that had been intended as a scream.

She hurried into the bedroom to grab a blanket. She got him well wrapped up so he wouldn't make more of a mess.

PART THREE

22

Ken knew all the alleys and used them to get clear of the downtown area. The voices of the cleaning crew seemed to follow them for blocks, shrill as sirens.

The town still slumbered. In not too many hours, daily life would start all over again. Lots of people here still got up at five, even when they didn't have to. It was just the way they'd been raised. They felt slothful if they slept as late as, say, 5:45. Getting up *that* late was for people who lived in the fast lane.

Every time they passed a street light, Darcy looked at another clipping. Six clippings over the past eight years. She still hadn't divined any similarity in them except that they dealt with the accidental deaths of local folks. Why would Judge Carmichael find that so interesting? And was there any connection between these clippings and the list of names the Judge had sent her in prison?

'Where're we headed?' Ken said.

'Somehow, I've got to talk to Cindy.'

'About what?'

'Well, for one thing, her name was on the list the Judge sent me. And he may have confided in her – you know, told her why he contacted me and everything.'

'I'm not sure how we're going to reach her.'

'I'm not either,' Darcy said. 'That's the problem.' Then, 'You know of any place we could go through these clippings?'

'I know where there's an old warehouse. Place I use sometimes to store feed.'

'Let's go there. Driving around is too dangerous.'

When Mary left her apartment, she assumed she left a dead man behind. But Ted Foster was still alive. He crawled slowly from the blanket wrapped around him and lifted the phone. He couldn't

171

speak. His hands and face were streaked with blood. He was sucking, gasping and crying all at the same time.

He dropped the receiver, missing the rest.

Then he turned around, still on his hands and knees, and worked his way to the front door. Going was slow. Twice, he collapsed.

It took all his strength to reach up and grasp the doorknob. His bloody hand streaked the door three times before he was able to seize the knob.

All the time he did this, his throat and lungs made pathetic wheezing-bubbling sounds, tears mingling with the streaks of blood on his cheeks.

Had to get to the hallway.

Jumbled thoughts of Amy and Megan; of his two youngest girls. Tumbling images of Brad shouting in his face about what a drunk and incompetent he was. Amy holding him after love-making, gentle and tender in the darkness, both of them high-school kids again with their shining futures ahead of them. Ted was going to be a successful doctor, the pride of his small home town. Then Brad screaming in his face again. And Ted throwing up in the driveway, glimpsing Megan's horrified face as she turned away, humiliated, from her friend Lara.

Had to get to the hallway.

That was his only hope.

The hallway.

His hand was on the knob now. Turning it. Or trying to. It did not turn easily. Gasping, he managed to get both hands on the knob. That helped. He could feel the knob working beneath the sinewy strength of his long hands.

There. He felt the knob give, felt the door tug open an inch or so.

The gasping got worse now and he fell forward, his arm wedged between door and frame.

Then the gasping ceased. As did his crying. As did his attempts to scream for help.

For the next ten minutes, nothing moved in the hallway of this respectable, upwardly mobile apartment house. Most of the residents, being responsible workers, were in bed watching Jay Leno or David Lettermen. The only people still awake were the newlyweds in 1-H. They were making love and, though Jay Leno was watching them, they weren't the least intimidated. They thought the show they were putting on was more entertaining than his.

Then the downstairs door opened and an attractive blonde lady came in. Paula Dayton's red London Fog coat was still damp from the earlier rain. Her eyes were damp, too. Her boss, Frank Lathrop, had broken it that night. He claimed he was too guilty about their affair and that he couldn't face his wife and kids any more. But Paula knew better. Frank was hitting on the new girl in the accounting department. Age had just suddenly descended upon Paula the last couple of years. Her weight was up twenty pounds; she had little pads beneath her chin; and tiny wrinkles had appeared around her mouth and eyes. Paula had gone into the work world at twenty, right out of junior college, and had always been the femme fatale at every place she worked. Somehow, there hadn't been time for a family or a decent savings account or any real advancement. She'd had too much fun seducing her bosses. She'd had a twenty-year run as the workplace seductress. A twenty-year run. Now it was coming to an end.

She trudged up the steps leading to the first floor – and that was the right word, too, *trudged*. She was so f – – ing weary (Paula did not like to use the entire f-word, it being so unladylike). As she reached the top step, she saw the hand sticking out of Mary's door. She knew Mary from the laundry room and liked her all right, even though there was something remote and a little bit spooky about the beautiful young woman.

But this wasn't Mary's hand.

Paula went closer, peered down.

A man's hand, streaked and caked with blood.

Instinctively, she stepped over to the door and pushed it open.

She recognized the man immediately: Dr Ted Foster. One of the doctors on her HMO.

She was no expert but it appeared that his throat had been cut. She didn't scream – she wasn't a screamer except when she thought her lovers might appreciate it – but she did recoil and feel a churning in her stomach.

He was dead, and horribly so.

She wondered if Mary was inside the apartment somewhere, dead, too.

The vestibule door opened and another woman came in. Ms Sanders, the optometrist. She was plump and plain and never seemed to get excited about anything.

'There's a dead man up here,' Paula said.

'You're kidding,' Ms Sanders said, walking up the stairs.

'No,' Paula Dayton said, 'no, unfortunately, I'm not.'

'My God, imagine that,' said the unflappable Ms Sanders, 'a dead man. Imagine that.'

When Cindy came in the back door, Gary was in the TV room in his recliner. He was going over his Rotary Club speech, one his secretary had typed up from his handwritten version. The title of the speech was 'Family Values: Why Parkhurst is the Safest City in the State.' Gary was one of the mucky-mucks at Rotary and was always put forth to give the speech whenever somebody from the national Rotary Club was expected to pop in for a visit.

Gary had all sorts of questions for Cindy when she came into the TV room. Her clothes were covered with thistles, stained with grass, and smudged with brown stuff, the true nature of which Gary did not really want to know.

'How you doing about your Dad?'

She was brusque. 'Just read me your speech.'

She had, as she saw it, four primary wifely duties. One: keep her checkbook balanced. Two: make sure the kids maintained an A average (Gary had Harvard dreams for his brood). Three: spread her legs without complaint on those two nights a month when Gary's little pecker got all in a tizzy. Four: listen to (i.e., endure) Gary's speeches.

'On second thoughts, how about letting me take a shower first?'

'All right. That'll give me time to go over it a little more. Make it bright and shiny.' He'd heard that at a seminar – How to Make Your Communication Skills Bright and Shiny – and had been using it ever since. Drove her absolutely fucking crazy.

Fifteen minutes later, after stripping out of her clothes and opening the window so she could sneak a smoke, Cindy reviewed her body in the full-length mirror that comprised the entire west wall. She knew she should be thinking about everything that had happened tonight but it was difficult to concentrate when you were looking at terminal tit-sag. My God, all those women with breast jobs she'd laughed at over the years. Was it time to get into her Mercedes and drive into Chicago and have the wondrous Dr Ralph Wexler do *her* breasts? It was sure looking that way.

She turned around. Her butt wasn't looking that good, either. It wasn't sagging as much as her boobs but it sure wasn't that fetching, insolent little bottom it used to be. A Country Club butt. She'd once read that description in a novel and decided that it suited her. She had a Country Club butt – a little uppity, a little arrogant. Drives the boys crazy. Now it was sagging just like her boobs. Life was unfair sometimes. Mother Teresa always used to bitch about the poor people in Africa. But most of them were young and at least had good butts. It was better than nothing.

She got into the shower. She wanted to pamper herself, put the events of this ghastly day behind her.

She lathered, shampooed and masturbated. She'd never been able to understand women who had trouble with orgasms. She could practically *look* at somebody – if he was the *right* somebody – and get off. Hoping to prolong the moment of ecstasy, she slumped against the corner of the shower and very delicately used the tip of a fingernail. God, this was so good. The heat and cleanliness of the shower. The beautiful explosion of her orgasm.

Faintly, behind the blasting shower, she heard the phone ring.

Who would be calling this late?

Whoever it was would probably wake the kids and she really wasn't up for the kids tonight. What she was really up for was several hours in the rack with Evan. Yes, indeed.

After drying off, she wrapped a towel around her head, put on her sexy blue silk robe, and returned to the TV room. Gary now had his speech on a clipboard and was going over the pages with a red pencil. He was chunky and earnest.

'Who called?' she said.

'They hung up.'

'Oh.' She wondered idly if it might be Evan. Maybe he was as eager to see her as she was to see him.

'I'm just about ready with this speech.'

'Oh, great.'

He looked up. 'Was that sarcastic?'

'Sarcastic? God, that's not too paranoid.'

'I listen to you – the least you can do is listen to me.'

'I'm listening, I'm listening. Don't get one of those hairs up your ass.'

He put his red pencil down on his clipboard. 'What's that supposed to mean?'

'You know how you get a hair up your ass sometimes.'

'Well, isn't that a nice way for a mother of three to talk?'

175

He hated it when she talked dirty.

She sighed. 'You just get dippy sometimes is what I mean.'

'I don't even know what dippy means.'

'It's like – oh, it's like *weird* only not as serious. A lot of nice people are dippy but not weird. You follow me?'

'I'd just as soon not have this conversation, if you don't mind,' Gary said.

'All right. Why don't I go into the kitchen and make myself a sandwich and then when I come back, I'll listen to your speech.'

'You've ruined the mood now, frankly.'

'Oh, God, Gary. You know I like your speeches. I *love* your speeches. They make me so proud of you. They really do. Women at the club are always complimenting me on your speeches.'

Despite himself, Gary looked flattered. 'They are?'

'Absolutely.'

'Well,' Gary said. 'Well, well.'

She went into the kitchen and fixed herself a ham sandwich on wheat toast with lettuce and mayo. Lots of mayo. It was her only self-destructive act of the entire night.

They didn't have any trouble getting into the warehouse. Ken had a key.

It was a small space, which had once housed a thriving business. There was an office at the far end and the smell of horse feed heavy on the air. They didn't turn on any lights. The place was bare, sounds echoed off the concrete walls. Not long ago it had been filled with feed bags and machinery for filling those bags.

They went back to the office. The furniture hadn't been moved out yet. There were two desks. The drawers were packed with office stuff. Darcy found a flashlight.

As she laid the newspaper clipping out on one of the desks, she started sneezing. She'd always had bad allergies and a dusty place like this was bound to give her trouble.

She dug around in the desk drawers and found some Kleenex.

With Ken holding the flashlight, she went through the clippings.

They told the following stories:

John Saunders 11 February 1992 Accidental death: electrocution
Lucille Page   19 August 1993   Accidental death: drowning

John Goodall	2 March 1994	Accidental death: car accident
Richard Kelly	21 February	1995 Suicide
Paul Tucker	3 June 1996	Accidental death: car accident
Mike LaVelle	16 February 1997	Accidental death: electrocution

'I knew two of these people,' Darcy said. 'Lucy Page and Paul Tucker. Lucy was a junkie – and didn't one of her kids die in mysterious circumstances?'

'Now that you mention it, I think so.'

'And we went to school with Paul, remember?'

'Yeah. He was a biker.'

'I heard he was a dealer, too.' Then, 'Oh, God.'

'What?' Ken said.

She showed him the clipping. 'Richard Kelly. Of course. Remember, he was a sort of strange guy with a limp and he asked me to sign my books to him. And then he sent me one of his stories.'

She remembered all this reluctantly. For all the misery of the past few years, her life had been a blessed one compared to that of Richard Kelly. He was one of those young men – he was maybe twenty-two, twenty-three – who you could barely stand to look at because of the suffering you saw in him. He'd been embarrassed to approach her, even though the setting was the local B. Dalton and she was there to sign books. He had long stringy hair that he didn't wash very often and hunted eyes trapped inside heavy glasses that kept slipping down his nose. He wore an old Army jacket and faded jeans – not fashionably faded, either. Just old. He smelled, too. She remembered how startled she was by his body odor. She would have romanticized him in her books – made him the noble nerd, the noble outsider. But in reality, there was nothing about him you *could* romanticize. He broke her heart – she saw the way her other fans smirked at him and made faces about his looks and his smell – but there was nothing she could do. She just signed his book. 'I never had an author sign a book of mine before,' he said. 'Well, I'm glad I got to be the first one,' she said. He smiled a quick sad smile 'Me, too.'

Three days later, a manilla envelope containing a short story by one Richard Kelly arrived in her mail box. He explained who he was, how she'd signed his book the other day and he was sorry to intrude on her, but would she mind reading his story? He'd even enclosed return postage. It wasn't much of a story – in fact, it wasn't a *story* at all. It was a journal, the thoughts of a lonely young man who'd grown up in a rough neighborhood in Boston where he was pretty much of a joke who boys beat up on and girls giggled about. When he was twenty, he got in some trouble. He saw a young woman at a mall one day and managed to get her name and then he wrote her a poem and sent it to her. To make sure she'd understand that he was not being a creep – that this was a sincere expression of his feelings – he wrote his name and address at the bottom of the poem. The next morning, two cops came to the door and scared the hell out of his mother. They took Richard down to the station and grilled him for four hours. Even though they told him he could have an attorney if he wanted one, he didn't see why he needed one. He answered all their questions. But they didn't believe him. The young woman he'd written the poem to, it turned out, was the daughter of a very prominent citizen. The young woman had been receiving threatening phone calls and believed she was being stalked. Richard was so scared, he started crying. He wasn't the guy they were looking for. He really wasn't. But the father showed up with the police commissioner in tow and it was decided that Richard would be charged with a simple misdemeanor. He was so charged and told by his public defender to plead guilty and was then put on six months probation by a bored-looking municipal judge.

A long time ago, when he was only six, Richard – the character in the story, of course – had visited relatives of his in Iowa one summer. For two weeks he stayed on a farm. It became the very best of memories. In his mind, Iowa was a place of rolling green land and beautiful chestnut mares running across open pastures and people more friendly than any place else he'd ever been. The people were the best part of all. Why, the time he'd been out here, they'd treated him as if he were their own nephew. Everybody had a smile for Richard. People had never treated him like that before. So as soon as his probation was up and he could travel, he came out here and got a job as a shipping clerk. But it was not as he remembered. The Iowa folks took one look at him and treated him every bit as badly as the folks back east. He lived in a tiny sleeping room and never seemed to make any friends. He went out to the mall cine-plex a lot but always felt that the ushers kept a particular eye on him, as if he was some kind of wild animal or maybe even a monster. The other patrons treated him that way, too. They made a point of isolating him, of never sitting near him.

'The poor guy,' Darcy said. 'I remember the night he killed himself. I felt real bad for him – but I felt a kind of relief for him, too. That he wouldn't have to suffer any more.'

Ken looked at the clippings, shook his head. 'I just don't see what all these have in common.'

'I don't either but I'll bet Cindy does.'

'Cindy?'

'I was thinking on the way over here,' Darcy said. 'She saw the Judge two or three times a day. If anybody would know why he sent me the list of names, she would. She'd probably also know what these clippings mean.'

Ken put himself on the edge of the desk. 'Even if she does – how do we get to her?'

'What if I called her and hinted that I knew what was going on?'

'She'd just call Amy.'

'Maybe not. She might want to handle this herself. Especially if the Judge is involved. You know Cindy. She deludes herself that people think she's above reproach.'

'I guess it's worth a try.'

Darcy looked down at the clippings. 'I'm real curious now. What could an innocent like Richard Kelly have in common with a predator like Paul Tucker?'

'Well,' Ken said, 'let's hope Cindy is willing to tell us.'

23

Amy once met an old cop at the Police Academy in Des Moines who told her a story she'd never forget. Cop is out in a patrol car and he gets this call about a car accident at a major intersection close to where he is. He goes there and finds his own fifteen-year-old daughter lying dead in the middle of the street. She'd been on her bike and some drunk sonofabitch ran into her, even though she had the right-of-way.

That story came back to Amy when she looked down at the dead body of her husband lying half-in, half-out of Mary Ford's apartment.

Beechler, her second-in-command, came up and said, 'You want me to handle this, Chief?'

She flared at him. 'You think I can't?'

'No, I was just thinking because it was Dr Foster and all—'

'You worry about your business, I'll worry about mine.'

Beechler, a swarthy man who needed to lay off the donuts, said, 'I was just trying to be nice.'

She continued to glare at him until he backed away and returned to his work of securing the crime scene.

There were at least a dozen witnesses to her little moment of drama with Beechler, mostly apartment house residents in the hallway. Usually, she'd worry about her public image. Right now, she didn't give a shit.

Ted was dead. She'd loved him since kindergarten. They had three children together. Later tonight, she would have to give all three of them the awful news. The one she was really worried about was Megan. Like many children of alcoholics, she had a protective attitude toward the alcoholic in her life. She would be devastated.

The ambulance pulled up, followed by an MD named Hollingsworth, a somewhat prissy man she'd never liked. But then, he'd

181

never seemed to like her much, either, so they were even up.

He came up the stairs, spent a minute or two watching five cops secure the crime scene and begin the searching and fingerprint dusting and photography necessary for a complete report.

'I'm sorry, Amy,' he said when he came over to her, his angular, handsome face appropriately dour.

'Thanks.'

He stepped up to the door and got his first look at Ted. He was a pro and so he didn't let any emotion show when he saw the slash across Ted's throat. But his shoulders slumped as if he'd just been hit in the solar plexus. Amy was a past master at reading body language. It was often far more expressive than the face and certainly more reliable than words.

He shrugged himself erect inside his houndstooth sport coat. In his tieless white shirt and black slacks, he looked like The Sort of Man Who Reads Playboy. The trouble was, not even a sports car and a silicone blonde on his arm could hide a certain mincing quality. She didn't mind feminine men – she had elements of mannishness herself – but she did mind men who compensated by playing out the macho role.

'I guess I'd better get to work.'

She nodded.

He looked at the corpse then back to her. 'I just realized the irony here.'

'Oh? What irony?'

'He was the medical examiner.'

'Yes, he was.'

'So *he* should be doing this instead of me.'

She wondered if he wanted to be congratulated for the subtlety of his mental processes.

'I've got to get back to work,' was all she said.

Then she went inside the apartment, stepping over her husband as she did so. She didn't look down.

She spent half an hour going through the bedroom. Whenever anybody tried to enter the room, she'd snap at them to go away. The other officers gave each other puzzled glances. Easy enough to figure out what they were communicating: is the Chief finally turning girl on us and cracking up? But then they couldn't blame her, not really. How would any of them like to head up the investigation in the murder of *their* spouse?

She found what she was looking for in a shoe box on the second shelf of the generous walk-in closet. The room itself was no-nonsense. No frills whatsoever. Inexpensive dark drapes, bulky bureau, small make-up table, and bed. Everything looked used, old.

She carried the shoe box out of the closet and spread the contents out on the double bed.

She didn't have to look long before she found the photograph.

Given the style of clothes, and their hair cuts, Amy dated the picture back to the mid-eighties. The boy looked maybe fifteen; the girl slightly older, maybe sixteen, seventeen. The boy looked pretty much as he had when he lived out here. The girl had gotten even more beautiful during the passing years.

She turned the photo over. On the back, in ballpoint, it read: 'Richie's sixteenth birthday, May 23, 1987.'

There were other photos of the two of them, at various ages, and seasons, but always the same neighborhood – a slum in a big city, with lots of black and brown faces hanging around the edges of the photos. You could smell the urban decay, feel the desperation. They were always together, the boy and the girl. She usually managed to have a protective arm around him. After Amy saw enough photos, she began to see the family resemblance, faint though it was: the girl and boy were brother and sister. There was no sign of a mother or father. Just the boy and girl – the boy always vulnerable, scared-looking somehow; the girl extraordinarily pretty, slender, yet self-possessed, too. She was tough, no doubt about it.

She found only one thing with their names on it, a citation from a library that they had both participated in a Summer 1984 Reading Program. Mary Kelly and Richard Kelly. Brother and sister.

Then it all made sense to her, the two Committee members who had been murdered over the past two months; and the murders of Judge Carmichael and her husband tonight.

Mary Kelly wouldn't be done yet. There were three more to go – Selden, whom she'd almost managed to kill at the cabin tonight – and herself. Oh yes, Mary Kelly would definitely have Amy on her list.

She felt somewhat better. She knew that the feeling wouldn't last long – she would slide into the anger and depression and remorse of finding Ted dead – but for now she could tell herself that she at least knew *why* Ted had been killed. It was a knowable universe, after all. Things happened for a *reason*. Somehow, human beings liked to believe that.

The rest of the box yielded only one more interesting piece of information: Mary Kelly had typed up their names neatly on a white sheet of typing paper. Every single member of The Committee. Nothing dramatic. She hadn't scratched their names off as she'd killed them. She'd simply typed their names up. Like goals to be achieved.

She emptied the contents of the box into her purse. She wasn't about to turn this over as evidence. Now that Ted was dead, she saw that there was only one way to handle this whole evening. She would have to move quickly.

She went out into the living room and walked over to her Assistant Chief Beechler. 'Sorry I snapped at you.'

'Oh, hell, that's all right. I'd be the same way.'

Beechler was a good and decent man. Too bad she'd turned him into her official whipping boy the past few years. There were times when she wished they had their old easy and equal relationship back. But he was used to being treated badly now, and resented her; and she was used to him *allowing* himself to be treated badly, and thus couldn't take him seriously as an equal.

'This is who we're looking for,' Amy said, handing Beechler some of the fake ID Mary Kelly had used in her role as Judge Carmichael's maid, Mary. 'APB. I really want to find this woman. And fast.'

'I'll get on the horn right away.'

'Thanks. I appreciate it.'

He nodded and walked away. He didn't look quite as resentful as usual. He was cutting her some slack because of Ted and she appreciated it. But he still needed to lay off the donuts.

Dr Hollingsworth came over. 'I've got everything I need, Amy. Again, I'm sorry. This has got to be a bitch for you.'

'Maybe it'll help keeping me sane. Having to work, I mean.'

'I've got a sedative if you'd like it.'

'No, thanks. I've got a long night ahead of me.'

He looked around the room. 'You've got some good people.'

'Thank you.'

'Wish we had them over at the hospital.'

'You've got some good people there, too.'

'Some, yes. But too many people who like to screw around too much. I'm always having to write somebody up.'

As he said this, she saw the mincing old-maid schoolmarm in him. 'I'm always having to write somebody up,' he'd said. And don't think he didn't enjoy it, either.

'Well, Amy, if there's anything I can do, let me know.'

'Thank you. When will I see your report?'

'Early tomorrow morning on your desk. I'm assuming from what I saw tonight that Ted was killed with a straight razor, which is kind of funny.'

'Funny?'

'I don't mean laughing funny. I mean, strange.'

'Oh?'

'All the years I've been working in hospitals, it wasn't until lately that I saw people getting their throats cut.'

He shook his head. A sheet had been draped over Ted's body. She felt cold, physically cold, and dead inside. Just plain dead.

He put his hand on her shoulder. 'I'll talk to you in the morning.'

He walked to the door, stepped smartly over the body, and was gone.

24

They finally talked about Cindy's father right before Gary went up
to bed. Cindy had showered and was in the kitchen fixing herself
some popcorn and opening a bottle of O'Keefe's Irish Beer when
Gary came out and said, 'Merle over at the funeral home called
while you were in the shower. I told him tomorrow morning would
be soon enough.'

She carried her turkey sandwich and beer to the breakfast nook
and he came over and sat across from her. There was a huge window
next to the nook so they could look outside. Moonlight traced a
huge, rolling backyard with a gazebo in the distance.

'You want me to cry?'

'What?' he said.

'You want me to put on a big theatrical production for you?'

'I'm not following you, honey.'

You never follow me, you fucking idiot, she thought. 'I should be
weeping. My father's dead.'

'I didn't break down and cry about *my* father for days after it
happened.'

'Yeah, well, there was a difference.'

'Oh?'

'Yeah. You loved your father; I didn't love mine.'

'Oh, c'mon, now, you had your differences sometimes but it
wasn't anything serious.'

'Not speaking for two fucking years wasn't serious?'

'Well.'

'And calling him a cold, pompous prick in front of a dinner party
at the club wasn't serious?'

'Honey, please, you're just feeling guilty. I felt guilty, too. You know,
I could've spent a lot more time with my Dad the last years of his
life but I was so busy working—'

'Maybe I'll never cry for him.'

'Someday you will.'

'Will you please fucking *listen* to me for once, Gary.'

He sighed. 'All right, dear.'

'And don't call me "dear". It makes me feel like one of those old menopausal bitches out at the club – one of those menopausal old bitches *I'll* be someday.'

'I just wish you wouldn't swear so much. The girls—'

But she ignored him. She didn't care about being *Parents' Magazine*'s Mom of The Year. 'So what happens – you're supposed to be so f – – ing smart, tell me – what happens if I don't ever feel *anything* for him. I mean, not ever?'

'You don't feel anything now?'

'No.'

'Not even a little bit of sadness?'

'I told you, nothing.'

He looked uncomfortable, and just a wee bit bored. Feelings were 'woman stuff' to Gary. Men dealt with the concrete; women with the ethereal. Thank God women had tits and pussies, otherwise they'd be totally worthless.

'Maybe you could ask Merle.'

'Merle-at-the-funeral-home-Merle?' she said.

'Yes. That's his business.'

'No, that's not his business. His business is selling people all kinds of bullshit they don't need for funerals.'

'He's a very nice man.'

'He's a Twinkie.'

She was exasperating him and she knew it and she loved it. She needed to beat the crap out of somebody tonight and who was more deserving than her husband Gary?

He sighed again. 'If you don't need me, I guess I'll go on up to bed.'

'Fine.'

'I'm sorry about your father.'

'Yeah, I know.'

'Merle really is a nice man. He's a big booster of Hawkeye football.' There were two things Gary took seriously: money and the University of Iowa sports program. Gary owned Hawkeye socks, Hawkeye scarves, Hawkeye jackets, Hawkeye seat cushions, Hawkeye hats of several descriptions. It was a good thing they didn't make Hawkeye condoms.

'And that makes him a nice man?'

'It makes him, you know, the kind of guy I like to hang out with. I mean, we really should support the Hawkeyes.'

'If you say so.'

He got up and came over and kissed her.

'You coming up?'

'Pretty soon.'

'I'll probably be asleep. Though I hope I can get some of that new Tom Clancy read. I really like him.'

She wondered idly if Tom Clancy was a Hawkeye Booster.

Then she was alone and listening to all the house sounds. Maybe the refrigerator talked to the kitchen table when the whole family was asleep. What a bitch Cindy is, can't even cry over her dead father. And what a dweeb that Gary is. Hawkeye socks, my God. And what spoiled little brats those girls are. Just like Mommy – beautiful but empty and very, very angry.

Oh, yes, the house probably had some very interesting conversations about them.

She thought she saw something move.

She was sitting there, thinking her ridiculous thoughts about talking houses, and she was idly looking out the back window and there—

She was almost sure of it.

A shadow-shape such as the one that f –– ing letch Reverend Selden said attacked him. Or was she imagining it? It had been a long and difficult evening. The mind, under such stress, was bound to misfire a bit. Probably nothing, just a shadow shifting in the moonlight; just some errant night movement.

She got herself another beer and came back to the nook. As soon as she sat down, she had the same sense again – that something on the rain-soaked lawn – something around the vicinity of the double-stall garage – something had moved.

Something.

A human being?

That, she couldn't be sure of. But this time she was definitely sure that something had shifted position.

She thought of animals.

But the shadow-shape she'd seen – or thought she'd seen – was too large for an animal. Far too large.

She looked at the yard again. In daylight, it was beautiful. God

knows they spent enough on gardeners to make it so. But at night
– well, there'd always been a tinge of the ominous about it to her. It
was so large and there were so many pockets of deep shadow, places
for people to hide . . . They had a security system but she'd heard
plenty of horror stories about them not working when they were
supposed to—

She was being silly.

She sat there like a big girl and enjoyed herself and fought off the
feeling that somebody was standing in the back yard watching her.

Then the phone rang.

Mary Kelly had barked her knee when she'd come out from behind
the garage and hurried over to the tree nearest the window of the
breakfast nook. The wound was still smarting but it only fed her
anger. She had been thinking about Richie again – about his short,
sad life – and then the fury had overcome her again, the fury she'd
felt ever since Police Chief Amy Foster had informed her over the
phone that Richie had committed suicide. No way: Mary knew
instantly that the story was concocted, a lie. Back then, she hadn't
known *who* concocted the story or why. Those truths wouldn't come
to her until she left the east coast and came out here, which she'd
done almost immediately, changing her name, and using her
authentic credentials as a maid to get herself a job in the splendid
home of Judge Carmichael. The man she'd murdered earlier tonight.

She took the straight razor from her pocket, got it ready. After
killing Ted Foster, she'd taken the razor into the bathroom and
cleaned it up. Miles to go before I sleep, she'd thought as she soaked
the razor and dried it. A favorite remembered line from her school
days. Miles to go before I sleep. For both the razor *and* herself. The
razor had been Richie's. They'd killed him with his own razor. Now
Mary was returning the favor.

There was a back door to the right of the breakfast nook window.
People didn't lock their doors out here until they were ready to go
to bed. Mary was fairly certain she still had time to sneak in the
door and up the stairs to the kitchen before Cindy could do anything
about it.

Then Cindy got up and went to the phone. Probably a relative
commiserating on the death of the Judge. An inconsiderate call,
though, coming this late, no matter *who* it was from.

Mary watched Cindy in pantomime. The thing was, the

expressions didn't quite seem appropriate to a call of commiseration. If anything, Cindy looked pissed. Very pissed.

She began to wonder who Cindy was talking to.

'You killed my father. Don't try and tell me you didn't,' Cindy said.

'I want to talk to you.'

'You've got me on the phone, Darcy, so go ahead and talk.'

'No, not on the phone. I want to meet you.'

'No fucking way.'

There was a pause. 'You know what I have in my hands, Cindy?'

'I don't want to play any stupid games.'

'I have in my hands several newspaper clippings that I took from your father's office earlier tonight.'

She had to admit, the mention of newspaper clippings caught her attention. 'What kind of newspaper clippings?'

'I'll read you some names.'

Cindy needed a Tums. Her stomach was starting to give her trouble. She had a terrible stomach, something she'd inherited from her mother's side of the family. Tums-junkies, to a person.

Darcy read some names. Three, four, five names.

'What happens if I turn these clippings over to the state bureau of investigation, Cindy? You think they'll be interested?'

'You don't know anything about those names.'

'Don't I?'

'You're bullshitting, Darcy. You're just trying to scare me.'

Then Cindy said, 'All right. How about *these* names?'

As she listened, Cindy scanned the kitchen countertops for signs of Tums. She left them scattered all over the house in case of emergency.

Darcy was reading the names of The Committee members.

'So I take these names and the other names I read and then I turn them both over to the state bureau of investigation. Then what happens, Cindy?'

'Nothing happens,' Cindy said. 'Except that they catch you and put you back in prison where you belong. And one more thing while we're at it, the only reason you were ever popular in high school was because Amy and I let you hang around us. Otherwise, nobody but the dip-shits would have paid any attention to you at all.'

'Believe it or not, Cindy, I was well aware of that.'

'You were?'

191

'Sure, I was. I didn't have your looks or Amy's personality. I just sort of tagged along.'

'Oh.' Which really pissed Cindy off. She'd meant the line to be utterly devastating. You know, like in a soap opera when Kimberly tells Rance that the baby he thinks is his was really fathered by Ash. But there was no satisfaction to be had from Darcy. She just admitted to the truth of what Cindy said.

'I'll meet you in front of Reeves Park in half an hour,' Darcy said. 'You'd better be there, Cindy.'

'You really knew we were carrying you, Amy and me, I mean?'

'Half an hour, Cindy. Reeves Park.'

Then Darcy hung up.

The pantomime continued.

Cindy replaced the receiver and stalked across the kitchen to pick up a roll of what appeared to be antacids. She tore the paper from the roll and thumbed three tablets into the palm of her hand. Then she popped the tablets into her mouth.

She vanished, then, somewhere into the dark regions of the house beyond the kitchen.

Mary watched this from the oak tree in the back yard. This was the perfect opportunity to sneak into the house. But she had to be careful. Cindy had left the light on and would obviously be returning. Probably soon.

Mary eased away from the oak tree. She ducked down, her dark ski mask, jacks, slacks and boots one with the midnight shadows.

She was just approaching the back door when Cindy suddenly reappeared in the kitchen. She was carrying a jacket and a baseball cap and car keys. Obviously, she was going out again tonight. But where?

After shrugging into her jacket, Cindy picked up the phone and dialed Amy's number. She'd probably wake up Amy's kids but so be it. At least she wouldn't wake up Ted. He'd be passed out as usual. She needed to tell Amy about Darcy's call.

The phone rang six times before a sleepy Megan picked it up. 'Hello.'

'Hi, hon. It's me. Cindy. Sorry to wake you but I really need to talk to your mom.'

Megan yawned. 'I'm sorry. She's not here.'

'Jeeze. She's not home at this hour?'

'She came home and then she got a call.'

'A call?'

'You know, from the station.'

'Oh.'

'And then she rushed out of here and told me to watch the kids.'

'Your dad isn't home?'

'No. He left earlier.'

'Well, I guess I'll try the station, then.'

'All right.'

'Sorry, I woke you up, sweetie.'

'That's all right. G'nite.'

'G'nite, hon.'

She had to look up the regular police number, which pissed her off. She hated looking stuff up in the phone book. Talk about your arduous chores. And you thought those slaves had it bad picking cotton in the sun-blanched fields.

She put the phone book on the counter top and started flipping through the pages for the Emergency section. She could call Information but at this time of night, they took forever.

She got the number and dialed.

'Is Chief Foster there?'

'I'm afraid she's not.'

'This is Cindy.'

'I thought I recognized your voice.'

She wondered if this was the cute one with the tattoos.

'I really need to talk to her.'

'Did you hear about her husband?'

'Her husband?'

'He was found dead a couple of hours ago.'

'My God. Where?'

He gave her the name of the apartment house.

'What happened?'

'All I know so far is that his throat was cut.'

'His throat?'

'Yes.'

'Is there any way you could patch me in to her?'

'I'm not allowed to do that. I can call her and ask if she'll call you right away.'

'Tell her it's very important.'

'All right. Do you just want to hang on?'
'Sure. Thanks.'

The garage was dark and filled with all sorts of things to bump into. Mary moved very carefully.

She'd need a place to hide.

A place that would conceal her entirely.

She started looking around.

'Cindy?'
'Yes.'
'Thanks for waiting.'
'Of course. Did you get a hold of her?'
'Yes. But I'm afraid she can't call you right now.'
'Why the hell not?'
'I guess they're in the middle of going over some evidence and she can't be called away.'
'For Christ's sake, this is an emergency.'
'I'm sorry. I did what I could.'
'I know you did. And I appreciate it.'

She wondered again if he was the cute one with the tattoos.

Amy thought: maybe I should have taken Cindy's call.

Then she thought: it would probably be some hysterical horseshit that didn't amount to anything.

Then she thought: how am I ever going to tell the girls? For all the problems he'd caused, the girls had loved their father. And now she would have to go home and set them down around the dining-room table. And she would have to be dry-eyed and somber, yet loving and nurturing at the same time. And she'd have to tell them—

Assistant Chief Beechler had just started going through the evidence he had collected and was displaying it for her. He was commenting on each piece he felt was significant in some way. He was doing this in front of the other cops and it was important to give him his moment to shine. The officers actually looked interested, too. It wasn't often that they got to use their homicide training. Made them feel like big-city cops. The real thing.

Still, as she feigned total interest in Beechler's presentation, she kept thinking about Cindy. Maybe the call *had* been important. Maybe she should have taken it.

Then she started thinking about Mary Kelly. Obviously, she'd figured everything out and if she ever got to the press – Not even Darcy mattered any more. Darcy hadn't had time to put things together, even with help from Judge Carmichael.

Mary Kelly was the one who mattered and Amy had to find her fast.

25

Several times, Darcy leaned forward in her seat, thinking that she'd spotted Cindy's car. Sometimes a car would look like it was going to turn into the lane that wound through the park – but then it would keep on going, straight past the park entrance.

As always, Ken had more patience than Darcy. He sat silently watching the traffic flow. They were parked behind a copse of pines near the large stone lion that marked the beginning of the park grounds. Unlike Darcy, he didn't squirm around.

Darcy didn't have any clear plan of what she was going to say to Cindy. She was simply going to confront her with the list of names again and then push for Cindy to tell her the truth.

'Maybe she won't come,' Darcy said.

'She'll come.'

'What makes you so sure?'

'Because her father is involved in this. Anything about her family's reputation, Cindy gets very protective. She'll be here.'

'She's late.'

'Not by much.'

'God, I wish I could just sit there like you.'

'Annoying, isn't it?' he smiled.

'Yeah,' she smiled back. 'It sorta is.'

'Runs in the blood. They used to make jokes about my father, how everything could be falling down around him and he'd just sit there and say "I better think this through." He always said that. Used to drive my mom crazy, how he'd sit there like that. She was more like you. Got all hyper and everything. But I have to admit, it drove me nuts, too. I'd come home with some crisis at school or something and he'd just sit there with this pipe in his mouth while he brushed a horse and listen to me and not say anything. I always wanted to yell at him.'

'Thank God, you're not that bad.'

He reached over and put his arm around her shoulders. 'She'll be here, Darcy. She really will.'

'I just wish she'd hurry. I want to find out what's going on. If I get arrested, we'll never find out what those names mean. You know, on the list.'

Just then, an approaching car indicated left and started to angle toward the park entrance.

'She's here!' Darcy said.

'Oh, ye of little faith.'

'Smart ass.'

The car turned into the entrance, its headlights bathing the pines that hid Bernice's car.

The rap music told them immediately that this wasn't the car they were waiting for. The bass line thrummed, a group of rough voices talk-sang lyrics that neither Darcy or Ken could understand. Then there was laughter, boy-laughter, teenage-laughter.

The car, an old beater probably the same age as Bernice's but in much worse condition, continued its way deep into the dark park. The occupants out for a little beer drinking and marijuana smoking.

Darcy started feeling helpless again. The way she'd planned the whole escape, everything would fall neatly into place. She'd hand over all the facts to the proper authorities in no time and receive her pardon. Then she'd pick up with her life again, back with Ken at the stables, and back to work on her unfinished novel *The Silver Scream*.

Another car approached, headlights a rich golden color in the chill gloom. Despite herself, she felt a moment of hope. This would be Cindy. And Cindy would tell her the truth. And then Darcy's world would become sane and safe again.

It wasn't Cindy.

It was another car load of teenagers. The rap song followed them all the way down the winding park lane into the deepest darkness. The police usually patrolled the park but, with the search for Darcy and a murder investigation on hand, the teenagers probably didn't have much to worry about. The police would be very busy.

'It just isn't going to go together right, is it?' Darcy said, feeling tears sting her eyes.

She was glad when Ken scooted across the seat and took her in his arms.

* ★ *

'You did a nice job in there,' Amy said as Beechler walked her to her car. The night air revived her from the smothering, chemical-tainted air of the crime scene. But she didn't want to be revived. She wanted to sleep, perhaps forever.

The crime scene investigation was wrapping up. Her part of it anyway. She needed to free up as many people as possible. They still needed to look for Mary Kelly.

'Thanks,' Beechler said.

'I'm putting you in charge here.'

She could see a hint of a smile. Despite an occasional fit of belligerence, Beechler was a good man and he appreciated any sign of faith. He always walked a step or two behind her, as if he didn't have the right to bask in the same glory she did.

She looked around the parking lot. All the cars sleeping for the night, their owners asleep too. To them, this night with the dead man in Mary Kelly's apartment was just a cheap thrill. A few might be afraid that the same thing could happen to them. But for most of them it was just something to talk about down the years. They'd be telling this story for decades. 'Never realized before how much a dead man smells,' they'd say. And, 'I never saw so many cops before,' they'd say that, too. But Amy had to go home and tell her kids their father was dead. She envied the people who were sleeping, and felt grievously sorry for herself, something she rarely did. She never wanted another man to touch her. Not ever. There were widows who remarried right away. She would never remarry. Long ago, she had sworn to protect Ted, be one with him, indivisible. And she'd let him down. Hadn't protected him.

She looked at the somnolent cars again. Tomorrow morning they would carry happy people on their way to happy jobs. She would never be happy again.

'You all right, Chief?'

'Kind of a stupid question, isn't it?'

'Yeah, I guess it is. I wasn't thinking.'

'It's all right.'

'I'll do a good job for you here.'

'Sorry I have to pull so many people away.'

'That's all right.'

'I'll talk to you in a while,' she said.

She wanted to get in her car before she started crying.

* * *

Oh, great, Cindy thought as she opened the side door on the garage and stepped inside. The light isn't working.

The two cars in the garage were little more than swollen lumps in the blackness. The smells of motor oil and dead grass from the lawn mower disoriented her slightly. She felt the way she sometimes felt as a girl when she'd walked into The House of Horrors at the state fair. Wanting to go in – and yet *not* wanting to go in.

She tried the light switch next to the door again. She tried it three times, in fact, flipping it up and down. Still nothing but darkness.

Her car was on the far side, of course, meaning she'd have to wend her way through the shadows. Terrific.

Something moved. In the shadows on the far side of the garage. It didn't make any noise. But it moved. Slithered, actually. She was sure of it.

She froze in place. She thought of Reverend Selden in the dark cabin, getting cut up the way he had.

Her bowels felt terrible, cold and slithery. They always got that way when she was scared. And then she farted. Wasn't that great? She could be facing a killer in the garage and here she was passing gas. She'd like to see that in a horror movie, a horror heroine who cut a big one just as the murderer was about to come slashing out of the darkness.

She smelled wet lumber. The roof of the garage. The smell was sweet, and made her nostalgic for some long ago day of her youth she couldn't quite recollect. The odor distracted her from her panic.

Maybe she *had* imagined it. Maybe it was like in the breakfast nook a while ago, sitting there and imagining that she saw something moving out in the back yard.

God, her real problem was that she had to go meet Darcy. And here she was letting all this bogeymen stuff scare her. Ridiculous. She was a grown woman. Even without a light, the garage shouldn't be frightening to her. It was *her* garage, wasn't it?

Thus fortified with new courage – and damned proud of herself, too – she started to walk her way behind Gary's Lincoln and over to her own Volvo. She bumped her knee once but that was the extent of the injuries she sustained.

She felt better when she was inside the car and behind the wheel. She turned the dome light on for a time. It was just nice to have light, even faint and muzzy light.

She put the key into the ignition, fired up the engine and turned the headlights on, chasing the shadows, like skittering mice, deep into the corners. It was her own garage and perfectly safe and she now felt foolish for having been afraid. She hated wimpy women. That was one thing her father the Judge had given her: zero tolerance for wimpy women.

She thumbed the opener on her visor and watched in the rear view as the garage door lifted in sections.

She started to back out and that was when the back door opened and the woman – who seemed to come from nowhere – suddenly slid inside. She wore a dark wig and tinted pink glasses and at first Cindy didn't recognize her at all. The black trench coat, with the high, turned-up collar hid a good deal of her face, too. Plus which, most of her focus was on the bone-handled straight razor that the woman held in her gloved right hand.

'Oh, my God,' Cindy said.

'Where're you going?'

As soon as the woman spoke, Cindy knew who she was dealing with. 'You're my father's maid.'

'Believe it or not, bitch, I actually have a name.'

'I know you do, I—'

'Mary Kelly,' the woman said. 'I'm the sister of Richard Kelly. Remember Richard? The one you killed by mistake?'

'I was against it. I really was. You have to believe me.'

Mary Kelly grabbed Cindy suddenly, jerking her head back and laying the edge of the razor blade against the center of her throat. 'You saw what I did to your father. That's just how you're going to look, too, when I get done with you. Now tell me where you're going.'

'Please just take the knife away. Please. It scares me.'

'Good. I want it to scare you.' Then, 'Tell me, bitch. Who called you?'

Cindy told her. About Darcy. About the entrance to Reeves Park.

'Good. I can take care of both of you there. Her father died before I had time to take came of him – she'll do instead.' Then, 'Now I want you to back very slowly out of this garage. You understand?'

'Yes. Just please take the knife away.' Eyes bulging – spittle running down the side of her mouth – her entire right side twitching. Mary Kelly took the knife away.

Cindy let herself collapse against the steering wheel. A cold sweat gleamed on her face. Her right side continued to twitch. She wanted to open her car door and run for freedom. But she knew that Mary Kelly would be waiting for that. Mary would grab her by the back of the hair and then slash her throat.

'Get going.'

'I'm shaking.'

'I don't care. I said get going.'

'I didn't have anything to do with it.'

'Right.'

'I didn't Really.'

'By that time, your father was taking you to meetings. And you had a vote. You killed Richard by a unanimous vote. I got your father to admit that before I killed him tonight. He told me a lot of things tonight. Now get going.'

Mary Kelly sat back. Cindy was shaking so badly, she didn't know if she could drive. People thought it was so easy being her, with her looks and her money. How many people had to ride around with a knife-wielding maniac in the back seat? It wasn't easy being Cindy. It really wasn't.

She stepped on the gas so hard that they shot out of the garage and landed in the middle of the driveway before she got control of the car again.

She was crying and laughing at the same time, and it was really weird and she had no idea what it was all about, this laughing and crying at the same time, and she was saying, 'This really pisses me off, you know that?' and glancing in the rear view at Mary Kelly's crazed eyes. 'This really fucking pisses me off!'

Mary Kelly, of course, said absolutely nothing.

26

When Amy pulled into her driveway and shut the car off, she just sat there for a time. She was glad all the lights in the house were off. This way, she wouldn't have to tell the kids until morning. Driving over here from the crime scene, she'd rehearsed it a couple of different ways.

Kids, I have to tell you something but I just want you to know that I'm here and we're all going to get through this together. Your Dad died last night but you know how much he loves you and that he's always going to be with us in our hearts and souls.

Kids, you know that your Dad loves you very much. But last night something happened to him and he can't be with us any more. A crazy woman killed him but right before he died he called me and told me to tell you all how much he loves you.

Terrible stuff. Starchy and empty.

She couldn't prepare for a moment like this. All she could do was get the three girls sitting in the living room with her and then just start talking – see what came out of her own mouth. She'd be as surprised as the girls.

She got out of the car and stood looking at the side of the house where Ted had thrown up earlier tonight. She'd have to live with bad memories and good. They'd fight for dominance. What she always had to keep in mind was that alcoholism was an illness. God knows, she was no liberal. But she had been convinced of the illness thing by a number of doctors she'd met at the de-tox clinics where Ted had gone. And he'd tried to fight it. He really had. That's what had been so heartbreaking. If he'd chased women, or hurt the children, or hurt her, that would have been intolerable. But all he did was drink and suffer. He hated his illness as much as they did.

Well, she thought, at least he wouldn't have to fight any more. The battle was over.

She trudged inside.

She didn't make it past the kitchen.

She got the light on and set her purse down on the kitchen table and then she sat down, too, her head in her arms on the table.

She'd cry a little and then she'd stop and then she'd cry some more and then she'd stop again. She wished she'd been sweeter to him on the phone when he called her tonight. He'd found a way to redeem himself in the eyes of The Committee, which largely saw him as a pitiful drunk. He'd finally found a way to redeem himself and look what he got for his trouble, he got murdered for his trouble.

Then her mind wandered to mundane things, perhaps as a way of eluding the fact of Ted's death.

She wondered how much she could afford for the service. She wondered if she could get the Monsignor to say the mass instead of the new priest, who was just too swishy for her. She wondered if she could figure out a way to get a singer other than Mary Beth Wilson to sing at the service. Mary Beth was her niece, a sweet girl but a terrible singer. She'd much rather have Bunnie Hodgkins, whom she'd gone to school with, sing the funeral songs. And she wondered if Ruth Mae, one of her favorite aunts, would abstain from bringing her usual Texas Fifth of Old Grandad whiskey so everybody could get bombed. Over the years, the whiskey had caused a wife to slap a husband and two old grudge-holders to take swings at each other, not exactly decorous behavior for an after-funeral luncheon. She also wondered if she could get one of the doctors from the clinic to talk about what a good physician Ted had been. They owed Ted that at least. Even that prick Brad would have to admit that when Ted was sober, he was a damned good doctor. Then she wondered if her dark suit still fit her well enough to wear. She'd put on five, six pounds since her last funeral, a year-and-a-half ago. And finally she wondered if the kids at school would finally stop making cracks about Ted to her two youngest daughters. Maybe even kids, cruel as they could be, would be swayed by death, and show some regard for the girls' feelings. Maybe.

'Mom.'

She was so lost in thought that the single word didn't register at first. It had a dreamy, unreal quality to it. So she didn't raise her head from her arms.

'Mom.'

This time, the single syllable made sense. *She* was Mom and somebody was addressing her.

She looked up and there stood Megan, sleepy, blonde hair in her face. She always slept in one of her father's T-shirts. Even rumpled this way, she was pretty. She'd gotten Ted's good looks.

'How come you have your head down?'

'Oh, just tired, hon.'

'And you have your coat on.'

'Just forgot to take it off, I guess.'

Megan walked into the kitchen. She looked sleepy, yes, but there was also a hint of fear in her eyes and voice. She'd lived all her life with the dread that something was going to happen to her beloved father because of his drinking.

'I woke up to go to the bathroom and I looked in your room. And neither you or Dad were there and I got scared.'

'Oh, sweetie,' Amy said, putting her hand out. 'C'mere and sit down at the table.'

Megan stared at her. 'Mom, is everything all right?'

'Just c'mere a second, honey.'

She could see panic now in her daughter's eyes. She felt awful. How was she ever going to tell her? 'Where's Dad?'

Amy sighed. 'That's what we need to talk about, hon.'

'God, Mom, you're scaring me.' Hands flew to her face; her voice cracked; tears gleamed in her eyes. She looked young, terrified, paralyzed.

Amy took her daughter in her arms and just held her. She didn't say anything. She didn't know how. Megan had guessed the truth, anyway. Not the details, of course, but the simplest and most profound fact: her father was dead.

So they stood on the tile floor that Ted had put in two years ago during one of his four-month runs of sobriety, stood in the midst of paprika smells and Mr Coffee smells and the overhead fluorescent light that kept blinking and the sink that kept dripping and the kitchen table that needed clearing off – everybody came in the back door and just piled their stuff on the kitchen table – and the big rubber-handled can-opener which lay on the counter because nobody could work the electric can-opener Dad had bought Mom last Christmas.

Amy stood there and let her daughter cry. She cried so hard that Amy – knowing what was going to happen – eased her into the downstairs bathroom so she could throw up. Megan had always been afraid of vomiting and choking, so Amy held her over the toilet bowl and kept whispering to just let it go, that she would be safe. But even Amy was a little scared now because Megan couldn't stop sobbing. She seemed to be sobbing with her entire body, barely able to catch her breath.

Finally, she threw up, big hot chunks of vomit that made splashing sounds in the toilet bowl water.

Amy got the toilet flushed and then closed the lid. She gently guided Megan over to the sink. She slid one side of the mirror open so she could get at the Colgate toothpaste. Megan's toothpaste was upstairs. She ran cold water and then handed the toothpaste tube to Megan. 'Squirt some in your mouth, hon, and then get some cold water and swizzle it around inside.'

Megan did so.

Afterward, Amy sat Megan on the closed toilet lid. She sat on the edge of the bathtub. She leaned over and took Megan's hand. She kept hold of it as she talked. 'A woman named Mary Kelly – who was Judge Carmichael's maid – killed your father. She also killed Judge Carmichael. And the two others who were murdered in the last few months.'

Megan's eyes were brutally red. 'Did you catch her?'

'Not yet. But we will.'

'God, I just can't believe he's dead.'

Amy had hoped that vomiting would settle Megan down. She started crying again, though not with the violence of earlier.

'Where is he now?' she said.

'He's at the hospital. There'll be an autopsy.'

'Then they'll put him in the ground.'

'Yes.'

Megan looked at her, a truly lost child, her eyes begging her mother to make sense of this for her. But her mother was helpless and felt guilty for being so. 'That's what I can't stand to think of.'

'What's that, sweetie?' Amy said, holding Megan's hand tighter.

'You know, being in the ground. The cold and the worms and stuff like that. I mean, I loved him so much. He was such a good man. I didn't even mind his drinking, I really didn't. I wouldn't care if he drank all the time, just so he was alive.'

She was starting to cry harder now. Amy brought her over and sat her on her lap. She hadn't had Megan on her lap in a long, long time. She held her close and held her tight and rocked her the way you would a little girl. Megan just sobbed and held her mother around the neck the way she used to when she was a baby, just held on to her mother who could usually fix any problem you brought her. But not this problem. Not this time.

'You need to go back to sleep, honey.'

Megan forced herself to stop crying. 'I don't think I can, Mom.'

'You can. You just have to give yourself a chance.'

'I just keep thinking of him in the ground.'

'Oh, honey.'

And she started rocking her again, gently, and even humming an old nursery song that Megan used to like.

'I'll bet I'm killing your legs,' Megan said.

'You're just fine. I like holding you, honey.'

'It makes me feel like a little girl again.'

'That's fun sometimes, isn't it? Feeling like a little girl again. I do that sometimes, too.'

'You do?'

'Yeah. I've got this doll I keep in the bottom drawer of my bureau. I got her when I was five.'

'How come I've never seen her?'

'I guess I was just kind of embarrassed. You kids'd think it was corny. I wouldn't have told your father except one afternoon he came in when I was dozing off with this doll in my arm and he asked me about her and I told him. I'd just hold her and close my eyes and then I was a little girl again. And a lot of memories came back, you know, how things were a long time ago when I was little, and how light looked on the lake on summer afternoons, and how pretty the choir sang at midnight mass on Christmas Eve, and how the hay smelled in my Grandad's barn after the rain.'

'Wow, that's really neat, Mom. I'd like to see your doll sometime.'

'Are you serious?'

'Yeah. Truly.'

Amy saw that this was the first thing that had comforted Megan since learning about her father's death. Amy wanted to take advantage of it.

'How about if we go and see her right now?'

'Really?'

'Really?'

'Oh, Mom,' Megan said, and hugged her tight around the neck. 'God, I love you so much.'

They went upstairs and found the doll.

27

Every time Cindy speeded up a little, Mary Kelly said, from the back seat, 'Slow down.'

'I'm only doing the speed limit.'

'Bullshit. You're doing thirty-five and the speed limit is twenty-five. You want a cop to pull us over. But just remember this, I'll still have time to cut your throat.'

Cindy didn't doubt her at all.

The town dozed. Empty sidewalks. Window-dark little houses. Only an occasional dog looking lost and lonely prowling along the gutter. Cindy kept waiting for sight of somebody who could possibly help her. Maybe she could flip her brights on or off or something. Or, maybe, if the person was close enough, standing on a corner, say, Cindy could kind of incline her head and roll her eyes and the person would get the message that Cindy was in trouble.

They must have stopped at eight red lights and not a single car pulled up beside them. Every time they'd stop, Cindy would think about throwing herself out of the car. But Mary anticipated this. She always sat up close to Cindy, her straight razor gleaming and ready.

'If she isn't here in ten minutes,' Darcy said, 'we'll know she isn't coming.'

They still sat in Bernice's old car. It still smelled old and worn and sort of sad (if a car *can* smell sad); more faintly, it smelled of gas and oil and rain.

Darcy cursed herself for thinking it was all going to be so easy. Cindy would show up and confess and everything would be put to rights. Sure.

'She'll be here.'

Darcy smiled wearily. 'I'm glad *you're* keeping the faith. One of us has to.'

'She's going to show up and everything's going to be all right.'
Ken slid his arm around her again. 'I'm not going to let you get
away again.'

'Then you'd better start talking to Amy.'

Headlights. They both followed the course of the lights as they
came closer and closer. They watched to see if the left-turn light
started flashing. If so, it could be another car-load of teenagers – or
it could be Cindy.

'I don't want to go back to prison.'

'I know.'

'I have nightmares that I'll die in there.'

'You mean somebody might kill you?'

'Not that so much – I mean the nightmare isn't necessarily violent
– it's just that I die within the prison walls. It's hard to explain.'

'You're not going back.'

'Well, unless Cindy or somebody else starts helping me pretty
soon, I probably *will* be going back. And there's nothing either one
of us can do about it.'

The car went on, straight ahead.

Cindy was going to take the chance.

They were coming to a stop light. Just before she should bring
the car to a full stop – and without any warning whatsoever – Cindy
was going to open the door and jump out. The thing she had to be
sure of, when she bailed out, was to not stumble. She had to keep
running. If she stumbled, she was dead. She had no doubt that
Mary would slash her throat right out in the middle of the intersection. No doubt at all.

She would have to be quick, and she would have to be lucky, but
what choice did she have? Once Mary got her in the park, Cindy
was dead for sure.

They were half a block away from an intersection with an overhead light that swung in the wind. The light blinked red on and off.

Mary was lost in the shadows of the back seat again. Only her
eyes – her crazed eyes – shone in the rearview mirror.

Cindy started applying the brakes. Nothing too hard. Nothing
too sudden. Just the way she normally would.

She was sweating. A cold, greasy, dirty sweat. God, when this
was all over, she wanted to take a half-hour shower. Then she wanted
two or three really big, lovely drinks.

She was drawing near the intersection. Her foot was trembling on the gas. She continued to tamp the brake. She took the chance of glancing in the rearview again. As yet, Mary hadn't leaned forward the way she usually did when they drew near a stop light.

The car was traveling fourteen miles per hour.

Now. It had to be now.

She eased her hand over to the door and started to open it. She felt the lock trip. The door was open slightly.

And then Mary grabbed her hand and viciously jerked Cindy's head back.

'Put the brakes on!' Mary snapped, sliding the edge of the razor against Cindy's throat.

'Oh, God, please,' Cindy said. 'Please don't!'

'I said to hit the brakes!'

Cindy jammed the brakes on.

The car, ironically, sat just where it should, right on the STOP line painted on the roadway.

'I should kill you just for being so stupid,' Mary said. 'Did you really think you could get away with it?'

'I'm sorry. I really am. Just please take the knife away. Please.'

'You sound like a pathetic little child, you know that?'

'I'm sorry,' Cindy said.

Mary was angled in such a way that she could do it easily – she spat into Cindy's profile. Hot spittle foamed on Cindy's cheek and then slowly moved down to her jaw line.

'You really are pathetic, you know that?' Mary said.

But she took the knife away. That was all trembling Cindy cared about. That the gleaming knife was taken away from the long, lovely line of her patrician throat.

Only after Mary was lost in the shadows of the back seat again did Cindy realize that she had wet herself. Her whole crotch was damp and sickeningly warm.

When the light changed, she drove slowly across the intersection.

Megan slept with her grandfather's .38 beneath her pillow.

After coming upstairs, she'd headed right for the drawer where she'd kept it. Her idea was to go find the woman who'd killed her father, and shoot her. It wouldn't be hard. Not if she listened to the police radio Mom had downstairs. Not if she listened until Mom caught the woman. Then it would be as simple as going down to the police station and killing the woman right there. Right as they brought here in the back door, the way they brought in most prisoners, especially the important ones.

She'd taken the gun out of the drawer and filled her hand with it and stood there pretending to fire round after round into the woman. Mary Kelly was her name. Round after round into Mary Kelly.

Then the midnight wind in the trees outside her open window chilled her enough to raise goosebumps, and the cold brought her back to reality. She was a fourteen-year-old girl standing in a T-shirt and panties, no bra, no shoes, not even wearing her glasses or contacts, and she was going to shoot somebody?

Anyway, the gun wasn't even loaded, the bullets were all in her bureau drawer. Before he'd died, her grandfather had taught her all about firearm safety. There was no chance of it misfiring. But her father had died tonight, the world revealing itself to be the dark and terrible and ruthlessly surprising place she'd always suspected it was. Her little cousin dying of brain cancer at three. The girl at school in second grade getting AIDs from a blood transfusion. Bobby Thomas's father, perfectly sober, middle of a football Saturday afternoon, tripping on the top step of the basement and tumbling all the way down, paralyzing himself from the neck down in the process. A dark and terrible and ruthlessly surprising world. So, she slept with her grandad's gun under her pillow, the way she did whenever she felt particularly vulnerable. She cried sometimes, and then sometimes didn't, just thought of how sad and worn and old her mother had looked tonight downstairs in the blinking fluorescent light of the kitchen. She prayed sometimes, too, but she wasn't exactly sure to whom (would God really let her father be killed?) or for what reason (nobody was going to bring her father back to life) but just whispering the words of the Lord's Prayer comforted her. She tucked her hands between her legs the warm, oddly reassuring way she used to when she was small and then she kind of curled up into a foetal position and let all the energy drain out of herself. She wished she could shut her brain on and off, as if it was a light switch. And, failing that, she wished there was at least a Happy Switch in the mind. One you just flipped on and the very best memories of your whole life flooded your mind.

She was just about asleep – finally, finally – when her door opened up abruptly and there, silhouetted in the night light of the hallway, stood her smallest sister, Louise. Six years old. Hair mussed.

Sleeping in a shortie Minnie Mouse nightshirt. Then Megan saw Mom's note on the floor: BACK AT WORK. LOVE XXX MOM. She must've dozed off after all and Mom had left the note.

Megan sat up. 'You have a bad dream?'

'Uh-huh.'

'The dinosaur?'

'Uh-huh.'

'God, I don't know why you keep watching that movie.'

' 'Cause it's good.'

'Louise, it isn't good if it keeps giving you nightmares.'

'I looked in Mom's room. She isn't there.'

'She had to go out, hon.'

'How come?'

'Well,' Megan started to say. But there was no way, no way at all she could tell Louise what had happened to their father. That would be up to Mom. In the morning. For now, the thing was to get Louise back to bed. And to sleep.

'Did you go to the bathroom when you got up?'

'Huh-uh.'

'Why don't you go to the bathroom, then, and go back to bed?'

'Dad isn't there, either.'

'I know, sweetie. For now, you just need to go back to bed.'

'I'm scared I'll have that nightmare again.'

'You'll be fine.'

'The dinosaurs are so fast. They can outrun cars.'

'G'night, Louise.'

'Night.'

She wasn't a real great toilet-flusher, Louise. People were always flushing her toilet for her. So Megan knew better than to listen for the flush. Instead she listened for the pad of Louise's feet as she went from the bathroom to the bedroom she shared with her other sister.

Megan wondered if *she* could get back to sleep now. She was awake, wondering what Mom was doing. Maybe she'd caught the woman who'd killed Dad. One thing Mom hadn't explained was *why* she'd killed Dad. That bothered Megan. She always wondered why people did things. That was the most interesting part of human psychology for her, the *reason* people did things. Though sometimes people would tell you why they'd done a certain thing and you still couldn't understand. Sometimes, people were just totally

213

mysterious, and that's when they scared her the most, when she couldn't see anything recognizably human in their eyes, or hear it in their voices.

She yawned. She was more tired than she'd realized. She wished again for the Happy Switch.

Darcy said, 'We may as well go.'

'We could give it a few more minutes.'

'She's twenty minutes late already.'

'Anyway, where would we go?'

That, she hadn't thought of. And it was a weird feeling when she *did* think of it. There *wasn't* any place they could go. Even driving down the street was dangerous now. Anybody spotted them, they'd be sure to call 911 and turn Darcy in.

'I guess that's a good point.'

Headlights again.

Darcy said, 'I'm not going to get excited and think it's her coming because it *won't* be her coming.'

'Now, there's a positive attitude.'

They both saw it at the same time, the police department decal on the driver's door. The car that was approaching the park out of the night was a police car.

And its left-turn signal had just started flashing.

'Great,' Darcy said.

'Too late to get away. All we can do is sit here and hope they don't see us.'

They sat absolutely still as the police car entered the park. All they could hope for was that they were well hidden behind the trees. The car was going relatively fast as it approached them. The officers probably thought that nobody would try to hide this close to the entrance. Deep inside the park, those were the best hiding places.

The police car swept past.

'Thank God,' Darcy said.

'There's one problem I just thought of,' Ken said.

'What's that?'

'They're doing some construction work at the exit to the park. The police'll have to turn around and come back this way. When they're coming at us from that direction, they'll have a much better chance of seeing us.'

'What'll we do?'

He leaned forward and started up the car. 'I'll pull out on the street and park where it's legal. You hop in the back seat and get on the floor. I'll get on the floor in the front seat. If we have any luck, they won't notice us. They'll just drive on by.'

'We could always just drive away from here.'

Ken shook his head. 'I still think Cindy's going to show up.'

'If you say so,' Darcy said. 'I guess I may as well do it now.'

She crawled over the back of the seat.

Ken got the car going and pulled out from behind the trees. When he reached the entrance, he looked carefully around to make sure there weren't any other squad cars lurking about. Then he turned to the right, drove down a block and found a gift – a space between two parked cars. This car would fit in there perfectly. There would be nothing for the cops to notice. Just one of six or seven cars legally parked along the street.

'We lucked out,' he said to the back seat.

'I'm so exhausted, I could almost go to sleep.'

'Yeah,' he said. 'I know the feeling.'

'How're we going to know when the cops leave the park?'

'I'll sit up and check every car that passes.'

'I really appreciate you helping me like this.'

'My pleasure,' he said. 'I've always wanted to be a fugitive.'

'Yeah,' she said, 'me, too.'

Four blocks from the park, Cindy figured out what she was going to do. She still hadn't gotten over wetting herself. She felt like a child. She was glad that Mary Kelly didn't know about it. She'd gloat.

Cindy started watching the street carefully. What she wanted was a tree sitting very close to a corner. She would have to move very quickly. She would drive the car up over the curb at approximately twenty miles per hour and slam into the tree. She would then have to pop her seat belt and dive out of the car. The car hitting the tree would not only surprise Mary Kelly, it might well injure her. She wasn't wearing a seat belt. Cindy had a lovely image of Mary Kelly flying over the back seat and smashing her head against the windshield.

All of this go could wrong, of course. Even with a seat belt, there was no guarantee she wouldn't be hurt. Every once in a while you heard of people, who were wearing seat belts, getting killed in such minor accidents. But she'd rather die that way than having her throat cut. She thought of what her father had looked like earlier in the evening. The jagged bloody line across his throat . . . She'd definitely rather die slamming into a tree. She wondered if the tennis pro would miss her if she died. Then she decided she was being silly. Of *course* he wouldn't miss her. He'd be humping another Country-Club wife within twenty-four hours. That bastard. She allowed herself a luxurious moment of pique – it was so wonderful, pique, especially when it blotted out the thought that she might be dead at any moment.

She checked the rear view again. Mary Kelly had withdrawn once more into the shadows of the back seat.

Two blocks to go now. She started searching frantically for sight of a proper tree. There was a nice oak on a corner but to reach it she'd not only have to go up over the curb but then drive a seventh of a block. Too much could go wrong.

And then she saw it. A nice elm. Right on the corner. She was doing twenty-three miles per hour.

The corner street light painted everything in such soft kind colors, the large, well-kept houses along this street looking so charming and well-bred. Her kind of neighborhood.

She had to force her mind back to the task at hand.

She was half a block from the elm on the corner.

She checked the rear view once again.

Mary Kelly was still lost to the darkness back there; once in a while, when they passed beneath a street light, could she see the gleam of the straight razor that Mary Kelly held almost ritualistically in her black-gloved hand.

The corner. The elm.

Now. Cindy had to do it now.

'There they go,' Ken said, sitting up in the seat.

The police had come out of the park entrance a few minutes ago and driven straight past where Ken had parked the car. They took no interest in any of the vehicles there. They just continued on down the street.

As Darcy was sitting up in the back seat, Ken said, 'And believe it or not, here comes Cindy in her silver Volvo.'

'How can you be sure it's her?'

'A town this size, how many brand-new silver Volvos can here be?'

'I guess that's a good point.'

Darcy and Ken both witnessed it.

One moment the silver Volvo was moving down the street at a rather slow speed and then suddenly the car veered right, bounced up over the curb and slammed into the elm tree on the corner.

Even given the relatively low rate of speed, the impact was enough to crack the windshield down the middle and rock the tree back momentarily. One fender was completely crushed, its headlight pointing straight up at the sky, like a forlorn searchlight. The grillwork was snapped in half. The hood was partially sprung. Anti-freeze and water sprayed from beneath the hood.

Lights started coming on in the bedrooms of the surrounding houses. You could see people peering out of the windows.

The driver's side of the Volvo was flung open and Cindy emerged from the car, staggering, wobbly, blood streaming down the right side of her face.

Then the back door flew open and another woman staggered out, obviously shaken from the crash, too. Cindy was still trying to hobble away – she seemed to have damaged her knee – when the woman came up from behind her and grabbed her.

By the time they started struggling, Darcy and Ken were out of the car, running the quarter block to the lawn where the Volvo had crashed.

Now they were close enough to see that the woman held a straight razor in her hand and was trying to position herself so that she could angle the blade down across Cindy's throat. But Cindy was a worthy opponent. She stomped on the woman's instep and then hammered an elbow into the woman's ribs. Then, as the woman starting to fold in on herself, Cindy reached over and tore the wig away from the woman's skull.

But the woman surprised everybody by turning and running between the houses. This happened so quickly that nobody responded at first – especially with the police car pulling up, its emergency lights flashing and the shotgun cop already piling out of the vehicle. This was the same car that had just cruised the park.

Darcy knew she would be arrested immediately. All she could do was run between the two big Colonials the way the woman had done. She didn't even say anything to Ken. She just took off running. As she turned to look between the houses, she saw Cindy start to sink to her knees. Ken went over and helped hold her upright. This

217

actually helped distract the cop. He ran over to see if he could lend a hand. Apparently he hadn't seen Darcy.

Darcy ran.

The grass was so wet, she had to be careful not to run too fast and twist an ankle or break a bone. That's all she'd need. She had to find the woman and learn the truth. Why had she killed the Judge? Darcy sensed that in finding that out, she would learn everything else, too.

She ran on.

When she reached the alley, she looked down the narrow, gravel corridor for sight of the woman. Moonlight shone on the empty alley. Not even a stray tomcat could be seen roaming the midnight land.

She decided that the woman would have run east, not west. The police car – with more to follow, surely – had come from the west. She took another look down at the alley. The garages here were more like carriage-houses, meaning they'd been built many decades ago when buggies often sat next to automobiles. Maybe the woman hadn't run anywhere at all. Maybe she was hiding in the garages. It would take the police all night to search every one of these.

She started walking quickly, taking note of the garages on either side of her, listening for any sign of movement inside the buildings. Not so easy when an ambulance siren was waking the night a few blocks away. Cindy had looked as if she'd probably require at least a check-up in an ER.

Darcy spent the next five minutes moving swiftly down the alley. Finding nothing, she crossed the street, where another block of similar garages stood.

She was joined by a scruffy gray-and-black mutt who was still wet from the earlier downpour. He was good-sized but not especially threatening. He looked as if a single dog biscuit could buy his affection forever. He jumped up at her, streaking her pants with muddy paws, and then trotted along next to her as she proceeded down the alley.

She kept shooing him away. He was a distraction and, if she had to start running, he'd just get in the way, wanting to keep up with her and maybe tripping her in the process.

'Go on, boy,' she said, feeling guilty because he had such a sweet-sad face. 'Go on home, boy.'

At first, he wouldn't listen to her at all. He just kept proudly trotting along right beside her.

But, after she'd stopped a couple of times and kind of turned him around and gave him a little push, finally he seemed to get the idea and started trotting away from her, whimpering sadly all the while.

Guilt wasn't what she needed right now but she felt like a mother who had just deserted her child. Animals had always had a tremendous power over her. There had been times in her life when she'd much preferred the company of animals to humans.

She kept going down the moonlight-stained alley, looking between the large garages, staring back at the baleful dark windows, listening as alertly as she could to the night sounds.

Her walk took her near the end of the block. No sign of the woman at all. Once or twice, Darcy thought she'd *heard* something and froze the moment she had. She'd listened carefully and then walked toward the garage where the sound *might* have come from. But it hadn't. Because on closer inspection, there'd been nothing. Nothing.

She had two garages to go when she heard the dog barking at the far end of the block. She assumed it was her friend, the gray mutt who'd left his muddy paw prints on her trousers.

Now, in the gloom, she saw that he had trotted back up the alley toward her. He was halfway to her. And barking. If he kept it up, he'd lead the police here for sure. She had to shut him up.

Resentfully, she turned back. She should be searching for the woman. Instead, she had to take care of a dog.

She hurried down the alley toward him.

'Boy, am I going to kick *your* butt,' she said as she drew near him. The animal was prancing around and around, apparently happy to see her. As soon as she was close enough, he even jumped up and imprinted a few more paw marks on her trousers.

She really did want to kick his butt but she couldn't. Not with that sweet face looking up at her.

She settled for having a real heart-to-heart with him. She knelt down next to him and slid her arm around his wet neck.

'Now, listen, you've got to leave me alone. If you don't, you're going to get me in a lot of trouble, understand? Right now, you and I both need all the friends we can get.'

But as she talked, she noticed that he kept inclining his head

219

toward a large, white garage immediately to their right. At first, she dismissed this as coincidence. The dog was simply riled up. But then he broke from her and hurried over to the garage and started whimpering. She thought it odd that he didn't bark. Just whimpered. It sounded almost like a cry.

She decided to see what he was trying to tell her.

She stood up and walked over to where he stood next to the side door of the two-storey garage. The moon gave the white paint a strange glow. She walked up to the door. The mutt had settled into silence. He just looked up at her, then looked at the door. He seemed eager for her to go inside.

She put her ear close to the door. Listened. Heard nothing. She wondered what the dog was so excited about.

She put her hand on the doorknob. Turned it. Put her face inside.

The Blessed Virgin was her friend. The Blessed Virgin Mary would ask her divine son to forgive Mary Kelly for what she'd done. She should not have murdered those people and she knew it now. The blood still streaked on her hands seemed to burn with the fires of damnation.

The garage was silent. Mary Kelly stood next to the window, the moonlight streaming down upon her. She had not been to mass in many years, and perhaps she would not be forgiven now for her sins, for *any* of her sins, least of all the way she had killed those who killed her brother.

Her brother: images of him on his sled when he was seven; at the swimming pool when he was fourteen and wearing the new red trunks she'd bought him from working nights at Red Lobster while she went to college during the day; him riding the new bicycle she'd bought him when he was fifteen.

But the neighborhood boys had stolen it from him, and when she went to the police they didn't do much about it, not after the cop took one look at her brother. She still remembered the smirk on the cop's face when her brother came out of his tiny bedroom, tears in his eyes. This was the kind of kid the cop had beaten up when *he* was back in school. Geek. Slimeball.

There had been so many incidents like that. What the kids had done to him had been so intricate and subtle – and sometimes so crude and obvious.

Back in those days Mary had still gone to mass and she'd prayed and prayed that The Blessed Virgin would help her brother and make the kids quit picking on him. But it was as if Blessed Mother was so busy she didn't have time to help Mary. There were so many sad, broken people in this world, she probably didn't have time to get to them all.

Mary raised her head now and looked up at the moon through the dirty garage window – and there she was: The Blessed Mother's kind, loving face imposed on the moon.

Mary Kelly began to weep.

She would, after all, be forgiven for the terrible violence she had visited on the people of this town.

The Blessed Mother herself was smiling at Mary Louise Kelly, who was a good girl basically, she really was.

Oh, thank you, Blessed Mother, Mary Kelly thought as she prayed. Thank you for answering my prayers.

And then, on the floor below her, Mary Kelly heard the door creaking open. Somebody coming in.

But she was no longer afraid.

Not now.

Not with the Blessed Mother protecting her.

Darcy pulled the door open, peeked inside.

Darkness, and the smell of decades of dust and dampness, of trapped dead sunlight that had once streamed through the dusty windows, and timber and concrete flooring and rain.

But she heard nothing.

And then she heard something.

At first, she had no idea what she was listening to. At first, she wasn't even sure where the sound was, it was so faint.

There were two large new cars in the garage and they filled up the ground floor almost entirely. She wondered if an animal was trapped beneath or inside one of the cars. Her first assessment of the noise was that it belonged to an animal of some kind.

She moved into the garage. The dog wanted to come, too, but she had to shoo him away and close the door. At least, he wasn't barking.

The ancient smells were even stronger now that she was inside. Her eyes hadn't quite adjusted to this particular darkness. She moved along the side of a car, holding on to it for reassurance. By the time she reached the hood of the car, she could pretty much make out everything on the ground floor. At the back of the garage, neatly arrayed, were a variety of lawn and garden tools. There was a work table with peg board as a backing. Various hammers, saws, screwdrivers hung from the pegboard.

Then she heard the sound again. Coming from above her in the gloom somewhere.

She saw the wooden ladder leading to the second story. By now, of course, she'd recognized the sound for what it was. A woman weeping inconsolably.

Impulsively, she walked over to the ladder. Gripped it. It seemed plenty sturdy.

The weeping woman above her seemed unaware of Darcy below. Or, if she was aware of her, she didn't let on. She continued to sob without interruption.

Darcy seized either side of the ladder and began her ascent. She went one careful step at a time. She didn't trust wooden ladders, especially ones in garages this old. The rungs creaked as her weight was applied to them. She tried to be as quiet as possible as she climbed but only a deaf person could fail to hear her. She wondered what the woman was making of all this. But the weeping continued without pause. Somehow this didn't fit with the woman's murderous history. This only served to make her more complex and thus more dangerous in Darcy's mind. Simple people were a lot easier to deal with because it was easier to predict what they were going to do.

Then a creepy image filled her mind: what if the woman was weeping as a diversion? What if the woman was actually standing right next to the top of the ladder with her straight razor? Darcy gulped. She could almost *feel* the slash of the razor across her throat, her frantic gasping for breath, the jumbled thoughts as life flowed out of her . . .

But she kept going, one slow rung at a time, one foot at a time, one hand at a time. Only when she was near the top did she pause. She tried to measure the distance between the sound of the weeping and the top of the ladder. The weeping still sounded far away, off in a corner somewhere.

She took a deep breath. Two rungs more and she'd be on the next floor. Had to take a chance.

The second floor was wide and dusty and empty except for a couple of Victorian-styled trunks gathering cobwebs in a corner. Moonlight streamed through a high dusty window and fell upon the woman on the far side of the large room like a spotlight.

The woman sat on an old and dusty straight-backed chair, the kind in which criminals always sit in movies where the police are interrogating them. Except the woman was slumped forward. She was beautiful. Even from here, Darcy could see that – elegant, refined features, silken dark hair, and eyes that were gorgeously violet even in the frail moonlight.

The woman didn't even look up when Darcy came off the ladder and stood on the floor. Her weeping had become a moaning now and she rocked bar and forth, holding herself, the way she would hold an infant she was trying to comfort.

Darcy decided to risk getting closer. Gently, quietly as she could, she walked across the dusty boards of the floor toward the woman.

Then the woman raised her head and looked full into Darcy's eyes. Darcy felt as if the temperature had dropped ten degrees. She'd never seen a face that conveyed such a mixture of madness and sorrow.

At first, the woman looked as if she didn't quite know where she was. Or who Darcy was. Perhaps the woman didn't even know who *she* was.

Darcy stopped moving. It was as if the woman's gaze had immobilized her.

The woman said, 'You're Darcy, aren't you? And your father was one of them.'

Darcy paused. 'One of "them?" '

'The Committee. The people who murdered my brother. That's why I killed them all. Because of what the Committee did to my brother. I mean, I know The Committee started out to do good – to get rid of the drug dealers and gamblers and hookers and violent people in town here. But then they got carried away. After the man who killed the little girl was set free by the court, The Committee killed him and made it look like an accident. Then they started killing other people, too. And they decided to make this a white, Christian community. So they started pushing out blacks, Jews and Indians, people who weren't guilty of anything at all.' She paused, looked down at her hands. 'Then they killed my brother—'

'My father wouldn't do anything like that.'

An angry smile did the impossible – made the woman ugly. 'He wouldn't, huh?'

'No. He was a good man.'

The woman shook her head. '*You* may have thought he was a good man. And even *he* may have thought he was a good man.' She stood up. 'But he wasn't. No, he wasn't at all.'

Now, they stood facing each other, no more than a few feet apart.

'You know what they did?' the woman said. 'You remember there was a seventeen-year-old girl raped and murdered and thrown in Moon Lake one night? They found her the next morning, her blonde hair all tangled up in the pier. Well, somebody had seen my brother talking to the girl earlier in the evening. So they decided that my brother had to be the killer – especially since he had a record for "harassing" a girl back in Boston by writing her a letter. It was a completely innocent letter but they charged him. The Committee took a vote and decided that my brother was guilty. And so they killed him.'

That was when she brought the blade up. 'They killed him with this.'

'The same blade you've been using.'

'Poetic justice.' Then, 'That's why the Judge sent you the letters in prison. I was working as his maid – he told me more than he should have. He couldn't bring himself to come out with the truth but he thought maybe you could after he was gone. He thought because you 're a writer, you'd be able to put it all together. He didn't know I already had.

'But why did you kill Rick Kenton'

She shrugged. 'After my brother died, I came out here and started nosing around. Rick started putting the moves on me. He was sort of fun in a sleazy kind of way. He liked to boast about how he was in with the Country Club set. One night he told me about Judge Carmichael's daughter, Cindy, and what she'd told him about this Committee – you know how people spill secrets when they're in bed together. Turns out Rick was blackmailing the Committee. He went in through your father, made your father collect all the blackmail money from the others. I asked him for help. All I wanted from him was some background on The Committee so I could understand what it was all about – why my brother had been killed. But he thought I was trying to muscle in and threatened me. We had a row and I killed him. And you got blamed. I never did find the material he had but I'm sure Amy did, and destroyed it. She's kind of been running The Committee since her father died and Judge Carmichael got sick.'

The woman paused and looked down at the knife in her hand. She made a moaning sound in her throat.

And that was when she brought the blade up suddenly and moved toward Darcy.

Darcy screamed.

Amy had gotten a call shortly after seeing Megan to bed. The dispatcher was passing along a tip that Mary Kelly had been seen near 27th Street and A Avenue, a part of town known mostly for winos and the town's small homeless population. It was a perfect section to hide in, a maze of old apartment houses and deserted buildings.

Amy had gone over there immediately. There were two squad cars in attendance and patrol officers were interviewing the winos. As witnesses, the winos left a lot to be desired. Most of them wanted to know if there was a reward and would they be punished if they *hadn't* seen the woman the cops were describing.

Amy joined in the search for half an hour but she soon became weary of it. This was the worst job in the world, combing neighborhoods like this, especially late at night when people got out of bed grumbling and in no mood to be cooperative.

After several such visits she decided that they were acting on bad information. She went back to the streets, where her people were still interviewing the winos. They hadn't gotten anywhere, either. She said she thought the sighting had been bogus.

That was when the call came in about the car crash near the entrance to the park. Mary Kelly had been seen and a search was already underway.

Amy stuck her emergency light on top of her unmarked car and took off for the park. The two squad cars were right behind her.

By the time Amy got to the scene, the street was ablaze with cops, ambulances (two of them), TV reporters, and neighbors of every description, all of whom had been sensible enough to wear something heavy. With this kind of excitement, they'd probably want to hang around a long time. Sure wouldn't want to catch a head cold or anything. They tried to hide their disappointment that nobody – at least so far – had actually died, though they were glad to see that Cindy at least had had the decency to get some blood on her.

Amy pushed to the front of the crowd. Cindy was on a gurney

being loaded into the back end of the shining white ambulance.

Amy waited while they finished getting the gurney inside. Cindy looked pale and blood-streaked and tired. Amy noticed that, unlike the rest of her, Cindy's left hand was trembling. It seemed to be a separate part of her body. The ambulance was cramped, white, neatly arranged. It made Amy claustrophobic.

Before Amy could speak, Cindy said, 'She really hates us, Amy.'

Amy pressed her fingers to Cindy's mouth. 'Not here.' Anybody could be listening. She didn't want any talk of The Committee. 'I'll see you at the hospital later.'

'Where're you going?'

'I'm going to find her.'

'Darcy ran after her.'

'Darcy?'

Cindy told her about Darcy and Ken showing up and Darcy running after Mary Kelly.

'I'd better get going,' Amy said.

'What if it all comes out?' Cindy said.

'It won't.'

Amy looked for the officer in charge. Hastings seemed overwhelmed by the situation. He was inhaling angrily on a cigarette. He'd quit six months ago. Tonight was such that he had returned to his old ways.

Hastings told her how he'd sent six officers to search for Mary. They were still looking, checking in on their walkie-talkies. So far, no luck.

The crowd pressed closer. A lone female officer was trying to hold them back.

Amy needed to find Mary and quickly. 'I'll walk around myself, see what I can find'

'You want me to go with you?'

'No, you stay here.'

'All right.'

'I need a walkie-talkie, though.'

He pointed to the female officer who was dealing with the crowd. 'Karen's got one.'

'Thanks.'

Amy relieved Karen of her walkie-talkie.

'I'm sorry about your husband,' said the woman.

Amy spent the next fifteen minutes shining her flashlight into every dark corner in a two-block area she could find. The first sweep of a search was often careless. Officers got so excited that they occasionally missed the obvious. It was frequently the second sweep of searchers, the more methodical ones, who actually found the prey.

She found nothing.

Either the first sweep had been thorough or Mary Kelly hadn't been here to begin with. Or else she'd gone elsewhere.

She might not be a professional criminal, Amy thought, but Mary had intelligence, patience and cunning on her side.

Amy started down another lonely, dark block, seemingly unaffected by tonight's events. No house lights shone. Everybody was in bed, snug and comfortable. She thought of morning, of telling her two youngest daughters about their father. She'd have to handle it just as she'd handled it with Megan. No prepared speeches, just tell them simply and straightforwardly and then be there to help them.

She walked across lawns, looking between houses. Nothing. When she came to the end of the block, she saw the alley. That would likely be the first place the officers would have looked. Alleys offered all kinds of hiding places.

Without realizing it, she began to retrace the steps Darcy had taken earlier. The first alley yielded nothing. She checked each of the garages – still nothing. The first sweep of searchers had undoubtedly checked this alley out first and moved on.

She came to the street and looked across at the mouth of the next alley. The garages were even bigger in the next block. She remembered as a girl always thinking how neat it would be to have a garage this size. Kids could play a lot of interesting stuff in places like these.

But now, all these years later, when she finally got her chance to go through these garages, she wasn't playing. She wasn't playing at all.

She was just as assiduous with this block as she had been with the previous ones. Most of the garages were unlocked, so she could easily get in and look around. She kept her walkie-talkie in her jacket pocket, her gun in her right hand, and her flashlight in her left. Most of them were empty. They smelt of rain, damp lumber. A few had dirt floors and were tomb-dank. In one of them, she scared a bat. In its frantic surprise, the thing smashed against a window before finding a broken pane that allowed it to fly away.

Then she heard the voices.

At first she thought she'd simply imagined them. Maybe her battered mind was playing tricks. She would probably 'hear' Ted later tonight. The bereaved often spoke of hearing or seeing their loved one shortly after death.

She crept up to the garage in question. She was a good cop. She kept her gun at the ready. Even if her mind *was* inventing this, she didn't forget standard police procedure.

She eased open the door and went inside. Two cars filled most of the space on the first floor. She played her light around the walls and saw the wooden ladder leading to the second floor.

The voices were coming from the second floor.

She clicked off her flashlight and moved to the rear of the garage, to the ladder.

Darcy's first impression was that the woman was lunging toward her so she could stab her. But she did an unexpected thing – she flung the knife into the darkness surrounding them. Then she sank to the floor, outlined in the spotlight of moonshine, and began to weep again, her face buried in her hands.

At first, Darcy wasn't sure what to do. She looked over at the knife, the blade gleaming in the moonlight.

Should she grab the knife while she had the chance? But no, she thought, looking at the forlorn and shrunken thing the woman had become. The woman was no threat to her now, only to herself.

Darcy stood there for a few more uneasy moments. She should run and get the police. But the way the woman wept, the gagging, choking sorrow of it, moved her. How could Darcy leave her at such a time even if she was a killer? Even if Mary was the person who had put Darcy in prison. Right now anyway, Darcy couldn't hate her. She hunched down next to the woman.

'There'll be people to help you,' Darcy said gently. 'They'll listen to you.'

But it was as if the woman hadn't heard. 'My brother never hurt anybody! Everybody picked on him all his life because he was so odd! He came out here and he was so hopeful that things would be good for him – and then they killed him! The Judge said it was an honest mistake but that doesn't matter. They still killed him!'

And then she reached out and drew Darcy to her, held on to her

228

so tight that she pulled Darcy down on her knees. And Darcy held her. She was able to forget – at least for now – that this was the woman who had put her in prison. In the woman's grief, she could hear madness, could glimpse what had so driven her to murder. How could you hate anybody this pitiful?

Darcy helped the woman lie flat on the boards, then sat next to her, holding her hand. The woman's entire body was dancing with delirium. She sobbed and muttered things that Darcy couldn't understand. Darcy said softly, over and over, 'It's going to be all right. I'll stay with you. I promise I will. I'll make sure that they take good care of you. I promise.'

The woman's crying lessened for a moment and she looked up at Darcy as if seeing her for the first time. Though she still sobbed at least Darcy could understand what she was saying. 'I don't understand why you'd help me. After what I did to you, I mean.'

Darcy softly brushed hair from the woman's forehead. 'Because I didn't understand what happened until tonight – what made you do what you did.' She patted the woman's hand. 'I don't agree with what you did but I understand it. And I think a jury will understand it, too.'

'I felt bad about killing them,' the woman said shakily. 'I really did. I mean, I thought it would feel good. You know?'

Darcy nodded.

'But it didn't. I just felt – empty inside. It didn't bring my brother back, killing them. And now—'

Her voice trailed off.

'Will you wait here?'

'Where are you going?' the woman said. She sounded like a frightened child. Whose parent was going to desert her.

'I'm going to get the police.'

'They scare me.'

'I know they do. But like I told you, I'll stay with you.'

'Really?'

'Yes.'

She tightened her grip on the woman's hand again. 'What's your name, by the way?'

'Mary. Mary Kelly.' Then, 'He was a good man. My brother, I mean.'

'I'm sure he was.'

'He was just so sad all his life. When we were growing up, he'd

229

walk down the street and people would make fun of him – when he'd get back to our apartment, he'd close his door and he'd just lie on his bed and cry. It was the saddest sound I ever heard. I think I was the only person in his life who ever cared for him. I really do.'

This time when she started crying again, it was soft, almost imperceptible.

Darcy stood up. 'I know you're going to be scared when I'm gone but please don't leave here, all right? I'm afraid if you run, somebody might hurt you. Now, I'm going to get the police. I'll be back in a few minutes.'

She was turning toward the ladder when a familiar voice said, 'You don't have to go anywhere, Darcy. The police are right here.'

Then Amy stepped into the spotlight. She carried her police pistol and nothing else.

Darcy realized then that she'd been so caught up with Mary Kelly that she hadn't heard Amy come up the ladder.

'You won't need your pistol, Amy,' Darcy said.

'Oh, yes, I will,' Amy said.

She raised her weapon and pointed it directly at Mary Kelly on the floor.

Ken had just about given up looking.

He'd been distracted when Mary Kelly ran from the accident. By the time he'd seen to Cindy – checked out her wounds and seen that she was going to be all right – Darcy had disappeared.

He'd been searching the surrounding streets ever since with no luck at all.

He had another thing to worry about, too, and that was getting arrested. After eluding the police, and aiding and abetting a wanted fugitive, namely his wife, he was sure to stand trial on several charges. So, whenever he saw a cop or a cop car as he looked for Darcy, he did his best to fade into the shadows.

But now, as he turned a street-lighted corner, he saw he couldn't avoid the police any longer.

He recognized a cop named Ryerson. The man sometimes brought his daughter out to the stables. The girl had a natural ability with horses. Too bad she didn't get to come out more often.

Ryerson saw him immediately.

'Hey, Ken, over here.'

He sounded glad to see him. Hadn't Ryerson gotten the word

that Ken was wanted? Maybe they'd just roused him out of bed and hadn't filled him in on everything yet.

'Hi, Paul,' Ken said, walking toward the cop. 'I expect you've been looking for me.'

'For you?' Ryerson said. Then, 'Oh, you mean earlier? Yeah, about an hour or so ago, I guess. But we got the word to concentrate on this Mary Kelly. Apparently, she's the one we really want.'

Ken was stunned. 'You're not looking for me?'

'Nope. Just this Mary Kelly.'

'No luck, huh?'

'Not yet. But she's on foot as far as we know. She won't get too far.' His walkie-talkie crackled and he took it from his belt. He was wanted back at the scene of the accident. The crowd was swelling.

'Looks like I'd better head back.'

Ken nodded.

'I'll be bringing my daughter out one of these days,' Ryerson said, as he left. 'She sure loves those horses of yours.'

'Look forward to it,' Ken said.

As he watched Ryerson retreat down the block, he stood there a free man. The phrase sounded funny. He'd only been a wanted man for a short time but it had changed his perspective on a whole lot of things. For one thing, being a fugitive had made him feel less than human. He still didn't feel quite human, as if his short-lived experience had left some permanent scar on his psyche.

He went back to looking for his wife.

Darcy grabbed Amy's wrist just in time, knocking the gun from her hand. The gun landed with a loud thumping sound and then spun around and skittered a few feet across the floor. Mary Kelly just stared at it dumbly and made no attempt to grab it though it was only a few feet from where she sat.

With Darcy and Amy, it was another matter. Darcy shoved Amy out of her way and dove forward for the gun. Amy grabbed Darcy by the hips and threw her aside. But as Amy reached for the weapon, Darcy stomped on her hand so hard that she had to let go. But Amy fought back, lashing out with her good hand and knocking Darcy off balance, on to her butt on the floor. Amy bent to pick up the gun and Darcy threw herself on Amy. This time it was Amy who hit the floor, but she landed next to the gun. She swept it up, pointed it directly at Darcy, and then slowly got to her feet.

A hard smile crossed Amy's face. 'You learned a lot in prison.'

'I don't want you to hurt her.'

'Who?' Amy said, the same hard smile on her face. 'Your good friend Mary Kelly? The one who sent you to prison?'

'She needs help.'

'Somebody sent me to prison like that, I'd give her some help all right.'

'I don't want you to hurt her,' Darcy said again. 'And after you get her back to the station, I want to talk to you about The Committee.'

Amy shook her head. 'The Committee doesn't matter any more. The Committee's all over. History.'

'I still want to know about it.'

Amy sighed. 'Just calm down, Darcy, and let me handle this. Now, will you go, please?'

Darcy looked over at Mary Kelly, who was still sitting on the floor, just silently watching them. She seemed in a trance, her gaze not quite in focus.

'What happens to her?' Darcy said.

'I take her in.'

'I told her I'd go with her.'

'You'd go with her? Are you kidding? Why would you do that?'

'Because she needs a friend.'

'She isn't your friend, Darcy.'

'For tonight, she is. She doesn't have anybody else.'

'You know how many people she killed?'

'I hear you. But I'm staying here. With her.'

'What the hell are you talking about?'

'I promised her.'

'She's a fucking killer, Darcy. Can't you understand that?'

Darcy said quietly, 'I gave her my word.'

Amy and Darcy stared at each for a long minute.

'All right. I'll let you ride along in the car to the station. But for right now I want you to go downstairs and wait for us.'

'Please don't go,' Mary Kelly said.

Her words startled both women. They looked at her. She hadn't moved. But the vagueness of her previous expression had been replaced by fear. Her frightened-child look was back. 'Please'

Darcy looked over at Mary and then back at Amy. 'She's scared.'

'I know she's scared.'

232

'And you're angry about Ted.'

'You wouldn't be?'

'Of course I would be. But I'd probably have somebody else question her.'

'I'll be fine.'

They stared at each other again and then Darcy knelt down next to Mary.

'Please don't go,' Mary said. 'You promised.' She was starting to cry again.

'I'll be right downstairs. I'll be able to hear everything.'

She held Mary Kelly's hand and then embraced her, holding her for a long time. Mary was trembling like a kitten.

Darcy got up. 'Remember something, Amy.'

'Remember what?'

Darcy nodded to Mary Kelly. 'She loved her brother just as much as you loved Ted.'

Then Darcy went downstairs.

How inconsequential humanity seemed at that moment. How clean and bright and eternal the stars – and how baffling humanity could be. She couldn't even understand her own motives. She should hate Mary for putting her in prison, and yet she couldn't. Mary was acting, however insanely, to avenge her brother's murder.

The night had returned to a semblance of sanity. A freight train rumbled through the hills to the west. Traffic could be heard on one of the main drags a few blocks over. Dogs barked. A cat sat on a garbage can, watching her. You didn't know what you had till prison removed you from all the pleasant little sights and sounds of everyday life.

Darcy looked down the alley and saw a lone figure walking toward her. From here, she didn't recognize the figure. Probably a cop. She wished that Amy would finish up with Mary. Then she could make it official with everybody – that Darcy hadn't killed the blackmailer, Mary Kelly had. And Darcy could ride with Mary to the station, see to it that she got the kind of help she needed.

She wondered what was going on upstairs in the garage. Amy had been eager to get rid of her. She had never seen Amy as cold and quiet as this. Spooky, no doubt about it. And yet Amy was bound by the law, too. Being Chief of Police didn't give her carte blanche. She might threaten Mary but there wasn't anything serious she could *do* to an unarmed woman. Still, Darcy wished she hadn't left. Mary had looked so scared. Darcy felt as if she'd deserted a small child.

As the figure approached the mouth of the alley, Darcy recognized Ken. He carried a flashlight and was shining it right and left, right and left, as he made his way toward her.

She walked out into the center of the alley and stood there watching him. She felt good and safe and happy seeing him come toward her this way – friend, lover, brother. She liked the clean, sensible, purposeful kind of man he was. No games. He was what he was and you accepted it or you walked away.

He got pretty close before he saw who she was and then he immediately started running. The sound of his cowboy boots striking the gravel thrilled her. He clicked off his flashlight and opened his arms so that by the time he reached her, he was ready to swoop her up off the ground.

Which is exactly what he did.

She wanted to blurt everything out – especially the part about Mary Kelly confessing to the murder that had put her in prison – but that was hard to do with Ken's mouth clamped firmly on hers as he danced her around and around in his arms.

Amy walked and stood over Mary, looking down. Both of them were within the circle of moonlight that shone on the coarse old boards of this garage.

'Did you enjoy killing my husband?'

Mary Kelly just stared up at her. Watched her, warily.

'I have to go home now and in the morning tell my two little girls that their father is dead. Did you think about that when you were killing him?'

Mary Kelly just watched. Scared.

Amy started pacing slowly. She looked up at the window through which the moonlight shone. 'Their lives are never going to be the same again. Never.' She turned back to Mary Kelly. 'But I'm sure you didn't think of that, did you?'

Mary Kelly, silent. Mary Kelly, frightened.

It was a good kick, sharp and swift and perfectly placed. It caught Mary in the stomach and knocked the wind out of her. She fell backwards, sprawled on the floor. Holding her stomach.

Amy walked up to her and then kicked her even harder in the ribs. Mary began crying.

'Sit up.'

But Mary Kelly just kept quietly crying.

Amy raised her leg again. 'You don't sit up, I start kicking you again. You want that?'

It wasn't easy and it wasn't fast. The way Mary Kelly kept holding her side, you could see she suspected she had a broken rib. Pain laced her face, robbed her natural beauty.

When she was finally sitting up, Amy said, 'Now pick up the razor.'

Mary Kelly looked up at her. 'I don't want the knife. Not any more.'

'I guess you don't understand how things work here, Mary. I don't give a shit what you want or not. I told you to pick up that razor, and I mean it.'

Mary started to protest but Amy kicked her in the side. Hard.

Mary started crawling. Slowly, painfully, making her way across the moonlit circle until she reached the razor.

'Now pick it up and bring it back over here, Mary.'

The woman whimpered but when Amy took a couple of steps toward her, Mary picked up the weapon and clutched it in her right hand.

Amy shot the left sleeve of her jacket, showing a slender exposed forearm. Her right hand still held her gun.

'I want you to cut me with that razor, Mary. And I want you to do it right now.'

There was anguish in Mary's eyes. 'I don't want to hurt anybody anymore. I'm through with that.'

'No, you're not.' Amy shoved her arm up. 'I want you to cut me. Just slash me right across the forearm.' She slapped Mary hard across the face. 'Right now.'

'Please don't make me—'

Amy slapped her again, even harder. Mary looked confused, her eyes wild and unseeing.

'Bring the knife down, Mary. Now.'

Mary, moaning, raised a trembling hand and brought the razor down until it rested only an inch above Amy's forearm.

'Now cut me. And cut me good. You understand?'

'No,' Mary said. 'No, I can't—'

'Then I guess I'll have to help you.' And with that, Amy jammed her gun into her jacket pocket, grabbed Mary's wrist and brought the razor down on her forearm.

And then she guided Mary's hand until it slashed the knife deep and true into her flesh.

The pain was startling. Amy hadn't been expecting anything like this.

She let Mary fall back and the razor tumbled to the floor as she gritted her teeth and gave herself over to the pain. Accept it, she thought, and in accepting it, you'll conquer it. She cursed and drew her arm closer to her body. By now, blood was pouring from the cut.

She raised her head and looked at Mary.

'You tried to kill me,' she said, 'and I didn't have any choice. Self-defense. Pure and simple self-defense.'

Mary searched frantically for somewhere, anywhere, to hide.

But it was too late for that. Far too late.

Darcy was in Ken's arms when she heard the shot. She jumped as if she'd been shot herself.

She didn't say anything. She just turned around and flung the door wide. Ken was close behind her. The ladder was in the darkest shadows.

Darcy scrambled up the rungs. The first time she'd climbed these steps, she'd been careful, even nervous. But not this time. she reached the top of the ladder in seconds. The dust up here made her cough as she started to walk across the room.

The first thing she saw was the sprawled body of Mary Kelly. She had been shot in the forehead. Now, spread on her back, she looked rumpled and old. Death had taken both her youth and beauty. The moonlight made the blood draining from the wound look black.

Amy stood over near the window. She was wrapping her forearm in a handkerchief.

Darcy walked over to her.

'You killed her,' Darcy said.

Amy looked up at her. 'Yes, I did.'

'In cold blood.'

'In self-defense, Darcy. You see this?' She held up her bloody arm as if she was offering to Darcy as a gift. Amy glanced down at her arm and shook her head. 'She attacked me.'

'I don't believe you.'

'I was acting in the line of duty.' Amy's eyes strayed past Darcy.

'Ken, I want you to get Darcy out of here and right now.'

There were distant shouts, from the ally below. Ken met Amy's gaze.

'Your wife doesn't seem to believe that I was acting in self-defense,' she said.

Ken looked at the fallen body of Mary Kelly. 'Were you?'

Amy winced from the pain in her arm, notched her handkerchief tighter. She eyed both of them silently. 'I guess you folks don't recognize a gift when you see it. Kelly killed Rick Kenton – she confessed to me. Darcy's free. I even plan to make sure that she isn't charged for escaping prison. The warden's a good friend of mine.' She looked at Ken. 'She's free, Ken. Take her home now.'

Police officers were now hurrying through the downstairs door. Moments later, the first of them reached the ladder. Started slamming upwards.

'You killed her in cold blood,' Darcy said. 'You wounded yourself to make it look good.'

'Take her home, Ken. I'll bring her in tomorrow and we can get everything wrapped up.'

Ken glanced again at the corpse of Mary Kelly. Then at Amy Foster. Chief Amy Foster.

He slid his arm gently through Darcy's. 'C'mon, honey. I'll take you home.'

And then the other police were noisily filling the second floor, and Ken was getting her out of there.

28

Ken pulled up past the barn and the stables and swung the car into the open space behind the house. The house was dark. In the headlights, Darcy could see the familiar cream-colored curtains in the window, the lace curtains on their bedroom windows on the east side of the house. Home. How many nights she'd dreamt of this wonderful old place when she was in prison. But now . . .

'Well,' Ken said. 'We're home, honey.'

'Yes,' she said, her voice cold, 'Yes, we are.'

She could see him almost recoil. 'Isn't this what you've been wanting?'

'Yes,'

He smiled. 'Then how about a smile and a kiss or two?'

'Oh, sweetheart,' she said, pulling him into her arms. 'You deserve a lot more than that.' She kissed him deeply, putting as much of herself into the embrace as possible, hoping that the way she held him, kissed him would convey her love for him. Yet – Yet, a part of her was distracted. She couldn't forget Mary Kelly.

It was the same inside the house.

They lay on the bed. For the first time that night, they showed a bit of awkwardness around each other. They didn't kiss. They only held hands.

'She gave you good advice, honey.' Ken said at last.

'Who did?'

'Amy.'

'Oh.'

'I'm serious. You have to forget everything now. There'll be formalities – getting everything squared away with the warden and all – but then you need to get on with your life here and forget what happened.'

239

'The Committee—'

He stopped her. 'The Committee is all over. You can bet on that. Nobody's going to win by dragging it up again. Mary Kelly had her revenge. That's what she wanted. Now, the subject is closed.' He kissed her on the cheek. 'I'm being selfish and I know it, honey. And I don't care. I just want our lives to get back to normal.' He sighed. 'Don't you see? This needs to end – prison, courts, cops. You need to get back to work – and back to me.'

She'd needed to hear that. For the first time since leaving the garage, she started thinking about what 'home' meant. Home wasn't just a place, just a collection of buildings, it was a feeling of purpose and warmth and safety.

She slid her arms around his neck and brought him close. They kissed on the lips and rolled over. In less than five minutes, Ken was asleep, blissfully snoring.

Darcy wondered if she could sleep. Maybe she'd just lie here all night and mull things over and—

She fell asleep quickly, and slept well for almost two hours.

When she woke up, needing to go to the bathroom, she checked the luminous digital clock on the nightstand. 3:35 A.M.

She went quickly to the bathroom, washed her hands and then headed back to bed.

But halfway there, she stopped and looked at her clothes laid out on the straightback chair.

Just forget it happened. Just get on with your life.

Just go back to bed.

But she couldn't. She lingered in the kitchen, drinking part of a can of Pepsi, the caffeine effecting her almost instantly. This is what you've been dreaming of, isn't it? Forget it, and go back to bed.

A few minutes later, wearing the clothes Bernice had given her, she slipped out of the house.

29

She took the small Chevy truck with the automatic transmission but her driving was a little rusty. She killed the engine twice getting out of the garage.

First light was breaking as she turned around in the wide space of dirt in front of the out buildings. The pine trees to the east were silhouetted in jagged precision against the pinkish hue of the dawning sky. The air was exhilaratingly clean. None of the horses were stirring yet. It was a brand-new world.

She left the headlights off, hugging to the center of the lane that emptied out on to the county gravel road that led straight into Parkhurst.

The town was just waking, too, lights golden in about half the windows. A small city like this one, people were generally earlier risers, something they'd learned when they were young. Dawdlers and slackers might sleep in till seven or even (God forbid) seven-thirty. But not these hearty folk.

She knew just where she was going. There was little traffic. She went through the loop area. Then she was there. A simple right turn. Palmer Street. The houses were nice but not ostentatious, the lawns beautifully tended, and the street immaculate. A good place to live and raise kids.

She pulled into the driveway. The light was burning in the kitchen. She half expected somebody to come to the window and peek out at her. Nobody did.

She opened the car door and then sat there a moment. Did she really want to go through with this? Maybe Ken was right. Maybe just forgetting it all was the best thing. It was over and done with, anyway.

She slid out of the car, closing the door quietly behind her. No, she couldn't let it go. She had to set it right.

She went up to the side door and knocked with just two knuckles. Didn't want to wake the girls. There was no answer.

She noticed that the outside screen door was open an inch or so. She felt for the doorknob.

She pushed inward and stepped inside on a landing that led to the kitchen door. She went up two steps. The kitchen door was open, too.

She walked into the kitchen.

Amy was sitting at the kitchen table. She wore a white blouse. She looked tired. In front of her was a fifth of Black & White Scotch and two glasses.

'I've been waiting for you,' Amy said.

'You have?'

'I'd knew you'd show up. You'll always be a girl scout, Darcy. Champion of the underdog.'

'You killed her in cold blood.'

Amy shrugged. 'Have a drink with me, Darcy.'

'No, thanks.'

'We've been friends too long for you to be rude.'

'You were pretty rude to Mary Kelly.'

Amy poured herself a drink. 'You stop to count up how many people she killed?'

'That didn't give you the right to kill her in cold blood.'

'C'mon, now. Come over here and have a drink with me.'

Why not? Darcy thought. Isn't that why I came over here? To get the rest of the truth?

She walked over to the table, sat down.

'You want some ice?'

'I'll pass on the drink. I just want to talk.'

Amy smiled. 'Gee, I wonder what about?'

Amy took a sip. 'You remember what the town was like, the nice, safe little town we grew up in? All of a sudden, because of the Interstate, we had all these new people and new businesses we didn't want. Gambling, hookers, drugs. The crime rate was getting way out of hand just about the time I went on the force. My dad was still chief then and he didn't know what to do. Then that little girl was raped and murdered – and the killer went free. So your father and my father and some of the other town leaders got together and decided to clean up the town themselves. Since the law seemed to just get in the way, they decided to act outside the law. And they did. In four years, the crime rate was way down again.'

'The Judge sent me a list of people they killed.'

Amy looked at her steadily. 'People who deserved to die. People our esteemed county attorney refused to prosecute for lack of evidence. So we killed them. I say "we" because by that time The Committee had put both Cindy and I on as active members, so we could take over when our fathers got too old.'

Amy leaned forward. 'One of the men we killed beat his two-year-old to death but the crime lab couldn't quite prove it. Another was a drug dealer. Another was a child molester who'd molested at least six children in town. And so on. People who *deserved* to die, Amy. That's what you have to understand. We weren't doing this because we enjoyed it, we were doing it because we had to to protect the community.'

'You murdered Mary Kelly's brother and he was innocent.'

Amy sat back in her chair, put her head down momentarily. Then looked up again. 'And every one of us has felt guilty about that since the day it happened. I guess that's the price we had to pay for keeping our city clean.'

'That's easy for you to say, Amy. He wasn't *your* brother.'

'Just remember something, Darcy.'

'What?'

'Before you get too sanctimonious, your father was a part of it, too.'

'I know.'

'So let's just let it lie, all right? The whole thing, I mean. The Committee's going to be disbanded. My part in it will be a secret – and so will your father's.'

Darcy still hadn't made her peace with her father's role in all this. White of hair, steel blue of eye, a gentle and gentlemanly figure who had helped drag this state, kicking and screaming, into the modern age. Why would he ever have agreed to become part of a vigilante group?

'You don't seem to understand, Amy.'

'What?'

'I *want* my father's role to be exposed.'

'What the hell're you talking about? Do you know what that'd to do your family's reputation?'

'I know, Amy. But this was wrong. People need to know what happened here.'

243

'You'd destroy your family's reputation?'

Darcy stood up. 'That's what I came here to tell you, Amy. That I'm going to the press. As soon as I leave here, I'm going to call the state paper and tell them everything I know.'

'It'll take all of us down, Darcy. I've got three daughters to raise and no husband.'

Darcy sighed. 'I'm sorry, I really am. But the public needs to know what happened in this town so it won't happen anywhere else.'

And then Amy was up, her speed stunning Darcy. She grabbed Darcy and slammed her up against the wall.

It was part of a dream. That was Megan's first reaction. A dream in which a fight of some kind was going on. Shouts, curses, things being knocked to the floor, glass breaking.

She sat up in bed, spending a moment orienting herself to the darkness and the sounds. No, there really wasn't an argument going on downstairs. She looked at her clock. 5:28 A.M.

Who was down there? What was going on?

Amy pushed Darcy up against the kitchen wall, her hands around her neck. Amy's strength was overwhelming. Darcy could feel the hot, stinging blood in her face, could feel the way her windpipe was starting to fold beneath the pressure.

She kicked Amy in the shin but Amy only cursed and increased the pressure on Darcy's throat. Darcy tried to move right, then left, then to lunge forward. It didn't matter. Amy was not about to let her go.

Darcy's right hand dropped to her side. She made a fist that she was going to slam into Amy's ribs. Then Darcy's hand brushed against something long and and slender and hard in her pocket.

The switchblade knife the hobo had given her. She'd forgotten all about it, had transferred it from the hobo's clothes to Bernice's.

Now she brought it up, snicked it up open and pushed it roughly against Amy's side.

As soon as Ken rolled over and found Darcy's side of the bed empty, he knew something was wrong. She could be in the bathroom, or just sitting harmlessly in the living room. But, instinctively, he knew better. He moved quickly through the house, calling her name. She was nowhere around.

He dressed quickly, hurried out to the big truck, and jumped inside, the key finding the ignition even before the door had slammed shut.

There was only one place Darcy would head at this hour.

Amy gave up the fight. How could she win with the point of a switchblade in her side? They had reversed positions. Now Darcy held Amy against the wall.

'You're going with me, Amy.'

'Where?'

'To a phone booth so I can call the newspaper. And then we're going to your office.'

'For what?'

'You're going to resign.'

'No way, Darcy.'

'Oh, yes. That's exactly what you're going to do. You don't deserve to have a badge and a gun.'

'You smug bitch.'

Darcy shook her head. 'Mary Kelly didn't have the right to kill you people – but you drove her to it. You killed her brother. You're the smug one, Amy. You think you knew better than anybody else how to mete out justice. But it didn't work, did it?'

Amy said, slowly, 'This is going to destroy our lives, Darcy.'

'I know that.' Darcy pressed the knife in a little deeper. 'My car's in the drive. I want you to walk over to the door. I'll follow you outside.'

'Now?'

'Now.'

'I don't have any shoes on.'

'There's a pair of loafers right by your chair. Put them on.'

'I could have you arrested.'

'No, you couldn't. Now, hurry up and get your shoes on.'

Amy turned and said. 'I sure hope you've thought this through.'

'I have, Amy. No more talk. Go out to the car.'

As Amy went ahead of her, Darcy kept the knife right in Amy's back. That was when Megan walked through the kitchen door. She held her grandfather's gun in her trembling hand.

'Leave her alone, Darcy,' Megan said.

Darcy looked at her. 'I'm sorry for this, Megan. I'm only trying to do what's right.'

Megan started crying. 'Do you have any idea what Mom's been through? My dad was killed tonight. You can't come in here and do this, Darcy.

'This needs to be sorted out, Megan,' Darcy said. 'We have to do this the right way. Let the legal system do it. We can't handle this ourselves.'

'Put the gun away, honey,' Amy said.

'Put it away?' Megan sounded shrill, hysterical. 'I heard what she said. If she calls the newspaper, then you're going to prison, Mom. What'll us three girls do? What'll happen to us, then, huh?'

'Please, honey. Just put the gun down on the counter there. Please, honey.'

'No, I'm not letting her take you out of here. Grandad taught me how to shoot. Remember?' She raised the gun, sighted. 'I've got a clear shot at her. A real clear one.'

She did, too. All Amy had to do was throw herself to the left or right and Darcy would be a perfect target.

'Move aside, Mom.'

'Megan, please—' Amy said.

'I don't think you'll shoot me, Megan,' Darcy said quietly. 'You know deep down I'm doing the only thing I can.' She paused. 'C'mon, Amy, we've got to get going.'

'It'll be all right, honey,' Amy said to Megan. 'I'll be back here in a few hours. I really will.'

Megan sighted along her gun. 'You've got five seconds to walk out the door, Darcy. Alone. I'm not kidding, either.'

Amy looked back at Darcy. 'Are you satisfied now? Look what you've done to Megan.'

'This isn't about Megan and you know it.' Darcy glanced at the girl. 'Put the gun down, Megan. Please. This won't help your mother at all.'

Megan began sobbing, then she let the gun drop to her side. Perhaps the stand-off was over.

Amy started walking toward the side door.

'No!'

Megan raised her gun again, pointing it directly at Darcy's head.

'No, honey, please!' Amy shouted and leapt for the gun just as Megan pulled the trigger. Her leap placed her directly in the line of fire and she took the bullet full in the chest.

'Mom!' Megan screamed.

But it was too late. For a long silent moment, Amy hung in the air, then she collapsed to the floor.

'Mom! Mom!' Megan cried, hurling herself to the body on the floor.

Darcy was on the phone, dialing 911, shouting, 'Hurry! Hurry!'

Megan clung to her mother, sobbing.

Then came an awful silence.

After a time, Megan raised her head. Her eyes met Darcy's. She stood up slowly and crossed the kitchen to stand in front of Darcy.

She slapped Darcy with great force across the face. 'You bitch! You were supposed to be her friend!'

Then she threw herself into Darcy's arms.

And that was how Ken found them, a minute later.

30

The effect of all the emergency lights – police vehicles, ambulance, highway patrol – were lost in the shining new day. The beautiful spring morning was at odds with the grim reality of the emergency vehicles.

Darcy and Ken were talking to Beechler, the Assistant Chief of Police. He was saying, 'The girls will go to their aunt's for the time being. But you'd really like to take them?'

'Very much,' Darcy said. 'There's plenty of room for the three of them on the ranch.'

'Well, that's a good thing,' Beechler said. 'The aunt's pretty old. She'd never be able to handle those kids.' Then he looked at Darcy. 'I guess with all you told me about The Committee, our little town's going to be in the spotlight again, the way it was when we had all the gambling and drug problems.'

'I guess so,' Darcy said.

Beechler shrugged. 'I suppose we'll survive.' He nodded. 'Well, I'm sure I'll have more questions for you. But they can probably hold till tomorrow or so.'

'Thanks,' Ken said.

After Beechler left, Ken pointed to their separate vehicles and said, 'You ready to go home?'

She looked at him and smiled sadly. So much had happened; so many lives destroyed. And yet if the girls came to live with them at the ranch, some lives could still be saved. Darcy was sure of it.

'Yes,' she said, sliding her arm around her husband's waist. 'Yes, I'm finally ready to go home.'